LIEUTENANT STEPTOE SHOUTED, "FIRE."

As the crash of the carbines rippled along the line of attacking riders, Jacob Morgan fired at the Sioux he had in his sights. The man recoiled at the strike of the bullet, tried to catch himself, and tumbled to the ground.

Half a dozen other Sioux warriors were slammed from their mounts. Two Sioux horses went down in a jumble of kicking, thrashing legs.

Answering shots blazed from the rifles of the Sioux and two bowmen let loose their arrows at the white men. All along the line of the attacking force came the stutter of rapid firing pistols, scything down the remaining Indians.

Jacob knew the fight was almost won and looked to the side to see if his two partners were unhurt. Wolf Voice and the other two Crows scouts Steptoe had hired had fallen behind and were angling their mounts towards the three fur trappers. Jacob saw Wolf Voice's hostile eyes were fastened on him.

Wolf Voice jerked his rifle to his shoulder and fired at Jacob.

Other Books By F. M. Parker

SKINNER
NIGHTHAWK
COLDIRON
THE SEARCHER
SHADOW OF THE WOLF
THE HIGHBINDERS
THE SHANGHAIERS
THE FAR BATTLEGROUND
THE SHADOW MAN
THE SLAVERS
THE ASSASSINS
THE PREDATORS

WINTER WOMAN

F.M. Parker

Pinnacle Books
Kensington Publishing Corp.

http://www.pinnaclebooks.com

PINNACLE BOOKS are published by

Kensington Publishing Corp.
850 Third Avenue
New York, NY 10022

First Printing: December, 1996

Printed in the United States of America
10 9 8 7 6 5 4 3 2 1

For John Tumbleson

Prologue

The Creation of the Land

Only the primeval eye of the sun saw the birth of the mountains in that ancient time of orogeny on the northern continent of the Earth.

A compressive force of unimaginable power ushered in that age of mountain building. For a time span of millions of years, the crust of the continent was squeezed from the east and west, and the thick rock layers arched upward, bending until they stood at steep angles. A giant range of mountains was formed, stretching some three thousand miles north to south and spanning the continent. The stony mountain peaks stabbed four and five miles high, wounding the sky in scores of deep thrusts.

As the mountains rose, streams of a thousand sizes came to life and tumbled with awesome violence from the high ramparts. The myriad currents cut and tore at the steep flanks of the mountains, grinding the rock to sand and silt and rushing away with it to the lowlands. On the lower reaches of the streams, the grade became less steep and the currents slowed and wandered in meandering courses, dropping their load of eroded mountain debris. The valleys of the streams became choked with swamps and shallow lakes as thousands of cubic miles of sediment were spread in flat, ever-thickening layers.

Time ticked off the millennia, adding to millions of years. During the long epoch of deposition, a plain grew at the base of the mountain range and extended toward the rising sun for many hundreds of miles.

Far away at the extreme eastern edge of the plains, the streams coalesced to form a grand river. This stupendous flow of water poured in a never-ending current to the south, finally debauching into the salty brine of one of the great oceans of the Earth.

As time continued to whisper its passing, the climate of the Earth began to cool. Glaciers thousands of feet thick formed and marched across the northern portion of the plains, each time to retreat and die. In the harsh, frozen part of the cycles, the land was buried under an unbelievably large expanse of ice and swept by hurricane winds that never ended. Wet, warm, pluvial times, the interglacial periods, melted the ice, creating torrents that scoured the mountains and plains and sped off to add their volume to the prodigious south-flowing river.

A dramatic change occurred in the climate cycles of the Earth. The continental glacier retreated and the deluge came, but the next phase of the cycle did not arrive. Instead the land grew drier and drier. Broad forest died and the plains became a prairie, a sea of grass.

The great animals that had lived and thrived during the stormy glacial period, the wooly mammoth, the wide-horned bison, the saber-toothed tiger, and the vulture condor all died. However, the bison left a legacy, for in its genes there existed the potential for change. As the plains became ever more dry, each succeeding generation of the bison grew smaller and smaller, adapting to the changing climate and the decreased availability of food. It became a miniaturized replica of its ancestor, weighing a mere ton or less. This new breed of bison flourished by the millions on the grassy prairie.

In this warmer, drier time, a brown-skinned man came onto the plains and stalked the bison herds. The man was skilled and killed the animals he needed to survive. Only the white buffalo wolf competed with the brown man as he journeyed where the buffalo journeyed and lived in harmony with the herds for twelve millennia.

Then a new clan of man, one with white skin, came onto the broad prairie. The quiet tread of the moccasined foot and the silent bow of the Indian were joined by the hobnailed boot and thunderous rifle of the white man. The mountains were given the name Rocky Mountains and the prairie was called The Great Plains.

The two clans of man became enemies and fought savage battles in the mountains and on the prairie. The victor slew the vanquished without mercy.

This story takes place during that time of bitter struggle between the two clans of man.

One

The three white trappers and the young Arapaho woman forced their gaunt, long-legged mounts through the deep snow choking the bottom of the narrow mountain valley. The trappers led four packhorses heavily loaded with furs. Dark, heavy clouds scudded past close overhead on the back of the stiff, cold wind. The clouds flung hard, flinty crystals of ice down on the men and the Indian woman.

Jacob Morgan and Glen Kinshaw rode in front, each leading a packhorse. Renne Chabot came next with the two remaining packhorses. The Arapaho woman trailed in the rear. Her face was strained with worry, for she knew what the men planned to do to her.

Each trapper held his Sharps .52-caliber carbine ready across the saddle in front of him. Their eyes moved constantly, warily scouring the pine forest on the mountainsides above them and the brush thickets bordering the frozen, silent creek. They wore long wolfskin coats, unbuttoned so they could quickly reach their Colt revolvers, and buckskin shirts and breeches. Elk-hide moccasins clad their feet. Brimmed hats crowned their heads and held their long hair out of their faces. Their beards were winter-long, and their skin was weatherburnt to a dark brown. Jacob was the youngest, lean and blond. At nineteen years, he was less than half the age of the other two men.

The Arapaho girl was dressed in a long buckskin dress, and a wolfskin coat with a hood that was pulled up over her dark head. Her age was two years less than Jacob's. She appeared even younger, with a childlike, innocent face. Her large black eyes steadily watched Jacob's back.

Jacob turtled his head deeper into the collar of his coat, for the wind and ice crystals had teeth. It was a mean time to travel, but without a doubt wise. He scanned the forest on the mountainsides, at least what he could see of it. The clouds, sweeping past only a couple hundred feet above his head, hid all of the towering peaks of the Bighorn Mountains, and capped the stark, snow-filled valley with dark gray.

He caught movement in the forest ahead. Four ravens, seeking shelter in the brushy crown of a large pine, had taken alarm at the approach of the trappers. The black gang, cawing loudly to each other and with wings pumping powerfully, had launched themselves from their perch. They kited away riding the turbulence of the invisible river of air.

Jacob saw tracks in the snow where a band of six elk had come down into the valley and crossed to climb into the timber on the opposite side. The big pad marks of a pack of wolves were on top of the elks's tracks. The savage hunters were hungry.

He turned to Glen. "This'd be a bad place for us if the Crows jumped us," he said.

"They could sure bottle us up in here," Glen replied. "But I think we've left early enough that we'll catch the braves still wrapped in their blankets with their squaws and not out looking for trappers to rob."

"They probably won't bother us up high here in the

deep snow, but down below things could be different," Jacob said.

He twisted in the saddle to check Renne's progress. The man acknowledged Jacob's look with a lift of his hand. Jacob looked at the Arapaho girl, Moon Mist. She smiled wistfully at him.

Glen spoke again. "If it wasn't for the Crows being so damn ornery, all this country would've been trapped out by white men long before now."

"We found virgin fur country all right," Jacob said.

He looked ahead down the snowy valley. The creek was a tributary to the Powder River and ran east to join with it. Indians camped on the lower Powder during the cold winter months. In the early spring, the warriors became restless after being snowbound for weeks and set out looking for trouble, for white trappers to kill and rob.

The trappers and Moon Mist rode downward through the day with the flanks of the mountain gradually pulling back and the valley widening. The snow on the ground grew ever thinner until five thousand feet lower in elevation, it finally fell away behind the travelers. When the day grew old, the valley ended and a broad prairie stretched before them as far as the eye could see. The snow had turned to a cold rain that fell without sound on the gray, dead grass of winter.

Glen reined his mount in and Jacob and Renne halted their horses beside him. Moon Mist stopped several yards behind, for she knew what was about to happen and was reluctant to come close.

"The country's open from here on," Glen said. "Time we stretched these horses out and covered ground."

All three men twisted in their saddles and looked at

Moon Mist. Her eyes locked on Jacob's, holding him
with a pleading expression.

"Get on your way, girl," Glen said and pointed to the
south. "Your people are in that direction about five suns
riding."

Moon Mist sat her mustang and moved not at all. She
continued to stare through the rain at Jacob.

"Did you hear me, girl?" Glen's voice had an edge
on it. "Stop watching Jacob and answer me."

"Don't be too rough on her," Jacob told Glen. He
spoke to the girl. "Can you find your way home, Moon
Mist?" He saw the sorrow at her leaving in her face. He
felt a tinge of regret himself. But she was Glen's woman.

Though Glen had not shared her with him, or Renne
for that matter, her presence, her girl's voice, and her
woman's laughter had made the long, snowy winter the
most pleasant of any he had spent in the mountains.

In the fall of the year just past, the three trappers
had journeyed to the Bighorn Mountains along a route
through Cheyenne country lying to the south. At a
Cheyenne village on the Sweetwater River, Glen had
traded a spare pistol he had for Moon Mist, a girl the
Cheyenne had taken captive in a raid on the Arapaho.
She had wanted to go with the trappers and escape the
cruel slavery the Cheyenne had forced upon her. She
had promised to do anything Glen wanted of her. In
the long black nights in the cabin, and little more than
an arm's length away from him, Jacob had heard her
carrying out her promise to Glen.

The group now numbering four had continued warily
on into the land of the fierce Crow Indians, built a cabin
in a hidden valley in the Bighorns, and trapped furs all
winter. Tending the traplines required two men, one
working up the valley removing the animals caught and
rebaiting the traps, and one performing the same chore
downstream. Running the traplines rotated among the

men. The third man remained at the cabin with the Indian girl.

Moon Mist kicked her mustang forward and brought it up close to Jacob. She reached out and caressed his bearded cheeks. "Take me with you, please. I will be no trouble to you. When you go into the white men's village, I will stay out on the prairie and wait. You can come back to me when you are ready. No matter how long, I will wait for you."

"Don't listen to her," Glen said. "You don't need a permanent Indian squaw." He knew the girl had fallen in love with Jacob. However, he was certain Jacob had not touched her when they were alone in the cabin together. Youth was calling to youth, and he was a dashing young fellow.

"That's right," Renne added. "You couldn't ever forget she slept with Glen. And we don't know how many Indian bucks she laid with back there with the Cheyenne."

Jacob caught Moon Mist's hand and gently removed it from his face. During his few young years his experience had brought him to the conclusion that one woman was very much like any other. None had held him for long. He knew he did not want a woman tagging along after him. "Go home. We will give you a rifle with plenty of shot. That is something the people of your village can use, so they'll be glad to see you return. You are pretty and with a valuable rifle to give, you can find a husband."

Moon Mist jerked her hand free of Jacob's grasp. Her eyes narrowed and took on a hard sheen. "Give me the rifle," she said sharply.

"Can you find your way back?"

"What do you care?"

"I do care." He thought he understood her feelings. She had wanted to escape from the Cheyenne and had come with the trappers willingly, knowing full well what

Glen expected of her. In fact she probably thought that all of them would make demands on her. But now, months later, Glen was sending her packing and she did not want to leave. Actually, she did not want to leave Jacob. He felt some guilt at that; maybe he shouldn't have been so kind to her. "I want you to make your way safely back to your people without the Cheyenne catching you again."

"Give me the rifle," Moon Mist said sharply.

"All right." Jacob stepped down to the ground and extracted the spare Sharps from the pack on one of the packhorses. He handed the rifle to the Arapaho girl.

The instant Moon Mist's hand closed on the rifle, she cocked the hammer and swung the barrel to point at the center of Jacob's chest. She squeezed the trigger.

Two

Jacob saw the rifle's hammer fall and heard the metallic snap it made striking the unprimed iron nipple. He jerked back by reflex, and knocked the barrel aside, knowing even as he did so that there was no danger in the weapon. If there had been a cap on the nipple, he would be dead now, dead by Moon Mist's hands.

He looked up into the girl's angry eyes, and studied her for several seconds. "Travel safely," he finally told her.

He jumped astride his gray horse, reined it to the east, and raised it to a trot. He glanced back once at Moon Mist and saw her sitting dejectedly on her mustang in the falling rain. Then the Arapaho girl shook herself, as if coming out of a trance. Her head came up, and looking straight ahead into the wetness, she rode south.

"You did right," Glen said from where he rode his horse beside Jacob.

"Now let's get our prime pelts to St. Joe," Renne said. "And hope to hell we can do it without having to fight our way clean across Crow country." He raised his head and shouted out full-mouthed and happily across the plain. "St. Joe, here we come."

"Do you want Indians to hear you?" Glen asked with a grin.

"There's no one around for miles," Renne replied

and swept his arm across the empty prairie. He struck his horse with his whip and the animal broke into a ground-devouring gallop.

Glen and Jacob raised their mounts to match that of Renne's horse.

Jacob pushed away thoughts of the Arapaho girl and concentrated on the danger that lay ahead. He knew the horses were not strong. They had not been ridden since the first heavy snowfall of the past November, when the men had switched to snowshoes. Worse still, the deep winter snows had hidden much of the mountain grasses from the horses. Though the men had chopped down cottonwoods and willows so the horses could eat the bark and smaller limbs, the bones of the animals showed painfully through their skins. They would have little stamina in any race. Still, the willing horses ran at their masters' commands, their legs swinging, devouring the miles.

Jacob kept his eyes moving, searching for enemies. The danger of being discovered by the Crows was much greater here on the plains where a horseman could be seen for a very long distance. Still, the land was big and trappers could sometimes cross it without seeing an Indian.

As they hurried east, they saw several small herds of buffalo. The dark, shaggy animals stood motionless, like fields of boulders washed by the rain. They barely lifted their heads to watch the horsemen ride past.

The rain stopped as the day wore down. Jacob was glad for that. Perhaps they could find some dry wood and have an evening fire.

"Indians!" Renne called sharply from his position on the right, and thrust his arm out to the southwest.

Jacob snapped a look to the right past his comrades and in the direction Renne pointed. Horsemen, miniaturized by distance, tiny men on tiny horses, had come up from some low area and onto the skyline. Even as he watched, the horsemen broke into a run directly for the trappers.

Renne called again. "There's too many of them for us to fight, and we'll never outrun them with the pack-horses."

"Couldn't even without them," Jacob said, his pulse quickening with dread. Soon there would be a battle and they were dangerously outnumbered.

"But we've got to give them a damn good run and hope we find a place to fort up," Glen said.

Renne took another turn of the packhorses' lead rope around the pommel of his saddle. "I'm ready. Let's make tracks."

"You take all the packhorses," Glen directed Renne and handed him his lead rope. "Jacob, tie yours to mine. Hurry!"

Jacob swiftly fastened his tow rope to one of the straps that held the packs on Glen's packhorse. He let the rope long so that the animal could run behind Glen's.

"Ready," Jacob said.

Glen spoke quickly to Renne. "Jacob and me'll hold behind. If the Crows get too close, we'll see if we can slow them down. Now ride man, ride for your hair."

Renne did not question the plan, for he knew Glen and Jacob were better marksmen than he was. He raised his whip and lashed his mount. The stung animal bolted, dragging the packhorses on taut ropes.

Jacob slapped his gray horse smartly on the neck. In two strides, the big horse was in a run on the heels of the packhorses. Glen reined his mount into station beside him.

The trappers ran their horses across the gray plain and into the growing dusk of evening. Now and again, Glen or Jacob darted forward and laid their whip on the rump of one or another of the packhorses that was lagging and slowing the group.

Jacob often looked to the rear, watching the Indians as they steadily closed the gap separating the two bands of men. He clearly counted fifteen warriors. He could see their arms rising and falling as they whipped their mustangs onward.

The Crow warriors began to cry out, their voices rising shrill and eager, and as threatening as that of a pack of hunting wolves that sensed their quarry weakening.

"Trees ahead," Renne cried out over his shoulder.

Jacob heard Renne's shout over the thundering pound of the horses' hooves. He stared hard to the front and could make out two objects rising above the horizon. They were darker than the gray grass of the prairie and could indeed be small groves of trees.

He checked the Crows again. They were now only three hundred yards behind. He doubted there was time to reach the trees before the warriors would be within gun range.

His nerves tightened and began to strum. This would be a fight to the death, no quarter given or received. But for the next couple of minutes he rode with his friends, and they and he were still alive. He savored the cut of the cold wind on his face. He focused on the sensation of riding, the knotting and stretching of the gray's muscles between his legs. He listened more keenly to the suck and blow of the horse's deep lungs. *Run, you big brute. Run until your heart bursts.*

Jacob turned toward Glen riding beside him and found the man looking at him. They had ridden thousands of miles together, and had fought through many battles. They grinned at each other with grim humor, simultaneously, as if each read the other's thoughts. The terror of death was lessened when a comrade faced it with you.

Glen watched his young friend. His blond looks made him appear younger than his age. That appearance was greatly misleading, for Jacob had a streak of pure, hard metal in him and was a fierce fighter. Then Glen nodded.

At the signal, both pulled their Sharps from their scabbards and looked to the rear to measure the gun range to the Crow warriors.

Muskets began to boom out from the band of Indians. A bullet tugged at Jacob's coat. Another whizzed by close to his face. He tensed, waiting for one of the hurtling lead balls to hit him.

The guns of the braves fell silent and Jacob knew they had emptied their single shot weapons. He flung a look at Glen and Renne. Both seemed unhurt. The Indians had fired before they were close enough to strike a target from the back of a running horse. He felt relief that neither his friends nor he had been hit.

"The trees! The trees!" Renne cried out. "We're going to make it!" He pounded on, lashing his horse toward the nearer and larger grove of trees.

As the racing trappers drew closer, the grove of trees broke apart, becoming thirty or so huge, leafless cottonwoods growing in a shallow swale. Renne drove his horses straight in among the cottonwoods. Jacob and Glen plunged in beside Renne and jerked their animals to a sliding halt. All three men swiftly sprang down to the ground with their rifles in their hands. They jumped behind the thick trunks of trees for protection.

The Crows pulled their mustangs to a stop two hundred yards from the trappers and began to fire in among the cottonwoods. Jacob heard bullets tearing past with a whirring sound. One hit a tree trunk near Jacob, peeled bark, and ricocheted away with the snarl of a small deadly animal. Jacob swiftly raised his rifle. He caught one of the warriors in the sights of the weapon and squeezed the trigger. The gun crashed and bucked against his shoulder.

The Crow tumbled from the back of his mustang and hit the ground, all slack-muscled and hard hit. Glen's rifle cracked an instant after Jacob's. A second warrior was hit. He dropped his rifle and slumped forward across his mount. He gripped the neck of the animal to keep from falling to the ground.

"My turn," Renne said. He stepped out from behind his tree and raised his weapon.

Jacob saw one of the Indians fire his gun. An instant later, he heard the crush of a lead ball hitting flesh and bone, and a guttural gasp of pain. He whirled to see who was hit.

He saw Renne drop his rifle and clutch his chest. He had a surprised, disbelieving expression on his face. He fell backward to the ground.

Jacob jumped to Renne and knelt beside him. Renne's face was twisted with pain as he stared up at Jacob. He tried to speak, his lips moving, but no sound came. He felt his strength draining out the bullet hole with his blood, draining so fast that in a few seconds he couldn't see Jacob's face. Renne's eyes went blank and his head rolled to the side.

Glen threw a look at the Indians to see if they were going to charge now that they had downed one of the trappers. He saw they were whirling their mustangs to ride out of rifle range. He hurried up beside Jacob and squatted beside him.

"We're safe for the moment." Glen said. "The Indians are pulling back. How bad is Renne hit?"

"We'll soon find out," Jacob said as he swiftly worked on the buttons of Renne's clothing.

He finished unbuttoning Renne's coat and shirt and pulled them open. The bullet had hit the man in the left side of the chest. Blood oozed steadily from the round, deep hole. A vicious wound. Jacob turned the unconscious man to look for a wound in his back where the bullet would have torn through. There was no exit wound. Jacob laid Renne on his back again.

"God! I don't know how he's still alive," Jacob said. "The bullet's still in him and must be right next to his heart."

"That'll make it dangerous to get out?" Glen said.

"I don't think we can," Jacob said in anguish. "I'm sure I don't want to dig for it. I'd kill him for sure."

"Goddamn thievin' Crows," Glen cursed. "They'd kill a man for a few furs."

Jacob cut the tail off Renne's shirt, folded it into a pad, and bound it over the wound. He buttoned the shirt and the coat around the injured man.

"We've got to keep him warm," Glen said.

He moved to the packhorses and dug Renne's buffalo sleeping robe from his pack. Then he and Jacob gently placed the injured man in the thick, soft hide, and pulled it snugly around him to keep out the cold.

Glen and Jacob straightened from their task and looked out across the prairie at the Crows sitting their mustangs out of rifle range. They were gesturing and talking among themselves.

"One of them is a damn good shot," Jacob said. "And that sounded like a Sharps rifle. Not many Indians got Sharps."

Glen spoke. "We're in a hell of a fix. Renne's bad hit and maybe dying, and the Indians got us penned down with no way out."

Three

The black night crept in under the overcast sky, and darkness, so dense that a man could catch a handful, congealed around Jacob. The cold north wind sounded a dirge, cut by the bare limbs of the cottonwoods. In the center of the grove of trees, the trappers' horses stood silent and unmoving, too weary to graze.

Jacob sat in the darkness beside Renne and looked across the three hundred yards of prairie to the grove of trees where the Crow warriors had made camp. The Indians felt sure they had the trappers caged and had built a leaping fire that threw a yellowish red light upon the boles of the cottonwoods. Now and again, Jacob could see one or another of the warriors moving in the firelight.

The Crows weren't taking any chances on the trappers escaping. Just as night fell, they had stationed three warriors at strategic locations around the grove of trees the trappers were using for protection. The remainder of the Crows had withdrawn to the trees to the north. Jacob knew that now with darkness shrouding the prairie, the lookouts would have stolen in close, lying in the grass just beyond the view of the trappers. They would be watching for movement against the faint light of the night sky and listening with keen ears for the sound of the trappers moving. Jacob knew the Crows did not like to fight in the dark, and perhaps these warriors would follow that custom . . . but come sunrise they would mount an attack.

Beside Jacob, Renne's shallow breathing stopped. Jacob turned quickly to look at his injured comrade. He could see only the outline of the man on the ground. He hastily knelt and whispered into Renne's ear. "Breathe, Renne! Breathe, damn you, and live! You promised me that we'd go to California to grow grapes and start a winery."

As if in answer to Jacob's command, Renne began to breathe again, but ragged and feeble. Jacob sat back on his haunches. How could the man live with such a terrible wound? Jacob wondered. Surely not for long. Something must be done, and soon. He looked through the grove of trees in the direction where he knew Glen was hunkered down watching the black prairie.

Glen and Renne were Jacob's only family. He thought of them as favorite uncles, or older brothers. He had acquired them in a strange manner five years before in New Orleans.

Jacob had been born in Cincinnati, Ohio. His mother died when he was thirteen. Her death had greatly saddened him. The effect on Oscar, his father, had been devastating. Oscar had always liked his whiskey; now he began to drink more and more.

As the months passed, Oscar became undependable at his trade of bricklayer, going on drinking binges and not working for days on end. The time came when he could not find anyone to employ him as a mason.

Oscar found a job firing the boilers of a steamboat that transported live hogs from Cincinnati downriver to New Orleans. The two top decks of an old and once grand steamboat had been cut away and converted, except for the wheelhouse, into one huge railed deck. The "pigboat" was crowded stem to stern with grunting, squealing hogs. Their shit was so rank that it burned Jacob's nose. The slop of shit and urine leaked through the deck to the boiler room below, and there in the heat from the boilers, stank even worse.

A "pigboat" was the lowest, the meanest of all the boats on the river. The noisy, stinking vessel could be heard and smelled for long distances. The other riverboat men laughed and shouted insults when they passed. The men who shoveled coal in the boiler rooms of the pigboats were considered the lowest of all workmen.

Oscar's drinking became even heavier. Oftentimes he would fall down dead drunk in the boiler room. Jacob would drag him out of the way and take up the shovel and keep the flames leaping in the fire pit beneath the boiler.

Several times a day, the captain would come down to the boiler room and check the temperature gauge on the boiler. He would look at young Jacob, ignoring Oscar drunk or sober, and point at the marker he had put on the gauge. He always growled the same words, "Keep the temperature right there boy, or I'll kick your ass and your old man's ass into the river."

Jacob would stare out from his face black with coal dust, grip his shovel, and say nothing. He wanted to swing the shovel and smash the hard face of the captain, his drunken father, and the goddamned temperature gauge. But he held himself in. The moment the captain left, Jacob would spring into the coal bunker, grab up the sledgehammer and pulverize the lumps of coal until the sweat streamed down his body and exhaustion cooled his hot anger.

By the time Jacob was fifteen, he had made many trips down the Ohio and Mississippi to New Orleans. His growing body was corded with muscle. His hands were as hard as the lumps of coal he shoveled. The women in the river towns had begun to take notice of his fair good looks.

One night while the pigboat was under way, Oscar fought his way up from a drunken stupor on the floor of the boiler room. He stumbled to the ladder and climbed to the upper deck. Jacob never saw him again. He knew the river had taken his father. When the steamboat docked at New Orleans two days later, he rolled his scant belongings into a bundle and escaped.

Evening arrived as he drifted through the growing shadows up from the waterfront and into the Vieux Carre, the old French Quarter of New Orleans. On Decatur Street, he turned and walked leisurely toward a restaurant he knew of that served good food at a reasonable price. He had enough money to last him for a few days. Before it was all spent, he had to find a job.

Half a block ahead of Jacob, a brown-headed girl of twelve or thirteen came out of a dress shop and crossed the street. She continued on in the same direction he traveled. She walked with an easy, free, swinging stride that Jacob found enjoyable to watch. He quickened his pace to get closer. Not that she would talk with a boy off a pigboat.

Further along the street, three young men of Jacob's age were loafing, leaning against the front of a building. As the girl approached the young men, they began to ogle her, and talk and laugh among themselves. When she was almost abreast of the fellows, they spread out across the sidewalk to block her path.

The girl slowed cautiously, watching the boys, then hastened her steps to go between two of them. Before she could pass through, the larger fellow caught her by the arm and stopped her. He said something to the girl. She shook her head vehemently and tried to pull free. But the fellow held her and shifted his hands to her shoulders, pressing her against the wall of the building.

Jacob increased his pace as he recognized the members of the River Rats Gang. Twice before when his boat had docked in New Orleans, he'd had trouble with the waterfront toughs. There was no use trying to talk with them; he had tried that and in the end still had to fight his way clear.

Jacob was close enough now to see the gang member's hands fondling the budding breasts of the girl, and to see her white, frightened face. He dropped his bundle on the sidewalk and leaped the last few feet, driving past the two Rats watching the girl, and straight at the one holding her.

He caught the Rat by the hair on the top of his head and yanked savagely backward. Instantly he crashed his hard right fist into the temple of the Rat, snapping his head to the side. He swung again, landing a hard blow to the Rat's face. The Rat's hands came loose from the girl.

"Run, girl! Run!" Jacob shouted.

She stood for a brief moment looking at Jacob, her large brown eyes staring into his gray ones. Then she sprang away from the wall and sprinted off along the street.

Jacob released his hold on the stunned Rat and let him fall to the sidewalk. He pivoted to face the other two Rats—just as they pounced on him.

Jacob knocked the closer gang member flat with a hard wallop to the chin. Then immediately he backed into a doorway of the building where only one opponent could get to him at a time. Three Rats against him were bad odds, but still Jacob's heart beat nicely at what he had done to help the girl. When her eyes had touched his, it had felt like a kiss.

The two Rats Jacob had knocked down regained their feet. They joined with the third and advanced on Jacob, with the Rat who had not yet felt Jacob's fist in the forefront.

Jacob exchanged blows with the fellow, giving more blows, and harder ones, than he received. Then the three pulled knives and he knew things were going to get ugly and bloody.

Before the River Rats could use their knives on Jacob, Glen and Renne came into the street a short distance away. They stopped and stood silently eyeing the situation. The River Rats halted their advance upon Jacob and watched the two trappers armed with pistols and knives.

One of the trappers, whom Jacob learned later was Glen Kinshaw, had called out, "Do you need some help, young fellow? A pretty girl said you did."

"Just take their knives away from them and then I can handle the rest," Jacob had replied.

Glen had laughed at Jacob's brave words and pulled his long-bladed skinning knife. He stepped toward the River Rats and made a round-house sweep through the air in their direction with his knife. "Run, you river bastards, before I cut off your little dicks and make you eat them."

The River Rats ran.

After that Jacob had just naturally tagged along with Glen and Renne. He had hoped to see the girl again, but never had that kind of luck. When the trappers were ready to go back upriver to prepare for the coming winter's fur trapping in the Rocky Mountains, Jacob joined them. In St. Joseph, they helped him buy a horse, a young gray stallion. He immediately named it Jubal, and it was the horse he rode today.

Jacob had never regretted joining with Glen and Renne. He recalled that he had earned only one-quarter share that first winter trapping pelts. He had learned from those rowdy, experienced men how to set a trap, skin an animal, to track and shoot with the best of men. Coming down from the mountains in the spring of that first year, the group had been attacked by Blackfoot Indians. Jacob had killed two men that day and grew from boy to man. There had been more battles during the next three years, and Jacob had brought death to other men.

Glen was from Tennessee. He was the oldest, nearly half a century, and there were streaks of gray in his hair. But he was strong and tough. He had first gone into the mountains in 1840, when beaver was still king of furs. He often spoke of those grand days of the mountain man rendezvous, when the fur buyers—bringing everything a man needed, from lead and powder to sugar and women—came to the trappers on the great plains.

Renne was a Frenchman from Canada. He had migrated down to the States several years before. He would not give his reason for leaving Canada. He was tall and wiry. At times he would go for days his face gloomy and never say a word. However, he was the best trapper of the three, knowing exactly where and how to set the traps to catch the wily mink, martin, and fox.

Glen and Renne were men you could steal horses with, men who would bravely fight to the death beside Jacob.

He rose to his feet and moved through the darkness among the trees toward Glen. As he passed the horses, one of the packhorses whimpered with weariness, complaining to Jacob for running it so hard.

Jacob ignored the complaint and went on. He called out ahead in a low voice, "It's me, Glen." He didn't want to come up unexpectedly on the man, for he was damn quick with a knife and gun.

"Trouble over on your side?" Glen asked.

"No. I want to talk."

"About Renne?"

"We've got to do something. If we don't, he's going to die."

"I'm damned worried about him, too."

"There's an army surgeon at Fort Laramie. He must have had a lot of practice tending gunshot wounds and could take the bullet out of Renne. If we can get him there alive."

"That's a hundred-and-fifty miles from here."

"We could make it to the fort in three days, or even less if we didn't stop. I saw some young cottonwoods that'd be the right size for making a travois that we could haul Renne on." A hazardous idea like an excited bee was careening about in Jacob's head.

"We'd need stronger horses than we got. That'd have to be some of the Crows' mustangs."

"That's exactly what I've been thinking. All we got to do is kill the Crows first."

Glen stared through the darkness at Jacob. His young comrade made an excellent friend. But he was brave, brave to the point of being dangerous to himself. Still, Glen had been considering the same action so maybe it wasn't such a bad plan after all.

"There's fourteen of them against the two of us," Glen said. "However, one of them might be bad wounded."

"Three are watching us. And I think you hit that Indian you shot damn hard, so that leaves only ten against us at first. That's just five for each of us to kill. We'll take care of the others when they come running to help."

Glen laughed low in his chest. Jacob made it seem so damn easy, as if the Crows weren't mean fighters. Glen turned and studied the distant camp of the Indians.

"They won't think two men would be stupid enough to attack ten," Glen said. He looked up into the dark sky. "And the night's black as tar."

"We'll crawl up close," Jacob said. "Then just stand up and walk straight at them. It'll take them a few seconds to figure out we're not two of the guards coming into camp."

"We'll shoot them all to hell," Glen said. "You take Renne's pistol along with yours. I'll take my rifle and pistol. If we shoot fast enough, and don't miss too much, we might get it done and not get shot up too bad ourselves."

"Glen, I don't plan on missing. I'm going to be right in their faces before I start shooting."

Four

Jacob and Glen stopped worming their way through the dead prairie grass. Slowly they raised their heads and surveyed the camp of the Crows. They had removed their brimmed white men's hats, which would have been a dead giveaway, and now wore bands of buckskin tied around their heads. In addition, Jacob had pulled his long yellow hair back and tied it behind his head. There was nothing they could do about their white men's beards.

Two hours had elapsed since the two men had crawled out of the grove of trees and inched their way over the prairie. Fortunately no Crow lookout had been encountered. Now they were less than a hundred feet from the enemy.

Jacob began to count the warriors sitting in the flickering light of the campfire. The Indians were silent, their faces hanging like masks. Some were cleaning their rifles, others stared with black eyes into the flames. One lay wrapped in a sleeping robe. He would be the man Glen had wounded, Jacob judged.

"I count eleven," Jacob whispered.

"Those guns being cleaned won't be loaded," Glen whispered back. "Shoot those fellows last."

"I know that," Jacob whispered tersely.

"Keep your pistols out of sight. I don't expect the Crows have any and they'd make them suspicious."

"Right."

"Are you ready?"

"Let's get on with it."

Glen climbed to his feet and walked slowly and deliberately toward the camp of the Crows. He carried his rifle at the trail in his right hand.

Jacob walked beside Glen. He held his two cocked pistols along his legs and slightly behind, out of sight. He felt the tension in every muscle. His heart pounded against his ribs. Two men against ten, maybe eleven, was sure as hell tempting fate. One piece of bad luck, a gun to jam or misfire, or the Indians reacting too swiftly, could be Glen's and his death.

The two trappers closed the distance to seventy-five feet. Seventy feet. One of the Crow warriors picked up a piece of wood and tossed it onto the fire. As he straightened, he looked across the flames and into the night.

The warrior stared intently at the men coming out of the darkness. He saw the heavily bearded faces. One beard was almost yellow. The white trappers! He sprang to his feet and opened his mouth to cry out a warning to the other Crows.

Glen saw the expression on the Indian's face. He jerked up his rifle and fired. The lead ball plowed into the Indian's chest, burst the throbbing heart, and exploded out his back. The .52-caliber bullet slammed the man backward to the ground. Glen swiftly switched the empty rifle to his left hand and pulled his pistol.

The crash of the rifle and the fall of the warrior brought every Crow, except the wounded man, to his feet and grabbing for his weapon.

Jacob jerked up his right-hand pistol and shot a brave snatching up a rifle. He brought up his left-hand pistol and killed a man reaching for a bow. He knew with certainty, as only a truly skilled marksman can know, that his pistol balls had gone true to their intended marks.

Jacob cocked both pistols as he continued to advance. Strangely, the sound of gunfire and the startled cries of the Crow braves faded away, becoming distant and muted. Every second of time expanded, lengthened. The movement of the enemy seemed to be in slow motion. He pointed his right-hand pistol at the chest of a big warrior who had jumped to his feet and was raising a trade musket to his shoulder. Jacob fired. The man dropped his musket and fell.

Jacob and Glen were now well inside the ring of firelight. The range to shoot was but a few short steps. Still they moved closer, their revolvers exploding. More men staggered under the strike of bullets and fell in crumpled forms on the ground.

Jacob halted with the fire at his feet. He brought a pistol to bear on the Crow just beyond the fire, the only enemy still on his feet.

The man had been one of those who had been cleaning his rifle. He was swiftly reloading. In the few seconds since the battle had begun, he had poured powder down the barrel and rammed a ball down on the powder with a rod. Now he held a cap between his fingers and was ready to press it onto the nipple.

The warrior looked across the fire at Jacob and saw the pistol leveled straight at his heart. He raised his eyes to Jacob's, and studied their deadly sheen. His lips pulled back showing his teeth, and a mocking expression of contempt came over his face. He dropped his partially loaded rifle to the ground and spread his arms to expose his chest.

Jacob hesitated pulling the trigger. Not one of the Crow warriors had tried to run. Brave men, every one.

"So be it," Jacob said. He shot the warrior directly

through the heart. Brave men should be killed quickly. Just as he would have wanted to die.

Glen moved to the warrior he had wounded earlier in the day. The man had crawled partway out of his sleeping robe and lay with his hand almost touching his rifle, but too weak to reach it. He painfully raised his head and looked up at Glen.

"I'm going to leave you live, for you'll slow down the others," Glen said. "And you don't need that rifle." He kicked the weapon out of the reach of the wounded man.

"We'd better get out of the light," Glen said to Jacob. "The others might come running to help."

"I'll go guard Renne and our furs," Jacob said.

"All right. I'll wait here in the dark for a spell. Might get a shot."

Jacob stole away into the darkness.

An hour passed as Jacob crouched with loaded guns beside Renne and watched the night in all directions. The fire at the Crow camp had died and darkness had closed in to hide all the land. He had expected to hear a shot as one or more of the Crow warriors returned to their camp to investigate the shooting. However, the only sound was the rustle of the grass and the drone of the wind among the trees. And Renne's labored breathing. Jacob waited on, staring into the blackness.

A rifle exploded near the camp of the Crows and ripped a hole in the silence of the night. Jacob knew by the sound of the gun that it was a Sharps. He hoped it was Glen's gun and not that of their enemy.

After a time, two low, short whistles came out of the night's murk. Jacob answered with the same signal. A moment later, he heard a noise on the prairie and the dark outline of a man and three horses appeared. Glen came into the edge of the grove of trees.

"I heard you shoot, so I guess the Crows came?" Jacob said.

"Two men came sneaking up. One of them moved like a white man. But it was damn dark out there. Anyway, I took a shot at the one I thought was white. I think I hit him, but he ran off with the other fellow."

"That could've been the one with the Sharps that wounded Renne."

"Maybe so."

"I see you took some Indian mustangs to help us get to Fort Laramie. If you'll keep watch, I'll chop down those saplings and build that travois for Renne to ride on."

"The noise of chopping might bring the others."

"I'll be watchful."

Jacob dug a short-handled ax from one of the packs and went into the darkness among the trees.

Wolf Voice watched the white man Shattuck, a big man with a long, lank face, bandage the gun wound on his arm by the light of the small fire. He had been with Shattuck when the rifle shot had exploded out of the darkness as they crept up to investigate the battle at the Crow camp. It would have been fitting had Shattuck been killed.

Wolf Voice was angry because the white trappers had escaped with their valuable furs. It was Shattuck's fault, for he had misjudged the trappers' actions and gave bad advice. The trappers had been run to ground and were surrounded by many Crow warriors. Shattuck had told Wolf Voice that the trappers would abandon their furs and packhorses so they would make less noise as they slipped away in the night. Wolf Voice had wanted to believe that, for he knew several of his braves would

be killed in an attack on the well-armed trappers in
their fortified position.

Shattuck looked across the fire at the Crow War
Chief, and the warrior Long Running. They watched
him with black, savage eyes. Shattuck knew the bone-
deep malice the men bore him. "Now look, Wolf Voice,
you can't blame me for what the trappers did," he said.
"How could I know they'd come shooting instead of
running like any sane man would to save his skin?"

"You judge other men by what you would do," Wolf
Voice growled. Still he felt his own guilt at not preparing
his braves for an attack by the trappers.

Shattuck hid his scowl at Wolf Voice's insult in his
long beard. He wanted to pull his pistol and shoot the
heathen bastard. But he needed the Crow chief and his
several other bands of warriors patrolling the prairie
searching for trappers to rob of their furs. In turn Wolf
Voice wanted the trappers and every other white man
permanently out of his land. To drive them out and
keep them out, he needed new modern rifles instead
of bows and arrows and old trade muskets to arm his
braves. Shattuck would provide the guns, and in return
he would get the furs at a small fraction of their value
on the market in New York City.

Wolf Voice turned away from Shattuck with contempt.
He looked at the bodies of his dead followers that Long
Running and he had placed side by side near the mustangs that still remained in their possession. The
wounded Black Feather was unconscious and lay as still
as the dead.

Wolf Voice had unwisely depended too much on the
words of the white man. His braves had died because
of his failing as a chief. There would be much sorrow
in his village when the wives and relatives learned of
the terrible thing that had happened here this night.
It would have been much better had he fought and

died with them, then they all could have gone together
into the next world. But he was still alive and now must
try to atone for his lack of leadership and recapture a
little of his honor. To accomplish that, he would kill
the white trappers. Wolf Voice would also kill Shattuck,
after he had delivered the new rifles.

"Long Running, we will take Black Feather and our
dead comrades back to our village," Wolf Voice said.
"There we can give the dead the proper ceremony to
send them as warriors into the next world."

He faced Shattuck. "Do you know the names of the
trappers?"

Shattuck shook his head. "I never got close enough
to see them plain." A foxy look came into his eyes. "But
I see that you want to even the score with them."

"I want you to follow the trappers and find out who
they are. Meet me at Fort Laramie half a moon from
now and tell me what you have discovered."

"What does it matter who they are? Killing one white
man is the same killing any other."

"Do you really believe that?" asked Wolf Voice. He
cocked his rifle and half raised it toward Shattuck.

Shattuck looked at the gun in the Indian's hand, and
he saw Long Running become suddenly tense and alert,
ready to back his chief's action. "No, there's a difference," he said quickly.

"I'm glad you understand that I must kill those same
men. And that I must know how to find them."

"If I do that, do we still have our agreement?" Shattuck had ridden with the Crow chief to fight in an attack
on trappers to seal the agreement. Now it was in danger
of coming apart.

"Yes."

Shattuck did not want to waste time chasing after the
trappers. However, he knew that he must do what Wolf
Voice asked if he wanted more furs at a dirt cheap, give-

away price. "All right. They'll stop at Fort Laramie. I'll catch up to them there."

"Do it," Wolf Voice said. He motioned at Long Running. "Let us load our comrades on the mustangs and leave."

The two Indians moved toward Black Feather and the corpses. Partway there, Wolf Voice stopped and looked back at the white man. "Go, Shattuck. Discover who the trappers are. But don't kill them. That is for me to do."

The night reluctantly unravelled, giving up its dominion over the valley of the North Platte River. The day crept in and broke over Jacob and Glen staggering with exhaustion along the riverbank. They had traveled for three days with but a few short stops to rest and one for two hours of sleep.

Jacob held the lead rope of the horse that pulled the travois carrying Renne. The wounded man had not once regained consciousness or uttered a word. At the brief halts, Jacob had lifted Renne's head and, careful not to strangle him, poured water down his throat.

Glen led four packhorses, struggling along wobbly-legged under their load of furs, and two saddle horses too weak to carry riders. Three other horses too worn down to travel had been released along the back trail.

Jacob raised his eyes and looked ahead into the growing daylight. Some distance away, a large wooden structure sat on a bluff above the river. He fought to focus the vision of his tired, strained eyes.

"Glen, look," Jacob croaked. "I think I see Fort Laramie."

Glen raised his head and squinted. "I see it too. 'Bout a mile."

Minutes later Jacob and Glen stumbled through the gate set in the log palisade wall of Fort Laramie, the most isolated outpost of the U. S. Army. They moved on across the wide parade ground that dominated the enclosed area of the fort. On the left and backed up against the wall of the fort were the enlisted men's barracks. Flanking that structure were the armory and a blacksmith shop. Set off by itself was a combined store and trading post. Two trappers wearing worn, dirty buckskin sat on the porch of the store and watched Jacob and Glen cross the compound. The officer's quarters were on the opposite side of the fort. Directly ahead of Jacob and Glen on the far side of the compound were the Commandant's Office and the duty officer's room. The infirmary was adjacent to the duty office.

An officer emerged from the duty officer's room. He stopped on the steps and surveyed the two approaching trappers. Jacob and Glen recognized Colonel Granger, Fort Commandant.

"You take Renne straight to the infirmary," Glen said. "I'll see the colonel and talk him into having the surgeon take the bullet out of Renne."

"Right," Jacob replied. He stumbled on with the travois.

Jacob reached the entrance of the infirmary and halted. He leaned against the wall of the building to keep from falling. "Surgeon." Jacob's voice came raspy and weak. He called out more loudly. "Surgeon, we need your help."

The two trappers jumped down off the porch of the store and hurried to Jacob. "Can we do something for you?" one of the men asked.

"Help me carry Renne into the infirmary," Jacob replied.

"You look plumb wore out, so just stand back," said the man who had spoken before. "The two of us is plenty to carry him."

The surgeon appeared in the doorway of the infirmary. He looked at Renne on the travois. "What's wrong with him?" he asked.

"He's got a bullet in his chest," Jacob replied. "He needs help fast."

"Then bring him inside," the surgeon said. He called out impatiently to the men lifting Renne from the travois. "Hurry it up."

Glen and Colonel Granger came up at a fast pace. "Captain, I told Kinshaw that we would treat the wounded man," the colonel said.

"I intend to, sir" said the surgeon. He hastily led the men carrying Renne into the infirmary.

Jacob and Glen sat on the porch of the trading post and leaned exhausted against the wall of the building. They worriedly watched the infirmary. They would not sleep until the surgeon was finished with the operation to remove the bullet from Renne, and they knew whether or not their comrade had survived.

The other trappers had taken seats on the porch near Glen and Jacob. One of them spoke. "Was it Crows that hit you?"

Glen turned weary, bloodshot eyes on the man. He didn't feel like talking, but it was a fair question. "That's right, we were in Crow country. Ran into them just south of the Big Horns."

"How'd you manage to get away with your furs?" asked the second man.

"Jacob thought we should shoot the damn heathens. I thought so, too. And that's just what we did. Walked up on them in the dark and began shooting. Killed twelve of the fifteen."

"Bullshit," said the second man.

"God's truth, but believe it or not just as you want. Makes no never mind to me."

"Me and my partners lost our furs over by the Tetons," said the first man. "A sizable bunch of Crows chased us. They were getting damn close and shot and killed old Jim Boot, and looked like they were going to catch the rest of us. But we cut our packhorses loose with the furs and the Indians stopped and took them."

"Did you mark your furs so that if they show up somewheres you can lay claim to them?" Glen asked.

"Yeah. I marked them with "TB" for Tom Branham, that's me. The mark is on the left rear leg."

"The Tetons and the Big Horns are a long ways apart," Glen said. "Must be more than one Crow party out looking for trappers to rob."

"Crows always have been mean, thievin' Indians," Branham said.

Jacob, still watching the infirmary, saw the surgeon come out of the door and start across the compound. He sat up quickly. "Glen, the surgeon is coming," he said. He tried to read the officer's face. How was Renne?

The surgeon stopped at the edge of the porch and looked at Jacob and Glen. "Here's the bullet. Looks like a .52-caliber." He handed it to Glen, who was nearest.

Glen gripped the bullet tightly in his hand. "How's our partner?" he asked.

"Alive, but just barely."

"Will he live?" Jacob asked, his eyes holding a hopeful expression. God, how he would miss Renne should he die.

"I don't know. It's a bad wound and he's lost a lot of blood. We'll just have to wait and see."

Five

Cora Dubois raced along the wet cobblestone street of the plague-ridden city that was New Orleans. She had raised the long tail of her dress and fastened it under her belt to free her legs for running. The precious bottle of laudanum was gripped tightly in her hand. Her father was very ill with the dreaded yellow fever. She hoped desperately that the laudanum would help him fight off the disease.

She had been gone from her home much longer than she had planned. The druggist had locked his pharmacy and retreated to his home to be with his family during the yellow fever epidemic. Fortunately Cora knew where he lived far out in the Garden District and had hastened there. The druggist had given her a bottle of laudanum from his private stock.

A warm, steady drizzle fell from the dark overcast sky and Cora was soaking wet. Water lay in broad pools covered with a green scum that looked like velvet and stank dreadfully. The slops and garbage of the past days added their fermenting filth, for the slave brigade of street cleaners had not been at their task since the yellow fever epidemic had worsened days ago. Some of the pools completely flooded the street and Cora ran splashing directly through them.

Mosquitoes rose up in black clouds from the foul liquid on the ground as Cora ran past. They swarmed about her and she batted at the blood-sucking pests with her free hand. She squinted her eyes to keep the ugly insects out, and breathed through her nose so she wouldn't swallow any of them.

The streets were mostly deserted. Many people had fled the city, going to towns upriver, Baton Rouge and others that were not bothered with yellow fever. Nearly all those people remaining were hidden away in their homes. The few that were on the street drew back and with worried, fearful faces watched the young woman race past.

Cora turned into the street where she lived with her father and sister, Maude. A funeral procession was coming along the street toward her. Two caskets were in the open-sided hearse. Both were marked with lampblack, as was the custom to show that Bronze John, the name given to yellow fever because of the color it gave to the skin of its victims, had killed again. Cora heard the wailing of the women trailing behind in the rain. The men were mute in their sorrow.

A man riding a sorrel horse came splashing past the funeral procession and halted at the gate to Cora's home. She recognized Carl Thurgood, a friend of her father. He tied his horse to the fence and stood waiting for her.

As Cora drew close, Thurgood shook his head in disapproval. "Cora, you shouldn't be out on the streets alone, for there are thugs, and thieves, and even worse skulking about," he said. He unbuttoned his raincoat to show her a pistol shoved in under his belt. "Even I don't feel safe without this."

"I had to go to the pharmacy for medicine for Father," Cora replied.

"It's closed."

"I know. I had to go to the druggist's house."

"You're lucky you made it safely. I heard about your father being ill. How's he holding up?"

"Not well at all. He had a terrible headache and a bad chill when I left. How bad is the epidemic, Mr. Thurgood?"

"It's very bad. Charity Hospital has thirteen hundred patients. The Marine Hospital has nearly two thousand. Beds of the sick are crammed in every ward, hallway, and storage room. At the Marine Hospital, hundreds of army tents have been set up outside. They are overflowing. People are dying by the hundreds every day."

"What's being done to stop the disease?" Cora cried out. "Why can't the doctors do something."

"They don't know what causes the disease. The mayor called a meeting of the city officials, the doctors at both hospitals, and the Commanding General from Fort Jessup. They have decided to try and drive the disease away with loud noises and smoke. The general will bring all his big guns, two hundred cannon and one hundred howitzers, into the city and begin firing them. A burning tar barrel will be placed at every major street intersection in the city and near the hospitals and sailors' boardinghouses."

"Do you think that will do anything to end the epidemic?"

"I doubt it." Thurgood pulled himself astride the sorrel "Tell your father I wish him a quick recovery from his ailment."

"Thank you, Mr. Thurgood, for coming by. I'll tell Father that you were enquiring about him."

"Goodbye, Cora." Thurgood reined his horse back the way he had come.

Cora hastened across the yard to the front door. She kicked off her dirty shoes and went inside the house and across the parlor to her father's bedroom.

Albert Dubois lay on his bed. He was covered by several blankets and still he was shivering. There was a bronze cast to the skin of his face.

Maude, Cora's sister and ten years older at twenty-six, was seated by the sick man's bed. She was a tall, heavy-boned woman. She got up quickly as Cora came into the room. "What kept you?" she snapped at Cora. "Father's gotten worse and needs the medicine."

Cora looked into Maude's worried, haggard face. "I ran all the way," Cora said. She was not angry at Maude's tone of voice, for she understood her sister's concern about their father. She hastened past Maude to the sick man's side.

"Father, I have the laudanum for you."

Albert opened his eyes and fastened them on Cora. He gripped the blankets with his shaking hands. "I was worried when you were gone so long."

"I'm here now. I'll give you some laudanum and perhaps that will make you feel better."

She pulled the cork from the bottle. She lifted Albert's head and placed the bottle to his lips. "Don't take too much now. Just one swallow."

The glass bottle rattled against Albert's shaking teeth as he dutifully took the laudanum. "Thanks, daughter," he said. He drew the blankets tightly around himself as Cora lowered his head. "Did you learn anything about how bad the epidemic is?"

"Mr. Thurgood was here asking about you. He gave me some news." Cora relayed what Thurgood had told her. She concluded with, "The doctors don't know what causes the disease."

"The doctors are a stupid bunch," Maude said in a harsh tone.

"They tried the cannon and tar barrels in '47 and '53 and I don't think it did one whit of good," Albert said.

"That's probably all they can think of to do," Cora said. "What shall I fix you to eat?" she asked.

"I can't eat anything," Albert replied. He was beginning to shiver more violently. "But give me another swallow of that laudanum. Maybe it will lessen my chill and headache."

Cora jerked awake and sat bolt upright in her bed. The ear-bursting explosion still rang in her ears. She sprang from bed and ran through the house to the front porch.

She hastily looked along the street. In the early dawn light, she saw men in blue uniforms moving around an army cannon stationed at the intersection two blocks distant. Dark gray gunpowder smoke still hung above the big gun. As she watched, one of the artillerymen hurried to the muzzle, dropped a bag of gunpowder in, and began to ram it down the barrel.

She smelled the acrid fumes of something burning. It couldn't be the gunpowder smoke from the cannon, for it was too far away. She looked in the opposite direction. At the far end of the block, a burning tar barrel shot red flames and black, oily smoke into the air.

"Neither the cannon nor the tar barrel will do a bit of good," Maude said, behind Cora.

"Maybe not," Cora said. "But I pray to God that it does."

"We'd better look at Father," Maude said. She hastened inside with Cora close behind.

Albert did not see his daughters come up to his bed. He lay gripping his head, squeezing hard against his skull to equalize the tremendous pressure building within. The echoing bass drum inside his temples was growing louder, the beats jarring and thunderous. Surely his skull was going to explode.

He began to shake uncontrollably, his muscles involuntarily fighting one another in the body's instinctive action to warm itself. The very core of him became frozen, as if his heart was pumping frigid blood. Blackness closed around him.

Cora sprang forward and grabbed her father's thrashing body. She tried to hold him under the blankets and on the bed. But he was a large man and even in his weakened condition, he was too strong for her.

"Maude, help me!" Cora cried.

Maude stepped close, pushed Cora aside, and took hold of her father's shoulders. She pressed him down, pinning him to the bed with her strength and weight. "Please lie still, Father, so I don't hurt you," she pleaded.

Cora moved away from the bed and stood watching. Her sister continued to hold their father, thrashing about in his feverish delirium. He shouted out an undecipherable babble of words.

Maude looked over her shoulder at Cora. There were tears in her eyes, and her face had a lost, helpless expression. "He's dying. The only person in this world who loves me is dying."

"I'm still alive, Maude, and I love you."

Maude stopped shaking her head and stared at Cora, considered her sister's words. After a moment she spoke. "He is the only one who truly loves me, loves me as I am."

"I do love you," Cora said again.

But Maude was turning away and not listening to Cora. She continued to hold her father, looking down with anguish upon her face.

Albert fought against the cold and the terrible drum beat in his head. He struggled to organize his thoughts, for there was something very important he had to say to his daughters. He felt a wet, warm drop of liquid fall upon his lips.

He opened his eyes and stared up with blurred vision.

Maude was leaning over him and holding him by the shoulders. Were those tears in her eyes?

"Please don't cry, Maude," he whispered weakly.

An expression of pure relief and happiness flooded Maude's face. She eased her grip on Albert. "It's wonderful to hear your voice, Father."

Albert struggled to hold onto consciousness. It was nearly impossible to see through the haze that filled the room. "Cora, are you there?"

"I'm here." Cora realized his vision was failing him. "Come close beside Maude."

Cora came forward and stood near Maude. "Yes, Father?"

Albert looked up into the blurred faces above him. He spoke, his voice a faint whisper. "The yellow fever has killed all of our line of Dubois except for us three. Now I think I will die."

Maude burst out with a heart-wrenching sob. Cora began to cry silently.

Albert stared at his daughters. His vision was becoming even worse, but he could see them in his mind's eye. They were so different, so very unalike. Cora was a gentle person, and outstandingly beautiful with fair skin, brown, lustrous hair, and large brown eyes that seemed to smile at you when she spoke. Maude had exactly the same coloring of skin and hair, but God had not been kind to her. She was large and plain and, worse still, had a violent temper if crossed.

"You must leave New Orleans at once, before Bronze John kills you." He rested a moment, gathering his fading strength. "My savings are in the bottom of my trunk, more than four hundred dollars. Take the horse and buggy and go to Baton Rouge, or Saint Louis."

"I'll never leave you," Maude cried.

"She's right," Cora said. "We'll not leave you here sick, and with no one to care for you." She saw her father was holding onto consciousness by only a slender little thread.

"But you must leave before you die too."

"There's no way you can make me go," Maude said vehemently.

Albert now saw only darkness around him. He dredged up the last remnants of his strength. "You must promise me that you will leave after I am dead. And you both must go together to look after each other. Do you promise?"

"We promise," Maude said. "But don't talk like this, for you're not going to die."

You are wrong, thought Albert as the drumbeat grew and the pressure rose inside his skull. A heavy blackness flooded through his mind and wrenched control away from him. He began to thrash wildly in delirium. The last thing he remembered was Maude's strong hands holding him gently and lovingly against her.

Six

"Get out of the hole and let's get him covered," said the gravedigger impatiently. "There's plenty of others that need to be put under."

"Right you are," said the second gravedigger. He had climbed down into the excavation to position the body of Albert Dubois. He grabbed hold of the lip of the grave and heaved himself out.

"This'll be a damn profitable day for us," said the first man as he grabbed his shovel. "Five dollars a grave is a hell of a lot better than the usual two bits."

The second man was embarrassed by the first man's words. He turned to Cora and Maude standing beside the grave. "I'm sorry about your loss, young ladies," he said in a kind voice.

Cora and Maude, sobbing silently, stared down into the grave as the two men began to shovel the raw, wet earth onto their father's blanket wrapped corpse. Albert Dubois had died in the early afternoon of the day. The two young women had dressed the corpse and then tried to find a minister to say a eulogy, and a hearse to transport the body to the cemetery. Neither the man of religion nor a hearse could be found due to the overwhelming number of dead in the city. There would be no dignified funeral that their father deserved. They shrouded his body with a blanket and placed it in the buggy.

They had hastily prepared to leave New Orleans as their father had directed. They dressed in pants and shirts and boots that they wore when going tramping in the woods north of the city. Extra clothing—mostly feminine articles—was packed. Albert's money was found in his trunk as he had informed them. A .36-caliber Colt pistol, a flask of powder, a small bag of lead balls, and a tin of firing caps were also in the trunk. Their father had taught them both to load and shoot. Maude took the weapon, for she was the better marksman. The money, consisting of gold coins and paper bills, was put into Cora's purse.

The sight and sound of the dirt falling upon her beloved father cramped Cora's heart. "Let's hurry away from here," she sobbed. She spun away and climbed into the Phaeton buggy parked nearby.

Maude climbed into the opposite side of the buggy and sat looking at the grave. "I believe this horrible city is damned," she said in a voice filled with anger.

"Father should have left New Orleans a long time ago, before the terrible scourge killed Mother and our two brothers," Cora said.

Maude struck out with the long buggy whip and popped it over the ears of the horse hitched to the buggy. The animal broke into a trot and swiftly crossed the cemetery to the entrance. Maude reined the horse into the street and headed north under a brooding, overcast sky.

Cora turned her eyes away from the long line of people with their vehicles waiting to enter the cemetery with their dead. When she and Maude had arrived with their father's body, they'd waited for hours until their turn came to receive the help of the gravediggers. The number of vehicles now lined up at the gate to the cemetery was even larger.

"Faster, Maude, get us of this hell-hole city of the dead and into the country," Cora cried.

Maude struck again, this time lowering her aim and cutting the horse on the rump with the metal tip fastened to the end of the whip. The horse sprang forward, increasing its pace. With the iron-rimmed wheels of the buggy rattling over the cobblestones, the two women sped away from the cemetery.

On all sides, near and faraway, the thunder of cannon fire rumbled and hammered the frightened city. The very air around the buggy seemed to buck and surge with the concussions. As the buggy passed a tall building, ancient bricks, softened by age and shattered by the explosions of the big guns, rained down with a clatter to the street. The horse was startled by the bricks tumbling across the street and tried to run. But Maude held it with a tight, sawing rein.

Tar barrels burned at many intersections and threw off clouds of acrid smoke that seared the women's lungs. Many of the wooden tar barrels had given way under the charring fingers of fire, spilling the tar to spread in a bubbling, flaming blanket that nearly blocked the street. At times the sisters encountered black swarms of mosquitoes that had fled the smoke zones and congregated in clear areas. The women covered their heads with cloth to ward off the attack of the insects.

In the early night, they came upon a large fire burning in the middle of the street. Pieces of wood, tables, chairs, a door ripped loose from somewhere, and other burnable odds and ends were used as fuel. In the center of the flaming, crackling mass, a human corpse was being consumed. Maude pulled the horse to a halt.

"Don't stop," Cora said, and flung a look about in

all directions. She remembered Thurgood's warning of danger.

Maude reined the horse to the side and guided it up on the sidewalk in front of a hardware store to get past the fire. The horse halted, balking at the leaping flames. She cut it smartly with the whip. The frightened animal whinnied loudly in protest.

"Get on with you!" Maude shouted at the horse, and cut the brute again with the whip.

The horse went fearfully forward into the opening between the fire and building.

The fire was close on Cora's side of the buggy, the flames leaping higher than her head. She shielded the side of her face from the intense heat with her hat. The smell of burning flesh filled her nose, and she shivered. Knowing it was from the burning corpse made her ill.

The buggy passed beyond the fire and Maude turned the horse back off the sidewalk into the street. Before the horse could pick up its trotting pace, two men darted from the black shadows in the mouth of the nearby alley. One grabbed the bridle of the horse and yanked the animal to a halt. The second man leaped close to the buggy and, reaching in, caught hold of Cora by the wrist. A third man ran from the alley on the opposite side of the street and charged at Maude.

"Give me your money," the first man ordered Cora. He squeezed hard on her wrist and twisted. "Where's your purse?"

Cora had been so startled by the sudden and unexpected attack that she had put up no resistance to the man grabbing her arm. But now she let loose with a wild cry and began to struggle to tear loose from the man's grip. Her free hand clawed at his face, and she felt her nails ripping skin and flesh.

"Goddamn you, bitch!" the man cursed, and slapped Cora savagely on the side of the head.

Maude, watching the man running toward her, hastily reached down for the pistol she had stowed away in the satchel at her feet. Frantically she rummaged through the contents, feeling cloth and a shoe. Before she could find the gun, the man had reached the buggy. His hand snaked out to catch hold of her.

Maude snapped up her booted foot and jammed it into the man's cruel face. She thrust out powerfully and sent the man crashing down on his back in the street.

The robber, his face twisted with murderous rage, jumped back to his feet. He snatched a pistol from a holster belted on his side and started to raise it to shoot.

Maude had found her gun and snatched it from the satchel. She felt the buggy rocking from the struggle between Cora and her assailant over the purse containing the money. Maude wanted to help her sister protect the money, but the man with the pistol had to be dealt with first.

She thumbed back the hammer of the pistol as she lifted it. She pointed it into the robber's face not ten feet distant and reflecting a demon-like red cast from the light from the funeral pyre. She fired and the iron weapon jumped in her hand. A round black hole instantly appeared in the man's forehead. He was slammed backward and down on the pavement.

With a feeling of satisfaction, and amazement, at how easy it had been to kill the man, Maude whirled to assist Cora.

The robber holding the head of the horse had seen Maude shoot one of his cohorts. Surprised at the strong, fierce resistance of the women, he quickly drew a pistol and shot at Maude. At the instant the man pressed the trigger of his gun, the frightened horse jerked its head and bumped the man. His shot went wild.

Maude spun toward the sound of the shot. She saw the man and swung the barrel of her weapon, firing back at him. The bullet missed her intended target for she had fired hastily without taking time to aim. The man ducked down behind the horse.

Maude held her pistol aimed at the spot where the man had disappeared. She felt no fear, only a burning desire to kill her enemy. Then the man's head appeared past the shoulder of the horse, and his eyes locked on hers. She shot and did not miss, the bullet catching the man in the center of his face. Again she was amazed at how easily a man could be killed. She wheeled around to the battle beside her.

Cora clung doggedly to the purse. She was determined that the robber would not get the money. In the struggle, he dragged her from the buggy and she fell on her knees on the stone pavement of the street. He continued to pound her with a fist, at the same time trying to wrench the purse from her now two-handed grasp. The blows sent pain rocketing through her head. She didn't know how much longer she could hold on.

"Maude, help me!" Cora cried out desperately.

Cora heard another crack of a pistol. The blows of the fist to her head stopped abruptly. The robber's hold on the purse came loose. He staggered away from Cora. Immediately Maude jumped from the buggy and stood beside Cora.

Cora threw a look at the man who had attacked her. He was holding his side and scampering away. Maude shot again as the man vanished into the shadows of the alley from where he had come.

"Run, you bastard! Run and hide before I blow your brains out," Maude shouted. She laughed in a high, shrill voice.

Cora looked up at her sister. In the light of the flames from the funeral pyre, Maude's face held a strange expression, one Cora had never seen before. The face appeared twisted, distorted as if by a touch of madness.

Then Maude turned her head and Cora could no longer see her face.

Cora rose to her feet. She must have been mistaken about Maude. The expression on her face was from the strain of the battle and the flickering light from the fire.

Maude hugged Cora close against her. "You did well, little sister. They didn't get the money."

"He hurt me bad. He split my lip, and my head aches awfully."

"We made them pay dearly for trying to rob us," Maude said. She turned Cora's face up and examined the bruises. "You're not going to be pretty for a few days," she said.

Cora thought there was a half pleased tone in Maude's voice. But that could not be. She must be mistaken about this, as she had been about the strange expression on Maude's face shortly after the robbers had been killed.

"Get in the buggy," Maude said. "The man wasn't badly hurt and he may get his courage up and come back shooting."

Cora climbed into the buggy. Maude went swiftly to the far side and jumped in. She whipped the horse to a fast pace. They plunged into the darkness beyond the light of the funeral pyre. As the darkness closed around her, Cora began to doubt they would escape alive from the city with its violence and deadly disease.

They came to the end of the paved streets of the central city and plunged on along wet, muddy ways. Several minutes later they reached the edge of the city and entered the countryside. On the top of one of the rare occurrences of high ground on the flat Mississippi delta, Cora caught hold of Maude's arm. "Stop here. I want to take one last look." At some primal level she knew that she would never again see the city where she was born, and her family buried.

Maude pulled the horse to a stop. Both women stood up in the buggy and stared back at the city. The thundering boom of the cannons was much weakened, the nearer ones lying more than a mile away. The flames of the many funeral pyres were dirty red splotches on the blackness of the dismal night. The larger fires, shining against the bottom of the low overcast sky, had turned patches of the clouds red.

"All of our family are dead, mother, father, and brothers," Cora said sadly. "All we have is each other, and a little money. What will we do now, Maude?"

"There's danger everywhere. But we'll make it all right." Maude touched the pistol that she now wore shoved under the belt of her trousers. Oddly she had not been afraid during the gun battle with the robbers. And they had died so easily. She sensed a power in herself that had not existed there before, and she liked it. She would keep this feeling a secret from Cora.

Rain broke loose, pouring down from the dark heavens. The young women hastily raised the canvas top of the buggy and pulled down the side curtains. Maude again took up the reins. The buggy with its two occupants went into the blackness of the rainy night, and towards a distant, unknown destination.

Seven

Dakota Territory, 1859

The trail left by the horses of the Sioux raiders ran straight north across the sun-scorched plains as it had for the past six days.

Lieutenant Steptoe, U S. Cavalry out of Fort Laramie, held his fighting force of twelve dragoons, three Crow scouts, and three mountain trappers at a grueling pace upon the sign of the Sioux war party. They had chased the band of Sioux, containing an estimated twenty warriors, north across the Niobrara River, the White River, and the Cheyenne River. Now the dark silhouettes of the Black Hills reared up on the horizon barely a day's ride ahead.

The Sioux had attacked a small wagon train camped on the North Platte River in the Nebraska Territory. Several immigrants had been killed and most of their horses stolen. A man riding one of the few horses remaining to the people had reached Fort Laramie with the news of the attack two days later. Colonel Granger immediately ordered Lieutenant Steptoe to take a squad of dragoons in pursuit of the Sioux and punish them.

The lieutenant checked the three Crow scouts riding point, Wolf Voice, Little Horse, and Long Running. They were dressed in buckskin breeches and blue army shirts. Strips of blue cloth were tied around their heads to hold their long black hair. The Indian warriors had appeared at Fort Laramie three weeks earlier. Wolf Voice had requested that he and the other two Crows be hired as scouts for the army. Colonel Granger had decided to try the Crow warriors. He had explained to Steptoe and the other officers that having some Crow scouts might lessen the warlike nature of the Crow nation. He replaced their muskets with army carbines and Colt revolvers, and put them on the firing range to practice. They quickly became skilled with the weapons. Wolf Voice could have qualified as an expert marksman, had he been a trooper.

Lt. Steptoe twisted in the saddle and looked to the rear. His troopers in their dust-covered blue uniforms rode two abreast directly behind him. His eyes caught those of Sergeant Hundley. The sergeant came instantly alert, awaiting an order. But the lieutenant looked past him without a change of expression.

The three trappers rode several horse lengths further back to stay clear of the dust kicked up by the troopers. Each trapper was armed with his own .52-caliber Sharps carbine in a scabbard on his saddle, and a Colt revolver and long-bladed skinning knife on his belt. They were garbed in worn buckskin breeches and shirts, and wide-brimmed hats.

Lt. Steptoe, because of the unknown loyalties and abilities of the Crow warriors, was glad the three trappers were riding with him. They had appeared at the fort after a winter's trapping in the Big Horn Mountains. Renne Chabot, near death from a bullet lodged in his chest near his heart, had been transported unconscious on a crude travois by Glen Kinshaw and Jacob Morgan.

Upon the promise of Kinshaw and Morgan to pay for the medical assistance, Colonel Granger ordered the post surgeon to operate on the wounded man. The bul-

let was successfully extracted. However, Chabot hovered
on the verge of death for days. Then he had abruptly
taken a turn for the better and rapidly recovered his
strength.

Jacob Morgan caught Lieutenant Steptoe's eyes upon
him and gave him a surly look. The lieutenant ignored
the trapper because he didn't care a damn for the man's
anger. He recalled how strongly Morgan and Kinshaw
had resisted Colonel Granger's attempt to enlist the
three trappers to help the army against Indian raids.
They'd wanted to pay the army with some of the furs
they had trapped in the mountains. But the colonel had
reminded them that they had promised to pay for the
service of the post surgeon and the use of the hospital,
and that it was his choice how that payment was to be
made. The trappers had argued loudly and heatedly
that they should be the ones setting the method of payment, and further that they had been in the mountains
all winter and should be allowed to ride on to St. Joseph,
Missouri. The colonel would have none of that, and
informed them the payment was a month of service
with troopers in the field. He told the men that they
would have plenty of time to whore, drink, and fight
and still get back to the mountains before the next winter's trapping season began.

Kinshaw had angrily informed the colonel that he
had a woman in St. Joe and she was no whore. Morgan
had cursed and stomped the ground. Chabot had said
not a word, very conscious that he was the root of all
the trouble.

Lt. Steptoe knew Colonel Granger had a second reason for forcing the trappers to ride with his dragoons.
Fort Laramie was dangerously under-manned. Three
proven fighting men were much more valuable than a
few furs. The colonel had been correct, for this was the
second campaign since the trappers had become part

of the army's fighters. Even though the trappers had been damned unhelpful in most things, once the actual combat began they fought like demons.

Jacob watched Lt. Steptoe turn back to the front. Glen and Renne and he should not be riding their horses' hearts out trying to catch the Sioux, but rather should already be in St. Joseph drinking cold beer and making love to pretty women. But they were committed to ride with the lieutenant for only five more days. Then they would hurry east.

Jacob continued to stare at the lieutenant's back. He could not understand why the man would want to be an army officer. How could he endure always being under sworn obligation to follow the orders of another man? And even worse, one whose orders might be completely wrong.

Jacob removed the battered old hat from his head and wiped the sweat from his face with the sleeve of his buckskin shirt. He checked the yellow sun burning its way across the heavens. Beneath the sun, a hunting hawk was soaring on the hot updrafts. It gave a keening cry. Foolish bird, thought Jacob, it must be young or very hungry, for its prey would be hidden away in some cool underground burrow.

He dropped his eyes to the flat plains. The heat-warped air shimmered and danced, distorting vision and distance. Mirages quivered and fumed on the horizon. A band of antelope stood off a ways in one of the mirages and watched the troop of horsemen pass. The heat-distorted air had melted away the legs of the antelope and their bodies floated spirit-like above the ground.

Jacob glanced to the southwest where a storm front of towering thunderheads was advancing swiftly. Rain would be falling before nightfall. Already a thin film of fast-scudding clouds was closing on the sun.

Glen, riding beside Jacob, noted him watching the

approaching storm. "By the size of those thunderheads, they could hold hail as well as rain," he said.

"Could be," Jacob said.

"I wonder what the lieutenant will do when it rains and wipes out the Sioux's tracks?" said Renne.

"Well now, he's a West Point graduate and I suspect they've got a book answer to that," Glen said.

The three laughed and rode on after the horse soldiers.

Jacob and the other men of Steptoe's force of fighters rode hard into the growing evening dusk. Jacob often looked to the southwest and watched the monster thunderheads, soaring five miles, six miles into the sky, advance upon them. One of the mammoth thunderheads was charging directly at the band of men. Already the frontal winds were whipping the grass and stirring the dust around them.

Thin streamers of rain began to leak from the dark bottom of the clouds. Lightning flashed orange and yellow, trapped within the towering cloud mass, lighting it internally with a smoldering, infernal glow.

The lightning broke free of the thunderhead and lashed out to strike the earth. The charge rebuilt quickly to uncontrollable level and slammed down a second time, skittering across the darkening plains.

"Better get our rain gear on," Glen said.

The three men extracted their rain slickers from the tarpaulin-wrapped packs tied behind their saddles and pulled them on.

The storm roared relentlessly closer to the band of men. Then it seemed to jump forward, pouncing upon them. The belly of the cloud split open and the rain poured down, big drops driving hard, slapping their slickers and pounding down the brims of their hats.

The weary horses lowered their heads and humped their backs as the chilling rain fell upon their flanks.

Lightning flared all around, hissing and cracking like a thousand bullwhips. The explosions of thunder deafened the riders, each blast of lightning temporarily blinding them.

Lt. Steptoe's arm came up, signalling a halt, and he shouted for the men to dismount and hold their horses.

Jacob swung down from Jubal and stood leaning against the big horse's shoulder. On the open prairie, there was no protection from the storm. A man and his horse just had to endure the cold, wet onslaught.

Jacob heard Steptoe calling through the rain. A moment later the lieutenant came leading his horse along the line of men. Wolf Voice trailed behind him.

Jacob straightened. He pushed up the wet brim of his hat and joined with Glen and Renne to talk with the lieutenant.

Steptoe stopped near the trappers and peered at them through the deluge. He shouted out above the noise. "What do you think the Sioux will do in this storm?"

"Ask Wolf Voice," Glen called back in a sullen voice. "He's Indian and would know what other Indians would do."

"He's already given me his opinion. Now I want yours."

Jacob was watching Wolf Voice. He saw the anger in the man. The Crow didn't like the lieutenant asking for the trappers' opinion after receiving his. Jacob grinned through the rain at Wolf Voice. The Crow's face became as fierce as the storm.

"We don't have to guess for you," Jacob said. "The Colonel ordered us to ride with you. And that's all he said."

"You're an ungrateful bunch of bastards," Lt. Steptoe shouted. "If it hadn't been for the surgeon at the fort,

Chabot would be dead now." He stabbed a finger at Renne.

Renne felt responsible for the conflict between the lieutenant and his comrades. He didn't want it to grow worse. He spoke to Glen and Jacob. "We got only a few more days to ride with the army. So let's help the lieutenant catch the Sioux. Then we'll ride back to the fort, load our furs, and strike out for St. Joe."

Lt. Steptoe focused on Jacob. "Morgan, which way do you think the Sioux went? Talk to me."

Jacob studied Renne and knew that he didn't want any more arguments with the officer. "All right, Renne," he said and turned to Glen. "What do you say about helping?"

"Go ahead," Glen said. "Tell him what you think."

Jacob spoke to the lieutenant. "First off, we're only half a day behind the Sioux, and they know we're chasing them. You can tell that from the short night camps they make and no fire. There's about twenty of them. Now twenty braves won't stop and fight this many white men. They'd only do that if they outnumbered us two to one, or better, three to one."

Renne's head bobbed in agreement. "Jacob's got it right."

Jacob continued. "Also, I'd guess they've been heading generally in the direction of their village, which should be north of us in the Black Hills. They wouldn't want to go any closer with us trailing them. I think the Sioux will turn and run with the storm."

"I think the same way," Glen said reluctantly. "By staying in the storm as it moves, they can travel fifteen, maybe twenty miles and have their tracks washed out soon as they're made."

"So if we ride all night, we might be close to the Sioux come daylight," Steptoe said.

"Or they could be long gone off in another direction and we'd never come close to them," Glen said.

The lieutenant turned away from the trappers and stared for a few seconds off through the rain. He pivoted back to Jacob. "Wolf Voice said the same as you. And I agree with both of you. We'll ride with the storm. We'll angle a little north across its course since the Sioux are half a day ahead of us."

He spoke to the Crow. "Wolf Voice, take up point."

Wolf Voice did not move. His eyes held a malignant look as he watched Jacob through the rain and growing darkness. "You think you are wise like a Crow," he said.

Jacob tried to read the Indian's real meaning and failed. "Maybe," Jacob said. "And maybe we're both wrong."

"I think soon we will find out," Wolf Voice said. He turned his back and stomped away through the rain.

Lieutenant Steptoe moved off toward his troopers. His voice rose, calling out his orders above the drum of the rain. "Mount up. We're moving out."

The Crow scouts again took up lead position. The troopers formed up and followed. The trappers fell in at the rear.

"I hope we've called it right," Jacob said. "Steptoe made his decision on what we said to him."

"He's the officer and gives the orders," Glen said in a flat tone.

"They should've let us go on to St. Joe," Jacob said.

"Steptoe's got a job I'd not want," Renne said.

"I don't think he trusts the Crows," Jacob said.

"I know that I don't trust Crows," Renne said, and touched his chest.

The band of men rode through the rain with the lightning ripping the sky and the thunder shaking the earth.

Eight

In the small, weary hours of the night, the rain storm outran Lt. Steptoe's band of fighters. It drove away from them to the northeast, its booming thunder weakening to a muted growl and the lightning flashes diminishing to the winks of fireflies. The three-quarter moon low in the west shone down on a drenched land of low, rolling hills covered with tall grass. Newly born rivulets muttered in the shallow valleys between the hills.

Jacob rode with his head turtled down between his shoulder blades and his hands shoved into his armpits. His rain slicker had only partially shielded him from the wind-driven rain and his wet buckskin was cold against his skin.

He looked to the side to see how Renne was holding up. He saw the man shiver.

"You all right?" Jacob asked.

"Yeah, all right," Renne replied. But he felt frail in this time just before dawn, when man's vitality is at its lowest ebb. Worse still, the old wound had come alive and was a dull ache in his chest. He needed a warm sun and rest, and something better to eat than rations of jerky and hard bread. "I'll be around to go to California with you to grow those grapes."

"And show me how to make wine," Jacob said.

"The very best of all wines."

"Good," Jacob said. He and Renne had been saving their money for that sole purpose. One more year of trapping and they would have enough. Glen was going to make St. Joe his home. He would open a gunsmith shop, and he had a widow in mind for a wife.

Jacob's horse stopped on its own volition as the troopers in front halted. A moment later Lt. Steptoe came riding along the column of men. Reaching the center of the column, he reined in his exhausted horse and swung down to the ground. He straightened his shoulders and ran his eyes over his men.

"Dismount and gather round," the lieutenant ordered in a low voice.

The troopers began to dismount. The trappers reined their mounts near the lieutenant and climbed out of their saddles. Wolf Voice and the other Crows rode up and swung down near the trappers. The band of men stood weary, stiff, and wet in the darkness.

"We'll stop here and rest our horses until daylight," Lt. Steptoe said.

"And rest our asses, too," Glen said.

The lieutenant glanced at Glen. Then he looked at Jacob, who had pulled his Colt revolver and was busy removing the lead balls and gunpowder from the cylinders.

"That was a damn hard rain and powder might be damp," Jacob said in explanation. *And you should order the other men to reload also,* Jacob thought.

Lt. Steptoe's eyes glittered with moonlight as he studied Jacob. Then the shine in his eyes blinked out as he looked away.

"There will be no smoking, no talking, no noise of any kind," the lieutenant said. "Rest but don't sleep. Keep hold of your horse. And every man reload rifle and pistol with fresh powder and caps. Get to it."

The troopers dropped down where they stood. Steptoe moved away from them a few yards and stood leaning against his horse.

Jacob caught Wolf Voice watching him with a calculating eye. After a handful of seconds, the Indian moved off after the other two Crows, walking toward the far side of the troopers.

"I think that Indian has taken a dislike for you," Glen said.

"For all of us," Jacob said. "Haven't you seen the way they watch us? What are they doing here?"

"Maybe they just want new rifles and pistols," Renne said. "You can bet the army'll never get the guns back when they leave."

The moon crossed the last arc of the western sky and fell into the bottomless pit behind the horizon. The rolling hills became blanketed in deep darkness. The wind lay dead in the shallow valleys.

Jacob sat on the ground on his slicker and rested. His horse stood beside him, its bridle reins hanging within easy reach of his hand. He held his carbine across his legs and stared out through the murky night.

An old memory, one that always brought a sense of loss, came again to him. He was in New Orleans and a beautiful brown-eyed girl with amazingly white skin was looking into his eyes. She seemed to want to say something to him, but had not. Instead she turned and ran off along the street. He could still feel how it was when her eyes touched his and it was like a kiss.

He pulled his thoughts back to the present and examined the shadows on the hillside in front of him, checking their position, shape, and size to detect any change that might be an enemy stalking the camp. Everything was as before.

Glen and Renne sat within a few feet of him but facing away at different angles. Together the three could watch the land in a full circle around them.

Jacob turned his head and scanned the troopers, and Lt. Steptoe, who was near his men but seated off by himself. Beyond the lieutenant, the Crow scouts sat as unmoving as stones. They would be alert, Jacob knew.

Lt. Steptoe rose and made his way through the night gloom and squatted beside the trappers. He said not a word, simply staring into the darkness.

Jacob sensed the tension in the officer. He considered saying something to him. But there was nothing to say that would lessen the weight on the man. He had the full responsibility for the success or failure of the campaign.

Lt. Steptoe spoke without looking at the trappers. "We need to find the enemy, if they are here."

"The only way to do that is to get off our asses and go look for them," Glen replied in a gruff voice.

Jacob spoke. "We could take the south half of the compass and the Crows the north half and scout out aways. Might find the Sioux that way."

"Just finding them won't be good enough," Renne said. "We got to hit them while they're still camped."

"If they've rode as hard as we did last night, they might rest a little in the morning before they ride on," Jacob said.

"We can't bank on Indians doing what white men might do," Glen said. "And we shouldn't be separated come daylight."

"Go see what's out there," the lieutenant directed. "Be back before daylight. I'll get the scouts started." He stood erect and moved away in the direction of the Crows.

"I'll go straight south," Glen said.

"Southeast for me," Jacob said.

"Then that leaves southwest for me," Renne added.

"Watch the sky and leave yourself time to get back here before sun-up," Glen said.

Jacob shoved his carbine into its scabbard on the saddle. He pulled himself astride and reined Jubal into the black night. The beast made not a sound, its hooves falling silently on the wet sod covering the ground.

Jacob tuned himself to the night and the land. His eyes searched through the feeble starshine faintly outlining the hills. The valleys were pits of darkness. His ears strained, reaching out for sounds that could be made by the Sioux. His nose tested the wind for the scent of men and horses. His enemies could be there behind the next dark hilltop, or in the darker valley beyond, and shoot him all to hell.

As he rode, he checked the North Star now and again and held it over his left shoulder. He set the course, but let the trusty gray with its night-seeing eyes pick the route up the hills and across the valleys. The North Star and the Big Dipper also told him the time. The Big Dipper rotated around the Pole Star once every twenty-four hours. Together they made a giant celestial clock ticking off the time.

Pre-dawn light gradually came alive as Jacob hunted over the land, and added its bit to the starshine. In the combined light, the contours of the hills acquired more solid form. He halted the gray near the crest of a hill and sat judging whether or not to turn back.

On Jacob's left, a great horned owl came flapping across the sky on his five-foot span of quiet wings. He tracked the night hunter's path by the line of stars it temporarily eclipsed. He knew the owl with its unbeatable ability to see in the night had easily spotted him. The owl continued its flight, angling up slightly to cross the ridge top beyond Jacob.

As the owl was about to disappear behind the hill, the beat of its broad wings suddenly increased. The owl climbed steeply upward for a few wing beats, then peeled away to the side. In an instant, the bird had vanished into the darkness.

Jacob's nerves tightened up. Something had frightened the bird. He quickly dismounted, stepped to the gray's head, and caught its muzzle. "Quiet, old boy," he said.

He listened, breathing silently through his open mouth. There was no sound that shouldn't be there. He dropped the reins to the ground. "Wait for me," he whispered to the horse.

Jacob crept up the last few feet of slope to the hilltop. Cautiously he peered over.

The band of Sioux warriors were on a shelf on the hillside below him not a hundred yards away. They lay on the ground with their horses standing beside them. Jacob caught the odor of men and horses on the slow breeze.

He scanned the camp. Where was the sentry? Then he saw him near a couple dozen horses tied to a picket rope. Those animals would be the horses stolen from the people of the wagon train.

He turned and crawled back off the hilltop. Below the crest, he rose to his feet and hurried to Jubal. He pulled himself into the saddle and walked the horse down the hillside, across the narrow valley, and over the next hill. There he raised the horse to a gallop. He had to quickly find the lieutenant and the other men and lead them back to the Sioux camp before they rode out.

Jacob led Lt. Steptoe and his band of fighters at a gallop through the dark, rolling hills. The rumble of the pounding iron hooves of the horses filled the night. The noise worried Jacob, but before darkness deserted them, they had to reach the camp of the Sioux.

He scanned the far eastern horizon where the dawn of the new day was weakening the night's hold on the land. A thick finger of clouds lay low across the sky and would delay the arrival of daylight a few minutes longer. Perhaps that would provide enough time for him to get the men into position for an attack on the Sioux.

Renne, riding beside Jacob, looked at his young friend. He sensed Jacob's desire to again find the Sioux. Young men didn't have the proper respect for danger. But Renne did. The memory of the ambush by the fur thieves came flooding back and he touched the old bullet wound in his chest. He recalled the punch of the bullet that struck him, and the pain that erupted like fire. He shivered at the remembrance. Never again did he want to experience such a wound.

Jacob glanced to the side at Lt. Steptoe riding beside him. The officer was looking straight ahead. Jacob moved his arm to catch the man's eye.

"We'd better walk our horses from here on, lieutenant" Jacob said. "We're getting close, not more than a half mile, and the Sioux might hear us."

Lt. Steptoe nodded and immediately reined his mount down to a walk. The body of men behind slowed to the same pace. The pounding hooves of the horses diminished to muted thumps on the wet sod.

The band dropped down into a shallow valley and Jacob pulled his horse to a halt. The others stopped with him. Leather creaked as the lieutenant turned to face him. But he said nothing, watching Jacob, waiting.

Jacob hurriedly scanned the low hill directly ahead. The red dawn was steadily brightening and the grass-covered hillside was plainly visible. Nothing moved within his sight. He turned to the lieutenant.

"The Sioux were on a bench on the far side of the hill," Jacob said in a low tone.

"We don't have much time to scout. Are you sure this is the hill? It was dark when you saw it."

What a damn stupid question, thought Jacob. "Hell no. I just stopped us here so we could talk," he whispered in indignation. Instantly he knew his anger was uncalled for. It was just the tension caused by the coming battle. He spoke in a softer voice. "I remember the shape of the hilltop, lieutenant, and this is the one."

Lt. Steptoe's expression was strained. "How far down from the top?"

"Less than a hundred yards. Camped on a bench on the side of the hill. They didn't want to be skylined."

"All right. We'll go have a look." He motioned to his sergeant. "Sergeant, form the men in one rank. Wait two minutes and then follow me. Come quietly."

"Yes, sir."

"All right, Morgan, let's go have a look."

Jacob and Lt. Steptoe walked their horses up the side of the hill. Near the top they dismounted. Crouched low, they stole up to the ridge line. Looked over.

Jacob's heart began to hammer. The Sioux were there, and readying their horses to travel. They would be mounted in a very short time. Nobody pulled a successful surprise attack against mounted and moving Sioux warriors. At best a running gun battle would be all that could be hoped for.

"Hurry," Lt. Steptoe said to Jacob.

He pivoted and scurried back down the hill. Jacob moved by his side. They jerked themselves up on their mounts.

The sergeant with the remainder of the men were just below them and quickly drawing close. The troopers stretched left and right of the sergeant. The scouts were at the far left end, Glen and Renne on the opposite end.

Jacob reined his horse and fell in on the right of Glen

and Renne. He would fight nowhere except near his comrades.

He watched Lt. Steptoe riding along the line of men. "Carbines first," the lieutenant ordered in a low voice. "Wait for my command to fire. Then pistols." He turned in the saddle and scanned the line of men. Jacob thought the lieutenant smiled with grim satisfaction as he took station in the center of the rank of troopers. He said something to the sergeant that Jacob couldn't make out.

Jacob turned to his comrades. "The Sioux are just below the ridge of the hill," Jacob said.

"Goddamn Colonel Granger for not letting us go on to St. Joe," Glen said.

"I've got a bad feeling about this," Renne said. "Let's watch out for each other."

"Right," Jacob said. The situation was going to get very dangerous in short order.

"Forward." The whisper ran man-to-man along the line.

The band of men rode up the hill. Jacob heard leather creaking as men readied themselves in their saddles for the charge, and the horses' hooves made soft thuds on the ground. He hoped the Sioux didn't hear the sounds and weren't lying in ambush.

The crest of the hill drew nearer and nearer and Jacob's heart pumped great pulses of blood. He gripped his carbine. One more battle to fight. A knot tightened in his stomach. He hoped he would live through it and be able to journey on to St. Joe to once again enjoy the pleasures of good food, a soft bed, and a woman.

He reached out with his left hand and petted the muscular neck of his faithful gray. *Let's both have luck and not stop a bullet*, he said silently to the horse. He looked down the line of men, and beyond them to the eastern horizon where the blood-red dawn had captured half of the eastern sky.

He saw the lieutenant again check the position of his men, and then raise his carbine above his head.

"Charge!" the lieutenant shouted. He raked his horse with spurs and the beast lunged over the top of the hill.

Jacob screamed a wild, shrill cry and kicked his mount into a run. All fear and doubt left him and the battle consumed every thought. Death was a thing that would come to someone else. He heard Glen and Renne and the troopers shouting their high, keening battle call beside him. But their voices seemed dim and far away. His every sense was focused forward toward the Sioux. He cocked his carbine and shoved the hammered-iron barrel out in front of him.

Nine

Jacob ran Jubal beside Glen's horse as Steptoe's fighters charged over the hill and plunged down the far side upon the Sioux. He held his rifle ready in both hands and his eyes raked the camp of the enemy.

He saw the Sioux warriors were nearly ready to ride out. Some were fastening saddles made from buffalo hides to the backs of their mustangs. Others, their mustangs already saddled, were chewing on jerky. Five or so braves, holding the bridles of their mounts, had gathered and were talking. Then in an instant, as one man, the Sioux whirled toward the sound of the running horses and screaming riders rushing at them.

The seasoned Sioux warriors did not panic at the sudden appearance of their white pursuers. Each brave swiftly reached for his weapon. Most grabbed up rifles, while a few raised bows and arrows. Several Sioux leaped upon the backs of their mustangs, more used to fighting from horseback than on foot.

Jacob and the others of Steptoe's fighters fell silent as the distance between the opposing forces rapidly shortened. He raised his carbine to his cheek and aimed at a mounted warrior. None must be allowed to escape by riding away from the battlefield. Above the pounding noise of the horses' hooves, Jacob heard Lieutenant Steptoe's shouted command.

"Fire!"

As the crash of carbines rippled along the line of riders, Jacob fired at the Sioux he had in his sights. The man recoiled at the strike of the bullet. He reeled, tried to catch himself, failed, and tumbled to the ground.

Half a dozen other Sioux warriors were slammed from the backs of their horses. Three were knocked off their feet. Two Sioux horses went down in a jumble of kicking, thrashing legs.

Answering shots blazed from the rifles of the Sioux. Two bowmen let loose their arrows at the attackers.

The top half of Jubal's left ear exploded as a round ball struck. Pieces of flesh, bone, and blood slapped Jacob in the face and chest. Damn the Sioux for shooting his horse!

He rammed his single-shot carbine into its scabbard and snatched his pistol from its holster. The distance to the enemy had closed to easy pistol range. Jacob brought his gun to bear on a Sioux leaping upon his mustang. As the man straightened and reined his mount toward his enemies, Jacob shot him through the chest. An expression of great pain swept over the man's face as he fell from the back of his mustang.

All along the line of the attacking force came the stutter of rapidly firing pistols. The concentrated shots were scything down the remaining Sioux. Horses and men fell screaming and kicking and bleeding. A frightened, riderless mustang bolted down the hill away from the tumult of the battle.

Jacob knew the fight was almost won. He looked to the side at Glen and Renne. Both men seemed unhurt. They were taking deliberate aim and shooting. Jacob threw a glance beyond them at the troopers.

Wolf Voice and the other two Crows had fallen behind the advancing troopers and were angling their mounts toward the three trappers. Jacob saw Wolf Voice's hostile eyes were fastened on him. Wolf Voice jerked his rifle to his shoulder.

Jacob flung himself forward on Jubal's neck. The damn Indian was going to shoot him. He snapped a pistol shot at Wolf Voice. Knew he had missed as he fired. He saw smoke spout from the barrel of the Crow's weapon. The shot passed over Jacob's back.

"Watch the Crows," Jacob shouted.

Only Glen, who was nearest Jacob, heard the warning. He twisted to look and saw the Crows bearing down on them. He swung his pistol and fired at Long Running, who was taking aim at him with his rifle.

Long Running flinched to the side at the punch of Glen's bullet. Long Running's shot went wild and hit the trooper beside Renne, knocking him from the saddle. Renne saw the trooper fall and whirled toward the sound of the shots coming from behind.

Wolf Voice gave a shout and reined his mount away from the trappers. Long Running, not badly wounded, also wheeled his mustang away. Little Horse fell in behind the other two men. Led by Wolf Voice, the Crows lashed their horses back to the top of the hill, and vanished behind it.

Jacob turned back to the battle. It was over with not one Sioux still on his feet.

The troopers yanked their excited horses to a halt and held them with tight reins. They shouted a high-pitched, triumphant yell. The battle was over and they were still alive.

Lieutenant Steptoe rode out in front of his troopers. "Well done! Well done!" he called out. He was silent for a few seconds as he soberly examined the battlefield. Then he nodded to his sergeant. "Sergeant Hundley, take some men and tend to our wounded comrades. Make the wounded Sioux prisoners."

"Yes, sir," replied the sergeant and saluted.

Jacob had stopped near Glen and Renne. They sat their horses and looked at the battlefield where death had been wasted. The sullen red eye of the sun had risen above the horizon and the crumpled forms of the dead men and dead horses were starkly visible on the ground.

Four of the Sioux were alive, but badly hurt. Blood was gushing from a large neck wound on one of them. He was trying to stem the flood of blood with his hand. As the trappers watched, the man's hand fell away from the wound and he died.

"A hell of a lot of dead men for a few stolen horses," Jacob said.

"More than stolen horses at stake here," Glen replied. "The land itself is really being fought for, and I think the Indians are going to lose. We're too many for them and got better weapons."

"Maybe so," Jacob replied. He looked at the top of the hill where the Crows had disappeared. "Wolf Voice and the other two Indians with him were waiting for a fight so they could catch us unawares and shoot us."

"I told you I didn't trust Crows," Renne said.

"They sure seemed bent on killing us," Glen said. "Do you suppose they were part of the Crows that hit us out by the Bighorns?"

"They sure must be carrying a big hate to track us this far," Renne said.

"That'd best explain why they tried to shoot us," Jacob said. "We'd better tell the lieutenant he doesn't have any scouts. And that they were responsible for wounding one of his troopers when they left."

"I'll tell him," Glen said.

Jacob did not listen to Glen and the lieutenant talk. He began to reload his empty pistol, pouring black powder from his flask into the cylinders, pressing lead balls down on the powder, and sliding firing caps onto the nipples. He accomplished the reloading without consciously thinking about it. His mind was on other matters. In the fall, Glen, Renne, and he would be going back into the Big Horns. That was the land of the Crows. That was Wolf Voice's land. If his hate was as great as it appeared, then he would be waiting for them.

The double-decked steamboat, painted a bright red and white, angled across the current of the Missouri River and approached one of the few empty berths on the waterfront docks at St. Joseph, Missouri. The big paddlewheel on the stern reversed its rotation and beat the water to a foam as it slowed the steamboat. As the vessel gently nudged the wooden dock, deck hands sprang ashore from the bow and stern and secured strong lines to metal cleats on the dock.

Jacob stood on the top deck with Glen and Renne. After the battle with the Sioux, they had returned to Fort Laramie with Lieutenant Steptoe and his troopers. That very day the three trappers loaded their furs on packhorses and hurried off along the North Platte River. Twelve days later, they arrived at Florence, Nebraska and caught the steamboat downriver.

Jacob had a pleasant feeling of anticipation as he swept his eyes over the waterfront crowded with mounds of cargo and bustling men. The railroad, reaching all the way from the east coast, ended at St. Joe and its cargo was transferred to steamboats going up and down the river. Steamboats for transporting passengers, and others for hauling cargo, a fast mail packet, and a U. S. gunboat filled almost every space of the rickety wooden piers that stretched for a mile along the river bank. Jacob did not see a pigboat and was not sorry for that.

He noted several of the dock workers were black men. They were being watched by a white man sitting under a large umbrella. Jacob judged the blacks were slaves, for Missouri was a slave state.

"At last we are in St. Joe, where a man can get a warm bath and a cold beer," Renne said with satisfaction.

Jacob grinned at Renne's words. He examined his friends. With their long unkempt hair and beards, and keen eyes swinging to catch every sight, they reminded him of the big white wolves that trailed the buffalo herds. Did he look as wild?

He raised his sight to the town. St. Joe sprawled along the east shore of the Missouri River for at least three miles. Though barely twenty years old, the town had a permanent population of nine thousand people, and was growing rapidly.

He could see the west end of the Blacksnake Hills, which lay north of Saint Michael's Meadow. He recalled the legends of the hills. Before the white men came, the Indians forbade bloodshed and weapons there because several tribes believed that God dwelt on the hills, making the soil sacred. Ailing Indian chiefs of the different tribes were brought great distances by travois to die there. They would be buried on the summits of the hills facing west, over the valley of the Great River. The sunsets from the hills were so fine that the Indians believed the rays of the setting sun provided an invisible bridge over which the souls of the departed took a direct road to the next world. This place, called Wah-Wah-Lanawa, was holy, a place of peace and plenty, a refuge and a sanctuary. The Platte Indians acted as custodians of the Blacksnake Hills until the white man crowded them out and built on the sacred hills.

Thirty or so tents were visible on a small, green meadow near the river. Jacob knew converts to the church of the Mormons gathered there each spring before sailing upriver to Florence to start their thousand-mile trek pulling handcarts to Salt Lake City. He had often thought of those people and their new religion, people who were shunned and sometimes treated harshly by other so-called religious people. Jacob did not give much thought to religion. There was a God, he instinctively knew that, but he went no further with the matter of religion.

"Looks like a Mormon handcart company is getting a late start this year," Jacob said and pointed at the tents.

"They'd better get on their way or winter snow will catch them in the mountains," Glen replied.

"They sure do always have pretty women among them," Renne said.

"Let's go sell our furs," Glen said and kicked his horse ahead.

They went down to the main deck and led their horses off the steamboat. They climbed the slanting street up to the center of town. The main street was dirt and lined with two- and three-story brick, stone, and wood-frame buildings. The sidewalks were thronged with townspeople, river men, and immigrants hurrying along. Two small boys, shouting happily to each other, ran past with wheel and pang. Wagons of the farmers from the countryside rolled along with families, the children excitedly ogling everything within view. Drivers of loaded drays popped their whips and cursed their horses. Buggies sped past, drawn along easily by high-stepping trotters.

Jacob felt his spirits rise as he watched the hustle and bustle of the town. His blood flowed more swiftly as he looked at the pretty women on the sidewalk, and even prettier ones on the green and white omnibus carrying passengers up from the waterfront.

He looked at the many homes of the townspeople on the streets running east up into the hills. Men lived in those warm homes with their families. While he fought the frigid winds and deep snows of the mountains. He

was tired of the cold and the snow. But a man could, if
he was a skilled trapper and the fur was of good quality,
make twice as much in six months as a town man could
in a year working at wages. He would go into the mountains to trap furs only one more winter. When the snow
melted in the high mountain passes next spring, he
would head for California with Renne. Maybe he would
find a wife among the pretty, dark-eyed senoritas there.

A few blocks later, Glen spoke. "I see Shattuck is still
in business."

The three men halted in front of the large building
with a sign identifying it as "Shattuck's Fur & Hides".
They tied their horses to iron rings set in the tops of
wooden posts.

Jacob looked across the street at the Territorial Bank.
His savings were being held there. Soon as the furs were
sold he would deposit more money, and also find out
how much interest he had earned during the past year.
He fell in behind Glen and Renne as they entered Shattuck's establishment.

Shattuck was working on a ledger at a battered
wooden desk near the entrance. He raised his long face
as the trappers came through the door and his eyes
fastened on the men. He abruptly came to his feet, his
face tightening and his hand jumping to the butt of the
pistol in a holster belted to his side. Then, just as
quickly, Shattuck's big face took on a businessman's
smile. He shifted his hand from his pistol to hook a
thumb in the waist of his pants.

"Hello, Kinshaw," he said. He nodded at Jacob and
Renne.

Jacob had observed Shattuck's expression and the
movement of his hand to his pistol. Damn strange reaction at seeing men he had bought furs from for years.
He would discuss it later with Glen and Renne. He
looked to the far side of the room where Aasland, who

was Shattuck's right-hand man, was closely watching the trappers. He was a skeleton, mere skin stretched over long bones. His face was sharp angles with sunken cheeks, all framed with black hair. A stiff mustache fanned out from beneath a long drooping nose. His eyes were set in deep holes under the ridges of his brows. Jacob had heard tales that the skeleton man was not to be crossed. The man stretched his lips across snaggle teeth in a gruesome grin at Jacob.

"Hello, Shattuck," Glen said, sweeping a look over the piles of furs nearly filling the large room. "I see you're still in the fur business. Do you want to buy some prime pelts?"

"I'm always looking for good fur. You're lucky you got here when you did. I've rented space on the railroad and early next week I'm taking all my furs to New York to sell."

"You've got enough furs to almost fill a railroad car," Glen said.

"It's been an excellent year."

"We'll bring our furs in and we can get to dickering," Glen said.

The three men returned to the outside, and in a short time they had carried all the furs inside.

"Where did you fellows trap?" Shattuck asked.

"Bighorns," Glen replied.

"Any trouble with the Crows?"

"A little coming east."

"How did you get past them?"

"Why, we simply shot them," Glen said.

Shattuck studied Glen with a flat, emotionless expression. "All of them?"

"No. I think two or three might've got away."

"Killing them is the best way to deal with Indians," Shattuck said.

"We thought so, since they were trying to steal our

furs," Glen said. "Let's do some trading. My partners and me have some celebrating to do."

Jacob wandered among the mounds of fur while Glen and Shattuck discussed the values of their last year's catch. Idly he began to look at some of the pelts. To his surprise, he found the initials "TB" on one. With growing interest, he checked several other pelts in the bale, and the two other bales near it, and found all had the same mark. How did Tom Branham's initials get on furs found in St. Joe that were stolen by Indians a thousand miles away?

"Jacob, we're finished," Glen called and held up a sheaf of bills.

Jacob turned and found the fur buyer was watching him. "Shattuck, who trapped these?" Jacob asked and pointed at the furs he had examined. "Damn fine pelts."

"I don't know. I can't remember who sold me every pelt in my store."

"I suppose not," Jacob said. He followed Glen and Renne out the door.

On the sidewalk, Glen turned to Jacob. "What was that all about with the furs?"

"They had Tom Branham's mark on them."

"Well, that's damn strange," Glen said.

"Exactly what I was thinking," Jacob said.

"Isn't Branham one of the men who lost his furs out near the Tetons?" said Renne.

"The same," Jacob said.

"Maybe you shouldn't have said anything to Shattuck," Glen said to Jacob.

"Could be, but how could we find out anything without asking him?"

"Well, it's done," Glen said. "Let's talk about it some more over a cold beer at Garveen's." He chucked his thumb in the direction of the saloon across the street.

Jacob glanced back inside the building. Shattuck was

in deep conversation with Aasland. Jacob wondered what they were plotting. He turned and followed after his friends past their tied horses and into the street.

"Watch out!" Jacob shouted. He grabbed Renne who was in the lead and yanked him backward.

Ten

Maude stopped the buggy on top of the hill close above the Missouri River and pointed west across the wide stream. "That is the way we will soon be traveling," she said.

Cora looked at the south-flowing river, and beyond it to the flat Nebraska plain that seemed to stretch away endlessly under the brilliant blue dome of the sky. She sensed the empty vastness of the land, so unlike the rolling farming country they had traveled through for many days.

Cora and Maude were drawing near St. Joseph. They had come hundreds of miles with the horse trotting and the buggy riding easily on its metal leaf springs. Four days after leaving New Orleans, they had reached Baton Rouge. They found the town overflowing with refugees from plague-ridden New Orleans. Every hotel and boardinghouse was filled. They had left immediately, striking out for St. Louis, a large city thriving from river trade and the rich farmland surrounding it.

As they journeyed north through the pleasant green countryside, they slept and ate at the inns located at the relay stations of the stagecoach lines, or at smaller hotels in the town. They had sufficient money to last for several months if they were thrifty, and for the first time in their lives, they were free to go and do as they pleased. Maude seemed to have no fear that harm would come to them traveling by themselves. Cora knew this was due to the successful defense against the robbers in New Orleans. However, she remembered how helpless she had been in the struggle with the attackers. Also, the blows she had received from the man had hurt much worse than she had let on to Maude. She never again wanted to depend on another person for protection. At a gun store in the village of Memphis, Cora bought a pocket pistol, a Colt .28-caliber revolver. Though it was a small weapon, at a close range it would be quite deadly.

As they approached St. Louis, they read in a newspaper of a large, new gold discovery in the Sierra Nevada Mountains of California. Cora told Maude that she felt they might have the Midas touch and would find a golden hoard in that distant land. Little discussion was required for both young women to decide to continue on to far-off California. So they had turned west at St. Louis and continued along the Missouri River toward St. Joseph, the staging point for the wagon trains going to California.

They entered St. Joe with their horse pulling the buggy along very briskly. Cora looked at the people and the large numbers of vehicles moving along the street. A lively town, she thought.

As the buggy came abreast of a group of horses tied in front of a fur and hide business, three men stepped out from behind the horses and into the path of the buggy. The buggy horse, frightened by the abrupt appearance of the men, reared and lunged to the side, whipping the shafts of the buggy sharply to the side. The buggy rocked up on two wheels.

Cora felt herself falling and grabbed at the metal frame of the buggy. But her hand slipped loose and she tumbled into the street. An instant later Maude landed with a thump beside her.

Cora looked up quickly. The buggy was directly above her, and falling.

A man suddenly appeared beside Cora. With amazing

quickness, he reached out and caught hold of the falling buggy. He groaned, and his legs almost buckled as he stopped the descent of the heavy vehicle. Then he straightened and heaved powerfully upward on the buggy. With a thud and a jangle of metal, the buggy fell back onto its four wheels.

Cora scrambled to her feet and flung a look at her buggy horse. One of the men had caught the animal by the bridle and mane and was holding the frightened animal with great strength.

Jacob looked at the pretty girl who had climbed to her feet. She seemed unhurt and he was glad for that. He turned to the other woman and leaned down to offer his hand to help her up.

Maude knocked Jacob's hand away. She winced with pain as she climbed to her feet. She turned angrily on the trappers. "You damn bunch of fools, why did you scare my horse?" she shouted.

Jacob whipped off his hat. "I'm sorry we caused your horse to spook," he said. He understood the woman's anger. He would have felt the same way had he been dumped in the street. However, he was more interested in the pretty woman and fastened his eyes back on her.

He watched her brush the dirt of the street from her trousers and shirt. Then she turned and rested her eyes on him, and his heart began to beat a wild tattoo against his ribs. She was more than pretty, she was truly beautiful, the planes and curves of her face were delicately carved, and her widely spaced brown eyes were bright, pure crystals. The woman's eyes seemed familiar. He had a haunting feeling that he had looked into them before. But he couldn't pull the memory to life of where or when.

Cora continued to look at the man whose gray eyes were locked on her with an intensity she had never experienced before. His lean body was taut within his stained buckskin clothing. A pistol and a big knife were belted to his waist. His face, though not especially handsome, was striking. His long blond hair and beard were tangled, and his face was burnt a deep brown by sun and wind. She caught his odor, wood smoke and horses and sweat.

"Are you hurt?" Jacob asked. Belatedly he swung his view to include Maude.

Before Cora could reply, Maude spoke sharply. "Because of your stupid action we could have been badly hurt."

"I'm not hurt," Cora said.

"I think your horse has settled down now," Glen said. He released his grip on the animal's head and stepped away.

"Get in, Cora, and let's go," Maude said. "I've had enough of these smelly men." She grimaced as she climbed back into the buggy. Without a word she took the reins Renne handed to her.

Cora stepped up into the vehicle and took a seat. Maude spoke to the horse and the buggy moved off.

Cora cast a glance back at the blond young man. He was standing motionless and staring after her with a quizzical expression.

"Don't look at those dirty trappers," Maude admonished Cora.

Cora laughed. "If that younger one had a bath and a shave, he might be presentable," she said. *And maybe not so wild-looking either,* she thought.

Glen moved to stand beside Jacob. "What are you thinking?" he asked.

"I feel like I've seen that pretty one before, but yet at the same time maybe not. Have you ever seen her?"

"Can't say that I have," Glen said.

"How about you, Renne?" Jacob asked.

"There is something about her that looks a little familiar. But if I ever saw her before, it must have been some time ago."

"Maybe it'll come to you later," Glen said.

They crossed the street and entered Garveen's Saloon. The room had a long bar, high ceilings, and was deep, stretching back into shadows. They took seats at a table.

"Three beers," Jacob called to the bartender.

Glen divided the money he had received for the furs into three equal piles. He passed one to Jacob and another to Renne. "There you are. Everything share and share alike."

The bartender brought the beers. Jacob paid for the drinks.

He raised his mug of beer to his friends. "Here's to being back in St. Joe with our pockets full of money."

The three men grinned at each other and clanked their mugs together.

Jacob took a long pull at his beer. The cool, tangy liquid tickled his tongue, and slid smoothly down his throat. He took a breath. "Ah, damn delicious after doing without for six months," he said.

Glen set his mug down and wiped his mouth with his sleeve. "Now about Shattuck, did you fellows see his face when he saw us?"

"He seemed damned surprised," Renne said.

"More than surprised," Jacob said. "He acted like a man who expected us to jump him. I thought he was going to grab his pistol and start shooting."

"How did Shattuck get Tom Branham's furs?" Glen said.

"Maybe he buys stolen furs," Renne said.

"Even if he does, that doesn't explain how he acted when he saw us," Jacob said.

"No, it doesn't," Glen said and pulled at his beard. "I think it best that we watch out for Shattuck. Whatever was bothering him at first may now be worse, for we know he has Branham's furs."

"If we run into Branham here in St. Joe, we should tell

him about his furs being at Shattuck's," Jacob said. He finished his beer and thumped the mug down on the table. "I'll see you fellows later. It's time for me to get a shave and haircut, and get out of these dirty buckskins."

"After you see the town for a few days, we'll get together and plan for next trapping season," Glen said.

Jacob went to a barber shop for a haircut and shave, and then registered at the three-story, one-hundred-ten-room hotel called the Patte House, He retrieved his large leather-and-wood trunk from the hotel storage. Kneeling in the lobby in his dirty buckskin, he dug a dark gray suit and hat from the trunk. He handed the clothing to one of the young bellhops.

"Take this suit and get it pressed, and have the dents taken out of the hat." He flipped a silver half-dollar at the bellhop.

The bellhop expertly caught the coin. Then he caught the silver half-dollar that followed.

"That four bits is for the presser," Jacob said. "Wait for him to finish, then bring everything back to me by the time I take a bath."

"Yes, sir," said the bellhop. Clutching the clothing, he trotted away.

Jacob turned to the second bellhop. "Bring one of those portable bathtubs up to my room. Fill it with five full buckets of hot water." He tipped the boy a quarter.

Jacob closed and latched the trunk. Hoisting it to his shoulder, he went across the lobby and up the stairs to his room.

Jacob scrubbed himself with soap in the large tub of warm water. He felt naked now, with his hair cut short and his beard gone. But that would pass. Finally feeling clean, he lay soaking, savoring his indulgence in the luxury of the hotel, and the pleasant evening that was coming.

Jacob climbed from the water and dried himself. He dressed in the freshly pressed suit. He took a shiny pair of boots from the trunk and pulled them on. He buckled his pistol around his waist under his coat. The hat was set rakishly on his head.

He returned to the lobby of the hotel. "Go get the bathtub out of my room," he told the bellhop. "And take the buckskins and have them cleaned." He tossed him a four-bit piece.

"Yes, sir," said the bellhop.

Jacob went out to the sidewalk. The day had ended while he bathed, and dusk was flowing in from the east to fill the streets. It was going to be a grand night. He stretched his arms out to the side, raised his head, and laughed.

He patted his billfold. He had deposited most of his money in the bank. What he carried was for spending. He walked off along the street, smiling in anticipation of the pleasures to come.

As he strolled along, he returned the greeting of two men he knew. One of the pretty young women from the River Palace Steamboat, a traveling brothel, winked at him as she walked by. In the next block, he passed a bakery and the smell of baking bread sent his hunger surging.

Then his hunger was forgotten, for coming along the sidewalk was the girl he and his friends had caused to fall from the buggy. She appeared more feminine now, for instead of the man's clothing she wore earlier in the day, she was now garbed in a dress of a golden color that set off her young woman's body and long auburn hair. She walked with a free swinging stride and a half smile was on her lovely face. Jacob felt his gambler's instinct rise and he decided to take a wild chance.

He whipped off his hat and stepped into the girl's path.

Eleven

Cora halted abruptly as a tall man stepped into her path along the sidewalk. She quickly looked into the face of the stranger to determine if he was a threat to her. Her heart was beating swiftly, for she remembered all too well the attack upon Maude and her in New Orleans.

The man was young, and was holding his hat in his hand and smiling boyishly at her. His face was oddly two-toned. Where a beard had been recently removed, and above the hat line, the skin was very fair, while a band across the middle part of his face was a weather-burnt brown. He almost seemed to be wearing a mask.

He ran his hand over the front of his suit coat. "I clean up pretty good, don't you think?" he said.

Cora dropped her view from the man's face down the nicely tailored suit to his polished boots. She looked back into his eyes. "It's you," she said in astonishment, recognizing the young trapper from the episode with the buggy. He had indeed cleaned up very handsomely.

"A barber, a bath, and town clothes did it," Jacob said with a laugh. He was enjoying talking with the girl and watching her pretty face. "My name's Jacob Morgan. What's yours?"

Cora considered whether or not to reply to the question. He seemed to be a pleasant sort, and he had kept the buggy from falling on her. She decided there could be no harm in telling him. "I'm Cora Dubois."

"I'm glad to meet you, Cora. I saw luggage tied to the rear of your buggy. From that I take it you're not from St. Joe."

"My sister and I are from New Orleans."

"I've been to New Orleans several times. I always found it a lively town."

"You wouldn't want to go there now. It has a terrible yellow fever epidemic. That's why we left."

"I was there one time during an epidemic. My boat docked for just a short time to unload our cargo and then we immediately shoved off. But mostly I had a grand time in New Orleans." *It's a town with hundreds of pretty girls,* he thought to himself. He recalled the special girl that he had fought for and couldn't forget. "The only time I didn't was when I had trouble with the River Rats Gang, but that was back when I was a boy."

Cora felt a sudden shock of remembrance of the frightening experience with the River Rats. If it hadn't been for the help of a brave boy, she would have been hurt, or worse. He had been blond-headed like this young man smiling down at her. She replayed the scene with the River Rats in her mind. Was it possible this was the boy, now grown to manhood? "I once saw a boy fight the Rats to help a girl they were bothering," she said.

Jacob felt a rush of blood through his body as the possible meaning of Cora's words registered. "Were you that girl? Did the boy tell you to run? Do you remember him saying that to you?"

"Yes, I remember those words! I am that girl."

"I know you are, for I see it now." Jacob's eyes traveled up and down Cora. "Well, I'll be damned." He had found the girl whose face had haunted him for such a long time. She was even more beautiful now, grown to a young woman.

"I was worried that the Rats would kill you. When I found the two trappers just a short distance away, I told them what was happening. They said they would go and see if you needed help."

"That was Glen and Renne. They ran the Rats off."

"I came back to thank you, but you were leaving with the men. Now I wish to thank you, even if it is years too late." Cora held out her hand.

Jacob clasped Cora's offered hand. He pressed the small, warm hand, feeling the fine bones within their covering of soft girl's skin and flesh. After all these years and for the very first time, he was touching the girl from New Orleans. He must not let her escape from him.

"I accept your thanks." Jacob reluctantly released his hold on Cora's hand. He was ready to take another gamble. "Now that we are old friends, would you have supper with me? I know a good restaurant."

"I'm sorry, I can't. I must take Maude some food. She hurt her foot in the fall from the buggy. It isn't that bad, but she didn't feel like walking on it just yet. Also, I must find a wagon train that will let us join them for the journey to California. Maybe you can help me locate one."

Jacob was disappointed at Cora's rejection of his invitation. And he had bad news for her. "The wagon trains form up on the far side of the Missouri River. But you'll not find one leaving for California this late in the summer. They head out soon as there's a little green in the grass, say early April. All of them have left by the middle of May so that they can get through the mountain passes before snow blocks them."

"No wagon trains?"

"Not until next spring. And you can't travel by yourself, even if you could make it through before snow flies."

"We can't wait a year. We don't have much money and need to go on now. Isn't there some way we can go at least partway this summer?"

"None that I know about."

Cora frowned with disappointment and Jacob didn't like to see that. Wasn't there some way he could help her get what she wanted? Then he remembered the Mormon camp. "There are some Mormons still here in St. Joe who I'm sure will go on to Salt Lake City this year. They might let you travel with them that far. You could spend the winter there and then could go on to California next spring." Jacob pointed down at the Mormon camp on the meadow near the river.

Cora looked at the village of tents where the gray-white smoke of several cooking fires rose into the air. "I'd better go and see them now. They may be ready to leave soon."

"Some of the rough men on the waterfront might hassle you. I could walk you to the Mormon camp if you want me to."

"That would be kind of you."

They moved off together, going a half block then turning down sloping Francis Street toward the docks. The grade was steep and Jacob offered his arm to Cora. She smiled up into his face and took his arm without hesitation. Jacob felt pleasure at the touch of her hand.

A score of rivermen who had finished their working day passed Cora and Jacob. A pair of men stopped and stared when they saw Cora. The larger man whistled through his teeth and poked his buddy in the ribs. "Ain't she the prettiest little doxie you ever did see?" He raised his voice and called out to Cora. "When you're finished tumbling that fellow, I'm next. What's your name, for I'm going to come and look you up for a little tumble myself."

Jacob's temper flared hot at the insulting words. Cora was no whore. He shook her hand loose and started for the man. Cora swiftly moved after him and caught him firmly by the arm. "Don't, Jacob. Don't start another fight."

"I'll teach them some manners."

"They think I'm one of the other kind of girls."

Jacob gave the men a hard look, but let Cora lead him away. Behind him the men watched in puzzlement.

"What did you mean by me starting another fight?" Jacob asked.

"Like in New Orleans." Cora smiled at him.

Jacob laughed. "You sure bring out the fight in me."

"You don't have to protect me anymore, for I'm a big girl now." Still, she was pleased at Jacob's reaction to the man's words.

"Yes, you are grown up and very beautiful," he said. "Sometimes a woman's beauty can be dangerous for her."

"How could that be?" Cora thought she knew, still she wanted to hear Jacob explain.

"Beautiful women are the ones men carry off," he said gruffly and fell quiet. At this moment he wanted to grab Cora, throw her upon Jubal and ride away with her to the mountains. He touched the hand that held his arm. He wouldn't ride off with her right now. Maybe later, and he smiled at the thought.

"Have you ever stolen a girl and carried her off?" Cora asked in a teasing voice.

"Just once," Jacob replied, in the same bantering voice that Cora had used.

Cora was watching Jacob's face and thought he might be telling the truth. She was shocked at the possibility. She would have liked to hear the details of such a thing, but decided it was better that she not press him further.

They reached the edge of the Mormon camp of some forty tents arranged in two rows across the meadow. The three young women at the nearest tent watched them approach. They seemed surprised at Jacob and Cora's presence.

"Who's your head man?" Jacob asked.

"Elder Clive Pateman is the company leader," a girl with red hair replied. "His tent is there in the center." She pointed.

"Is he there now?" Cora asked.

All three girls nodded in unison.

"Let's go talk with him," Cora said to Jacob.

They continued on past other staring people, mostly young women, and halted at the entrance of Pateman's tent. Jacob called out. "Hello inside. Is Clive Pateman there?"

A moment passed and a giant of a man came out of the tent, ducking his head to clear the top of the opening. He straightened and towered over Jacob's six feet by a hand width. His head was big and his chest broad. Jacob judged the giant's age at something in the middle thirties. He certainly wasn't old enough to be called "elder." That must be a church title.

"What can I do for you folks?" Pateman's voice was a deep bass. His black eyes checked Jacob with a man's glance, then moved quickly to range over Cora from her head to her feet.

Jacob saw the scrutiny Pateman gave Cora and didn't like it. In fact, he regretted having mentioned the Mormons to Cora. However, it was too late to stop what he had set in motion.

"I understand you are going to Salt Lake City soon," Cora said.

"That's correct. Why do you ask?"

"I'd like to travel with you."

"Go with us?" Pateman said in surprise. "Why, are you a Mormon?"

"Oh, no. But my sister and I want to go to California. All the wagon trains have already left. Jacob suggested that we might travel with your people to Salt Lake City this summer and then go on to California early next year. Is that possible?"

Pateman cast an enquiring look at Jacob. "You wouldn't be going with her?"

"No," Jacob said. At the reply, Jacob thought Pateman hid a smile behind his black eyes.

Pateman spoke to Cora. "We'll be taking a steamboat up-river to Florence. After that it's a long, hard journey overland, more than a thousand miles. Are you up to that?"

"My sister and I are used to traveling. We've just come from New Orleans. We survived storms and floods. Men tried to rob us but didn't succeed. You wouldn't have to worry about us. We can carry our own weight and not bother anyone asking for help."

"What kind of vehicle do you have?"

"A one-horse buggy. It's a good Phaeton buggy."

"Do you have money for supplies?"

"Yes, enough."

Pateman again looked Cora over thoroughly, and then nodded. "You and your sister can travel with us. What's your name?"

"Dubois. My given name is Cora and my sister's is Maude."

"Mine is Clive Pateman. The buggy won't do. It would never stand up to the trip, for it's all rough country with no roads. You must trade it for a one-horse covered wagon. One with good canvas that'll hold out rain. We're leaving early tomorrow morning, so you must make the trade today. I know a man who will give you a fair deal. We can go there now before it gets dark."

"Cora, I'll help you make the trade," Jacob said. "I have a friend with a yard full of wagons."

"Mr. Pateman offered first, Jacob, so I will go with him.

Jacob shrugged his shoulders and said not a word.

He didn't like being rejected again. Still, he knew Cora had to please Pateman for he could give permission for her to travel with the Mormons. He had seen the look in the big man's eye and didn't like the thought of her being with him for days on end as they journeyed to Salt Lake City. In fact, Jacob didn't like anything at all about Pateman.

"What about supplies?" Cora asked Pateman. "Should I buy them here in St. Joe?"

"Yes. All supplies are cheaper here than in Florence. Buy enough to last for three months. We will be taking along a herd of beef that you can buy a share in for fresh meat. Also, we'll kill buffalo as we go across the prairie. You can expect a short wait in Florence while we wait for the construction of the handcarts to be finished."

"Handcarts? You travel by handcarts?"

"Handcarts have been taking my people successfully to Salt Lake City for the past five years. It's hard labor, but true believers can perform nearly impossible tasks. Now we'd better get started, for it'll be dark in an hour."

"I'm ready," Cora said. She was glad she would have a wagon and not have to pull a handcart a thousand miles across the prairie and up over the mountains to Salt Lake City. She turned to Jacob. "Thank you for everything. Maybe you can come and see us off in the morning?"

"I'll surely do that." See her off, hell. He felt unsettled about how things had turned out. He had just found her and now she would be disappearing from his life after just a few hours. He should have kept his mouth shut about the Mormons and he could have enjoyed Cora's pleasant company for weeks.

Pateman offered his arm to Cora. She took it and fell into step beside him. She glanced back at Jacob. The brave boy who had fought the Rats for her in New Orleans had become quite a man. She gave him a little wave.

Jacob did not respond to the wave, merely standing and staring gloomily after Cora.

Twelve

Jacob could not resolve the problem that plagued him so tenaciously. His head was lowered as he moved through the frail moonlight on the footpath that fishermen had tramped out in the weeds along the edge of the Missouri River. He had walked the remainder of the evening after parting from Cora, and into the night, and still the question eluded an answer.

Always before now upon returning from months of trapping in the mountains, he would dress in town clothes, have a good meal, listen to some good music in the company of a pretty girl, and spend the night making love. The part about making love to some strange girl now seemed to require rethinking.

He halted and looked down the river across the black water a quarter mile to the docks at St. Joe. He stood on the outward bend of a meander of the river, upstream of the town, and the dark outlines of the boats tied up to the docks were plainly visible. Berthed at the upper end of the docks was the luxurious River Palace Steamboat. The pale light from coal oil lamps shone in the windows of the boat and fell in a row of tiny pools of yellow mist upon the river passing in the dark. He could faintly hear a piano and violin, but could not make out the tune being played. He had visited the

River Palace before and knew what pleasures awaited a man there.

The discovery of Cora had created his dilemma of whether or not to go the River Palace and seek out a lady-love. While Cora had been but a beautiful memory of the past, there had been no conflict in his actions toward other women. But now the doubts loomed large.

Think clearly and be reasonable about this, Jacob told himself sternly. Cora's presence in St. Joe was only temporary. Tomorrow morning she would be gone. He recalled how Pateman had looked at her with a desirous eye. Many other men would also surely find her beautiful. Soon she would be married to some handsome, lucky fellow. The odds were impossibly large that that man would not be Jacob. In reality, he probably would never see her again once she left St. Joe. She would continue on with her life, without consideration for what he did or didn't do.

He took a deep breath of the damp air heavy with the musty mud odor of the ancient river. He felt the ageless primal urge of a young man, long denied, for a woman. "So be it," he said out loud. He strode off toward the waterfront docks. He smiled sadly in the darkness, for he wished he was on his way to visit Cora.

Jacob slowed as he came to the river docks. A man Jacob judged to be an army captain from the post located north of the town walked ahead of him in the path of light cast by three storm lanterns hanging on a cable that stretched across the dock from the land to the River Palace. The army captain went aboard the riverboat and entered the huge main deck cabin.

The River Palace was famous for its beautiful women, excellent food and drink, all of it available among elegant furnishings and polite conduct and manners. She journeyed up and down the Mississippi River and its two main tributaries, the Missouri and Ohio Rivers. She began her voyage north from New Orleans in the early spring, stopping at the cities and towns along the rivers for varying lengths of time to ply her trade and then continuing on. As the autumn brought its cooler, pleasant temperatures, the River Palace turned south and returned back along its course, to end its journey in New Orleans where it spent the frigid winter months.

Jacob went on board the River Palace and entered the salon of the main deck to the sound of the piano and violin being skillfully played. At the right end of the long room five military officers, a mixture of army and navy men, were resplendent in full dress uniforms. Only their swords were missing. The navy officers would be from the gunboat he had earlier seen tied to the dock. The men sat holding drinks and talking with three blond women. One was the pretty woman who had smiled and winked at Jacob on the street. She was facing partially away and had not noticed his entrance. Several men in civilian clothes danced with women on the polished hardwood floor in the center of the room. Everyone seemed to be having a good time.

A young army lieutenant leaned on the end of the piano and listened to a woman, equally young, play a light, airy tune. A fat, bald-headed man accompanied her on a violin. The musical rendition came to a close, and the lieutenant caught the woman's hand. She smiled, stood up and led him from the room. The man with the violin placed it on top of the piano and went to the small bar against the wall and ordered a drink.

The woman he had seen on the street looked past the officers surrounding her and saw Jacob. She watched him a moment and then excused herself and walked to meet him. He doffed his hat and half bowed to the woman.

The woman's rouged lips formed a gracious smile. "I'm Corrine, and I welcome you." Jacob clasped the soft hand she offered. She had a slight French accent similar to Cora and Renne. Jacob liked it.

"I'm Jacob Morgan." He couldn't help but smile back at the pretty woman.

"May I have your hat, Jacob?" Corrine asked.

Jacob started to give his hat to Corrine when a man and woman came down from the upper deck by steps at the far end of the room. They walked toward the bar. Jacob's smile fell away as he recognized Wade Shattuck. He believed the man was a fur thief. If that was true, then Shattuck was as guilty of murder as were the Indians who had killed Branham's man in the mountains. Jacob knew Shattuck was his enemy without a word being spoken.

Shattuck said something to the woman with him and she left and went toward the four officers. He swung his view around observing the occupants of the room. He saw Jacob watching him, and recognized the young trapper of Kinshaw's band. The nosy fellow had found Tom Branham's initials on the stolen furs. Shattuck cursed silently and raised a hand to clasp his coat close to his shoulder holster. He should have examined the furs when Wolf Voice's braves had brought them to him. Why in hell hadn't Wolf Voice killed the trappers after Shattuck had identified them for him? The Indian must have had plenty of opportunities on the campaign after the Sioux.

Corrine saw Jacob look past her, and his eyes become frosty and hard. His hand moved to hover near the butt of the pistol showing under the tail of his coat. She twisted to look in the same direction. Wade Shattuck was poised on the balls of his feet. His face and body were taut as he stared back at Jacob. She sensed the deep enemity between the two men and wondered what had caused it.

"What's wrong, Jacob?" Corrine asked in a tone hardly above a whisper.

At her question, Jacob began to smile tight-lipped. He showed no worry or alarm. Just a readiness to fight. Maybe a desire to fight.

"Shattuck acts like he owns the River Palace," Jacob said.

"He's quarter owner. When the Palace is in St. Joe, he comes often to sample for free what is offered."

Some of the tenseness left Jacob as he mentally reined himself in. So Shattuck was a whoremaster as well as a murderer and fur thief. However, the quarrel about ownership of the furs was Branham's to take up with Shattuck. Jacob hoped he would soon encounter Branham so he could tell him about the furs. The battle between the two men would be something to see.

"Pour us a drink and talk a little with me," Jacob said. He would not let Shattuck drive him away from the pretty woman with the nice French accent.

They sat drinking red wine and talking about unimportant things. Then the woman who had played the piano came back downstairs with the young lieutenant. He looked at the other officers and grinned as if he was proud of having done something big, and left the Palace. The woman began to play the piano again. The violinist left his drink and came and took up his instrument and joined in with the woman.

The music was very pleasing to Jacob's ear. He took Corrine by the hand and went onto the dance floor with her. She was very practiced and made his effort to dance seem almost graceful. He focused on the woman in his arms and the delightful music. When in the mountains, he missed not only the music itself but the journeys the music took his imagination on, to lands and people of strange and faraway places he had read about. But there would be only one more winter of being deprived of those things, and a score of other pleasures that most men took for granted.

The music ended and Jacob guided Corrine back to their table. He saw Shattuck leave and his spirits brightened. He smiled at Corrine and lifted his glass to her and drank.

Corrine smiled in return, red lips parting. She clasped Jacob's hand, feeling the hard, strong bones inside their sheaths of muscle and tendon and the rough callouses on the palm. "I know a place where we can rest in a cool breeze and watch the fireflies light their little lanterns and search for love," she said.

The scene the woman described to Jacob was pleasing. Until that moment he had not been sure he would make love to her. He picked up the partially full wine bottle and two glasses and let Corrine lead him away.

Cora sat beside Maude on the seat of the small covered wagon as they waited their turn to go aboard the riverboat tied to the dock at St. Joe. The Missouri River valley was still cloaked in lingering morning dusk, for the sun had not yet risen above the eastern hills. The river flowed past silent and black.

The riverboat was a small side-wheeler with two decks and painted white. The captain stood near the pilothouse watching the passengers load. He had ordered the fires stoked beneath the boilers and smoke now streamed from the smokestack.

Mormon men, women, and children, carrying their scant belongings, climbed the slanting gangway that led to the upper deck. Pateman was helping the drivers of three large covered wagons, each drawn by two yokes of lumbering oxen and containing the tents and other supplies of the Mormons, board by a stout ramp to the lower deck.

Cora twisted on the wagon seat and looked at the town. A few rivermen were coming down Francis Street, returning to their boats after a night on the town. There was no sign of Jacob. She hoped he had not forgotten that she would be departing with the Mormons for Salt Lake City this morning.

Maude was watching her young sister and saw the frown of disappointment come over her face. "That trapper won't come to say goodbye," she said. "And you're better off for it. So forget him."

"Why don't you like Jacob?" Cora asked. "He helped me when I needed it." She had told Maude of the discovery that Jacob had been the boy who came to her rescue when the River Rats had been molesting her in New Orleans.

"Because he's not the right man for you. He's wild as any Indian, and has no prospects for becoming wealthy. In California, you will find a man with much property."

"Is that all you think there is to men, whether they are wealthy or not?"

"I want you to marry a man with money and property," Maude said firmly. "I will help you find men like that. Then you can choose among them for the one that most pleases you."

Cora looked at Maude and tried to read her sister's impassive face. *You are wrong*, Cora thought. *You are not my mother and I will choose my own husband. And he may be rich or he may be poor.* She turned again toward the town, and immediately broke into a happy smile. Jacob was hurrying with long strides down Francis Street in her direction.

He came up to the wagon and whipped off his hat. "Good morning, Cora." He spoke to Maude, who was watching him. "And good morning to you too, Miss Dubois."

A surly, disapproving expression came over Maude's

face. She turned away from Jacob without acknowledging his greeting.

Jacob was taken aback by the big woman's rudeness. He would have liked to be on good terms with her because she was Cora's sister.

He turned to Cora. "I was afraid I had missed you when I went to the Mormon camp and found all the tents gone and not a soul around." He was pleased about finding her before she left.

Cora was angry at Maude for being so impolite to Jacob, but she couldn't help but continue to smile at him. "Pateman woke us early. He said we might as well get used to it, for that's the way it'll be once we start west."

"As I remember, you said you were going to California. What town would that be?"

"We haven't decided. Just California for now."

Maude quickly looked at Jacob. "We've also been thinking of going to Oregon instead of California."

Cora was surprised at Maude's statement, for they had never discussed Oregon. "California sounds most interesting to me," she said.

Jacob had been on the point of telling Cora that he was going to California in the spring, but now he held his tongue. For some reason, Maude didn't like him and just might be contrary enough to actually convince Cora to go to Oregon.

Pateman helped the driver of the last supply wagon bring his vehicle up the ramp and onto the riverboat. "Set the brake hard," he told the driver. He pivoted around to scan the dock to check the progress of the people to come aboard. He saw the trapper Morgan standing at Cora's wagon. Both Cora and the man were talking and smiling at each other.

Pateman shouted out across the dock. "Maude, bring your wagon on board. We're ready to shove off."

Maude immediately lifted the reins of the horse

hooked to the wagon and slapped them down on the animal's rump. "Get on there," she ordered.

"Well, this is goodbye," Cora said, looking down at Jacob, who was walking along beside the moving wagon.

"I'm sorry to say that it is," Jacob replied. Wanting badly to touch her, he held up his hand.

Cora was warmed by Jacob's look. She clasped his hand. "Thanks for what you did in New Orleans," she said.

"Thanks for St. Joe," Jacob said.

The wagon reached the steamboat. Jacob released Cora's hand and stepped back. He stood on the dock as the wagon moved up the ramp with Cora looking back at him. He thought there were promises in her young woman's eyes, deep and dark. But again, maybe not, and he wished he could read the mystery of the secrets she carried in her heart. He held a sadness for her going, and a dark premonition that he would never look into those eyes again.

Cora stood with Maude on the bow of the steamboat transporting the Mormons up the Missouri River. She was looking ahead as the boat churned across the current toward the clearing visible in the thick forest on the riverbank. In the last rays of the setting sun, she saw a small dock, with large ricks of wood on the bank close by, and a cabin for the woodcutters.

Pateman, standing close beside the sisters, spoke to them. "We have to stop for the night and tie up to the bank. The captain would run aground, or hit a snag that could sink the boat, if he tried to run the river in the dark. But we'll be in Florence by noon tomorrow."

Other women and a few men and children came to the front part of the steamboat to watch the landing. Pateman moved closer to Cora to give them room, and his arm pressed against hers. Pateman had told Cora and Maude that he had been on a two-year mission to England for the Mormon Church. He had converted several hundred people to his new religion. One hundred and sixty had joined with him when he returned to America. They had come by steamship from Liverpool to New York, and then up the Hudson River by steamboat to Albany, where they caught a railroad train chartered by the church to transport them to St. Joseph. They were now embarking on the last leg, of their journey to Salt Lake City, to Zion, as Pateman called the city. Cora was surprised that almost half of those who had followed Pateman across the ocean were young, single women. From the actions and the looks the women gave Pateman, Cora judged most were in love with the man.

Cora moved along the boat railing away from Pateman. She felt suffocated by his almost constant presence with Maude and her. Jacob had come to the docks to say goodbye and see them off on their journey. Pateman had monopolized Cora's time while Jacob was there, showing her where to park the wagon on the deck of the boat and where to tie the horse Then he had talked on and on, describing in great detail the trip upriver and the overland trek by handcart to Salt Lake City. Jacob had finally just shook his head in irritation, lifted his hand in farewell to Cora, and walked away from the dock. Cora was angry at Pateman, for she knew his actions were deliberately aimed at preventing Jacob from talking to her. She was also angry at Jacob for giving up so easily.

Maude, in contrast with Cora, was beaming at the attention Pateman showered on the two women. Few men were larger than Maude and she revelled in the fact that Pateman towered over her. Cora had never seen her sister so happy, so talkative, often smiling up into Pateman's face. Once Maude had actually taken Pateman by the hand and held it, until he had pulled free.

The riverboat reached the dock and the deck crew tied the riverboat to the rickety, wooden structure. The captain halted the engine and shouted down from the pilothouse to the deck hands, "Get the boiler fuel loaded aboard before it gets dark."

The men hurried up the bank to the nearest rick of wood, loaded large chunks of wood across their shoulders, and turned back to the riverboat.

The two woodcutters sat on the sawed ends of short lengths of wood on the porch of the cabin and looked down onto the deck of the riverboat tied to the docks a few yards away and below them. They methodically chewed their cuds of tobacco, spat brown juice into the yard, and watched the women spreading their sleeping pallets on the deck.

"It's hot and some of them Mormon girls are going to sleep outside in the open," one of the woodcutters said.

"I can see that plain enough," said the second woodcutter. "They sure do have some pretty girls. See that brown-haired one? The one with that big cow of a woman?"

"Yeah. I see the one you mean. She's sure a beaut."

"I think God made Mormon girls just for me and you."

"You're right. Yes sireee, Bob. Every year he sends them along the river past us so we can take our pick of the prettiest ones. The rest of the stupid Mormons just think she up and ran away from their damned polygamy religion and don't do much looking for her."

"We never have had any trouble when one disappears. We'll take the brown-haired one when it gets dark."

"Right. I can't hardly wait for it to get dark enough for them to settle down and go to sleep."

The first woodcutter spat a large stream of tobacco

juice off the porch. "After we're done with her, we'll just slide her into the river like we did all the others before. There'll be no trouble for us." He fished a coin from his pocket. "I'll flip you for who gets the first go at her"

"I'll take tails," said the second woodcutter. He laughed coarsely at his joke.

Cora rested on her pallet beside Maude on the stern of the riverboat. The deck was warm, for it still held memories of the heat of the day. She was glad when a slow wind crept out of the darkness on the river and washed over her. She hoisted the tail of her dress to mid-thigh and unbuttoned the bosom to allow the coolness of the breeze to reach her hot body.

She listened to Maude's even breathing in sleep, and watched the stars, bright pinpricks of light moving across the dome of the ebony sky. What adventures waited for her in the journey with the Mormons, and later in faraway California? Would she ever see Jacob Morgan again? She hoped so.

A bullfrog began to croak on the bank nearby, a big one from the deep bass of his voice. Little wavelets created by the wind struck with wet lapping sounds against the hull of the boat. The black bats came in the deepening night and began their tumbling dance in the darkness. Cora watched one's darting flight in the pale moonlight for a time before it vanished in the gloom. She felt a cooler breeze on her body and went to sleep thinking the journey to California might not be bad at all.

Cora came awake with a feeling of dread. She sensed great danger threatening her. She sat up and looked at Maude lying beside her, and found her sleeping soundly. Then she swept her eyes in the opposite direction to the railing of the boat. The black form of a man was crouched on the deck just inside the railing and but a few feet distant. She started to scream, but before the cry could pass her lips, the man pounced, falling on top of her and clamping her mouth shut with a hard hand. Another hand caught her around the waist and yanked her roughly against him.

Cora began to struggle furiously, kicking at the man with her feet and clawing at him with her hands. He caught her flailing arms and clamped them to her side. He rose to his knees, lifting her easily from her pallet. Standing erect, he turned with her toward the boat's railing.

Then Cora saw the second man standing outside the railing on the boat's coaming and reaching out for her with both hands.

Thirteen

Cora fought her attacker with frenzied fury. In a few seconds she would be carried off in the darkness to some awful fate. She strained to free her arms, but could not break loose of the iron hold the man had on her. She kicked his shins with all her strength. He seemed not to feel the blows from her bare feet.

She twisted her head violently trying to free her mouth to cry for help. The powerful hands of the man vised down more cruelly on her jaws, and he crushed her ever tighter against him, her chest to his chest, and stomach to stomach. Cora thought her ribs and the bones of her face were going to break.

The man pressed his mouth to Cora's ear and whispered, "Buck and hump, gal, for I like 'em when they fight me."

Cora felt his hot, rancid breath on her face and a silent chuckle vibrating deep inside his body. He carried her toward the second man waiting with outstretched, claw-like hands beyond the boat's railing.

Cora ceased her useless kicking of the man's legs. With a last desperate effort, she swung her foot out to the side as far as she could reach. She could not see the deck, however she knew Maude lay there close somewhere.

Maude came awake with a cry of pain as Cora's foot

struck her sprained ankle. She sat bolt upright. Against the moonlit sky, she saw Cora struggling in a man's arms. He was lifting her to a second man leaning over the stern railing of the boat. Maude surged to her feet.

Maude's cry had awakened the women sleeping on the deck around her. Now a bedlam of startled, frightened voices erupted. "What's wrong? What's happening? Make a light."

Maude shouted out above the uproar of voices. "Clive help!" She sprang at the man holding Cora. She grabbed him by the shoulder and the hair of his head and yanked him to a stop.

The woodcutter thought a man had caught him with a powerful grip. He dropped Cora, twisted to the rear, and smashed his balled fist into Maude's face.

The cruel blow staggered Maude backward. She tripped on her pallet and fell hard on the deck.

Cora scrabbled away from the man on hands and knees. She would find her Colt revolver and shoot the man before he could hurt Maude and her anymore. Then she saw Pateman burst out of the darkness on the starboard side of the boat where the men slept. He hesitated for but a fraction of a second, sweeping his eyes over the stern of the boat, the strange men, one inside the railing and one outside, Cora frightened and backing away from the men, and Maude trying to rise up from the deck. With a growl, he charged upon the men.

Pateman rammed the nearer man up against the railing and penned him there with his huge body. At the same time, he reached and caught the second man by the throat, jerked him forward, and slammed him down with great force over the railing. The hard wood of the railing broke several of the man's ribs, and one of the broken bones pierced the man's heart. He went limp as a rag doll. Pateman shoved the man backward, and he fell into the darkness below the lip of the deck.

Cora shivered as she watched the giant Mormon destroy her would-be kidnappers. He turned on the second man, grabbed him by the hair, pried his head back and slugged him twice in the face, knocking him unconscious. With great ease, Pateman lifted the man and heaved him over the boat railing and into the river. Cora heard the man's body splash into the water.

A light came to life in the captain's cabin atop the upper deck. The captain, carrying a lantern in one hand and a pistol in the other, ran outside and down the ladder toward the throng of awakened converts on the stern of the boat.

Pateman looked at Cora, studying her with a worried expression. "Are you all right?" he asked.

"My face hurts where he held me, but I'm all right."

The captain halted on the stern and, lifting his lantern up high, scanned around. "What happened?" he asked and looked at Pateman.

"Cora or Maude knows best and can tell you," Pateman replied.

"Two men tried to carry me off the boat," Cora said. "Maude came to help me and they hurt her. Then Clive came and stopped them."

"It was the woodcutters—I recognized them," Pateman said.

"Where are they now?" asked the captain. "We'll arrest them to take to Florence."

"I threw them in the river," Pateman said. "One I'm sure is dead. The other may be too, for I never saw him come up. I'd say you'd better hire yourself more woodcutters."

"Saves us the trouble of taking them to the law for trial," said the captain. He spoke to the crowd of people who had gathered around. "It's all over folks. Everything is okay. Go back to sleep. I'll post one of my men on guard just in case someone tries to cause trouble. We'll be on our way at first light."

Maude moved to stand beside Pateman as the people dispersed. She took his hand in hers. "Thanks for coming and helping us," she said.

"I wish I could've gotten here quicker to stop the man from hitting you," Pateman said to Maude. But he was looking past her and intently studying something that held greater interest for him.

Maude turned her head to follow the direction of Pateman's stare. She saw Cora. Maude's eyes flattened with jealousy and her jaw became ridged and hard.

Jacob awoke to deep darkness in his room in the Patte House hotel. He lay listening to the curtains rustling with the wind in the open window. Twenty days had passed since Cora had left St. Joe on the journey to Salt Lake City with the Mormons. He almost wished he had not discovered the beautiful young woman. He felt a deep gloom from losing her and that made him irritable and unable to sleep.

He climbed from bed and went to the window and stared out into the murk of the moonless night. The wind, coming strong off the Missouri River, sang a plaintive song as it was cut by the corners and rooftops of the dark buildings lining the street. He looked up to check the position of the stars and judged the time past midnight. The remainder of the night belonged mostly to the rough rivermen, the trappers gathering to leave for the mountains, and the town toughs and rowdies.

He splashed water on his face from the basin on the washstand and dried himself. He buckled his pistol on and went out of the hotel and onto the sidewalk. The street was deserted. The streetlamp that should have been burning in front of the hotel was unlit. Only the stars, pale and faraway, broke the Stygian gloom.

He heard the music of a piano and violin carried by the wind up from the River Palace still tied to the dock on the waterfront. That brought the pretty little doxy Corrine to mind. He had encountered her on the street after that first night and she had asked him to come and visit her. He had promised that he would, but never did. Once each week, on Sunday, he went to the home of Glen and his woman, Henrietta, on the far east side of town and had dinner with them. Also in his rambles around town, he had met Renne several times and they had drunk beer and played games of billiards together. Renne's company had temporarily helped to lighten Jacob's gloomy, downcast mood.

Jacob stood solitary and motionless on the sidewalk. Since he couldn't sleep, how would he spend the remainder of the night? Maybe more poker at Garveen's Saloon? He played there practically every night. Strangely, due to his morose attitude, not caring much if he won or lost, he most often won and was ahead of the game by more than three hundred dollars. During the day he frequently made long rides up or down the river astride Jubal.

As he pondered his next action, some instinct penetrated his mood of discontent. He sensed danger in the night. His eyes swung to probe the darkness and he stepped back against the wall of the hotel.

A pistol exploded on his right. He heard the whizzing pass of a bullet and felt it tug at the front of his shirt. He whirled in the direction of the shot, dropped to one knee, and jerked his pistol from its holster.

He caught a fleeting glimpse of the tall, thin figure of a man leaping into the mouth of the alley just beyond the hotel. The shooting range for the man had been short. Only the absence of the light and Jacob's step backward had saved his life.

Jacob spun the opposite way and sprinted toward the first intersecting street. If he should follow the shooter into the alley, the man could be lying in wait and have all the odds in his favor to pull a successful ambush. However, if Jacob could catch him coming out of the far end of the alley, then he would have the advantage.

He reached the first cross street and wheeled left into it and raced the length of the block. At the corner, he came cautiously into the street that ran behind the stables of the hotel. A half block away, a shadowy figure of a man in a flat-out run was vanishing in the black night.

Jacob halted, breathing hard. The man covered ground like a runner, and there would be little chance of catching him in the darkness. Why had somebody tried to kill him? With the poor visibility, had he been mistaken for someone else? Or had Shattuck finally decided to kill him because he had seen Tom Branham's mark on the furs? If so, why would Shattuck try after all these days?

Jacob cursed as he holstered his pistol. Getting shot at had deepened his foul mood. He went off in the direction of the town center.

In Garveen's Saloon Jacob bought a mug of beer at the bar and carried it to a seat where he could watch the players at the poker table. He began to study the five men, watching their expressions as they examined their cards, bet, and finally showed their hands.

At the end of a hand, one of the players threw his cards down on the table. "Goddamn, that cleans me out," he said. He shoved back his chair and stomped away.

Jacob started to rise to take the vacated seat and join the poker game, when a man stopped at his table and thumped a mug of beer down.

"Hello, Morgan, I see you made it from Fort Laramie," the man said.

Jacob reseated himself. The man was dressed in a town suit and hat, and sported a close-cropped black beard. "Well, Tom Branham, I do believe. I almost didn't recognize you."

Jacob motioned to the chair beside him. Branham dropped into it.

"Same with you," Branham said. "Changing from buckskin to store clothes and getting sheared of a bushel of hair makes a whale of a difference in how a man looks. How'd your partner heal up? Or did he?"

"Renne healed, but I think the wound bothers him now and again. Still, he doesn't complain."

"Wouldn't do any good."

"Yeah, I know. Where have you been? I've watched for you around town."

"I haven't been in St. Joe. Drew out the money I'd saved from the bank and went downriver to St. Louis to have some fun. Now I'm back to put together an outfit to go to the mountains for fur."

"Talking of fur, I saw yours. Your mark, "TB", was plain on the legs, just like you told us at Fort Laramie."

Branham's eyes narrowed and he leaned across the table. "Where was that at?"

"At Shattuck's."

"Now how could Shattuck have my furs when they were stole by Crow Indians hundreds of miles from here, way out in the Wyoming Territory?"

"Same thing I asked myself."

"Did you come up with an answer?"

"My best guess is that somehow Shattuck is hooked up with the Crows to take the furs they steal from trappers."

"One of my friends got killed by the Crows." Branham's eyes narrowed until they were mere slits. "I saw

Shattuck earlier today when I got off the riverboat. He had that warmed-over dead man, Aasland, with him. They sure didn't look pleased to see me."

Jacob touched the hole in the front of his shirt where the bullet had cut it. "So Shattuck and Aasland know you're in town. That tells me Aasland is the man who took a shot at me. I should've recognized that bony sonofabitch, even in the dark."

"What do you mean?"

"Somebody took a shot at me a short while ago. Shattuck knew I had seen your mark on the furs. He must've sent that skeleton man to shut me up before I talked to you."

"Seems like both of us have something to take up with Shattuck and Aasland. My furs will be long gone back east to market. So I'll have to take my pay out of Shattuck's hide."

"Let's go run those fellows down. We'll start at Shattuck's office."

"It's way past midnight. Neither of them will be there."

"Maybe they are, for it hasn't been all that long since Aasland tried to shoot me. Shattuck would want to know right away if I'm dead, so maybe he told Aasland to report to him at his office. But if not, we'll check the River Palace next. Shattuck likes the women there."

"The place is dark as Hades," Branham said, staring in through the front window of Shattuck's fur buying business. " 'Pears no one is here."

"Let's go down to the River Palace," Jacob said.

"Sure. But first I want to look around inside." Branham struck the windowpane with the barrel of his pistol and the shards of broken glass fell with a clatter. He stepped over the sill and inside. A match flared as he scratched it on the wall. The cavernous room was empty of all furs. "Nothing here I can steal to make up for my furs," Branham said.

Corrine broke into a pleased smile and started quickly forward to greet Jacob when he and Branham entered the River Palace. She halted partway across the room when Jacob shook his head in the negative and looked past her. His eyes settled with a glacial expression on Shattuck playing solitaire at a table on the river side of the room. Shattuck had been there for an hour, and with unexpected behavior had rudely rebuffed the women's attempts to engage him in conversation. Corrine backed away to stand by the bar.

Shattuck glanced up from his cards as Jacob and Branham stopped at his table. A foxy look came into his mud-colored eyes. Without looking down, he raked the cards into a pile and began to shuffle them. "Care for a game of cards, gents?" he said.

Jacob saw no surprise in Shattuck at seeing the two trappers. He was expecting them, and that meant Aasland must have reported that he had missed Jacob. Or would Aasland have attacked Jacob without Shattuck's orders and then not tell him about it?

"Where's Aasland?" Jacob said, scanning the room.

"How the hell would I know?" Shattuck said roughly. "I haven't seen him since earlier today. If there's something you fellas want to take up with me, then let's go outside."

"You first," Jacob said. He motioned with his hand for Shattuck to lead.

Shattuck smiled a joker's thin-lipped smile. "Sure, me first. Why not?" He stalked across the River Palace, out the door and onto the dock. He stopped in the light of the first storm lantern hanging on the cable, pivoted to face Jacob and Branham, and set his feet.

"Well, what's on your mind?" Shattuck said in a loud voice.

"Where's my furs?" Branham growled and thrust his face forward, ready to pounce on Shattuck. "Morgan told me he saw my mark on furs in your place. Those furs were stole off me and my men by Crows and are still rightfully mine."

"Morgan's a liar." Shattuck snapped back harshly.

"You're the liar, Shattuck." Jacob's words were like pieces of metal hitting. He readied himself to draw his pistol and shoot, for there was only one way this was going to end.

Shattuck's eyes narrowed like those of a sniper. He put his hand on the butt of the pistol belted to his side. "Branham, I don't have any furs with your mark on them."

"Sure you don't, you've sold them. Now I want pay for them."

Jacob was disturbed by Shattuck's willingness, actually his quick suggestion to leave the River Palace with two men, both his enemies. Aasland had taken the shot at Jacob. Where was the skeleton man? With suspicion building, Jacob twisted around, searching the darkness that blanketed the dock outside the narrow strip of illumination created by the lanterns.

Nothing was visible in the dense murk. He examined the lighted windows of the River Palace, then raised his eyes to the windows of the second deck where the women took their customers. Still, nothing dangerous. He looked up higher to the open upper deck.

A man was silhouetted against the stars, a rail-thin man. He held a long, thin object to his shoulder and was pointing it down at the men on the dock.

"Branham, it's a trap!" Jacob shouted.

Fourteen

Jacob grabbed his pistol from its holster, cocked it as it rose, and pointed it up at the man on the upper deck of the River Palace. He fired, and the red lance of flame from his gun reached out.

The man staggered back at the strike of the bullet. Then he righted himself and again sighted his rifle down at the dock. Jacob had quickly raised his pistol to eye level and was taking deliberate aim. He fired a second time. The man fell backward out of view on the deck.

Behind Jacob, two shots crashed, so close together they seemed almost to be but one. A hot, searing pain burned along his left ribs. He flinched and spun to help Branham against Shattuck.

Branham was tottering on his feet. He fought to remain erect, failed, and collapsed onto the dock. Shattuck stood spraddle-legged and grimacing with pain. His wounded right arm hung at his side. He fought to hold the pistol in his hand. Jacob realized the two men had shot each other, and Shattuck's bullet had gone through Branham and creased him.

Shattuck's eyes burned with hate. He reached down with his left hand and took the pistol from his right. He started to raise the weapon.

Jacob felt the certainty of his coming revenge, as ele-

mental as water flowing downhill; he was going to kill
this tricky, thieving bastard.

"Too late, Shattuck," Jacob growled, and fired.

The bullet found the weakness between two ribs of Shattuck's chest, rammed through breaking bones, and
plowed into the lungs. It crashed onward into the spinal
column, nearly severing the pathway of corded nerves.
The heavy body fell, and bucked and rolled and twitched
like a berserk marionette. The booted feet hammered the
wooden planks. A deformed shadow of Shattuck, a black
ghost, mimicked his every movement. Then he abruptly
stopped his wild death spasms, quivered, and lay still.

Jacob knelt beside the motionless body of Branham.
Blood soaked the front of his shirt. The yellow lantern
light on the man's lifeless eyes made them shine like
gold coins. Jacob had gotten Branham killed by telling
him Shattuck had his furs. Still, he couldn't have kept
it from the trapper. A man had to protect what was his
no matter what the danger.

Jacob straightened and walked into the night as men
and women streamed out of the River Palace behind
him. He heard someone shout, "There's been a killing,
get the marshal."

Jacob moved quickly around the hotel room preparing for travel. He had half an hour at best before the
town marshal would have been rousted from his bed
and be at the River Palace investigating the killing of
Shattuck and Branham. His clean buckskins were
shoved inside his bedroll. He assembled his wolfskin
coat, the Sharps carbine, his canteen, and the leather
pouch containing ammunition for both the Sharps and
his Colt pistol. He placed two twenty-dollar gold pieces
on the dresser as payment for his lodging.

He blew out the lamp, went quietly into the hallway,

and down the stairs. The lobby was empty. He left the hotel by the rear door.

The darkness felt soft as soot and hid everything. The wind still blew from the west, and the odor of the hotel stables, hay and horse manure, were strong. He moved up the wind toward the source of the odors. When he came into the end of the stables, Jubal caught his scent and nickered a welcome.

"Hello, old fellow," Jacob said. "I'm thinking the marshal might make me stretch your legs tonight."

He saddled swiftly in the darkness. The bedroll and coat were tied behind the saddle. The carbine went into the scabbard, and the ammunition into the saddlebags. He swung astride, walked Jubal outside, and reined him down the street that ran parallel to the river.

A short sprinting distance upriver from the River Palace, and in deep darkness, Jacob dismounted and tied Jubal to a tree. He hurried along the riverbank toward the lights and the hubbub of men and women at the killing place on the docks.

Marshal Whitfield straightened from examining the corpses of Shattuck and Branham and scanned the faces of the dozen or so whores from the River Palace. Also present were half as many men. Whitfield judged twice that number of men, not wanting to be found at the Palace with the whores, had fled after discovery of the killing. "All right, who knows what happened here?" he asked in a hard voice that cut through the babble of conversation.

The people fell quiet. They watched the marshal. No one spoke.

"Somebody saw something," the marshal said accusatively. "So speak up."

Jacob was approaching the group and heard the marshal's question. He shoved his way to the front. "I can tell you what happened," he said.

Marshal Whitfield focused on Jacob. "I've seen you around town. Who are you?"

"My name is Jacob Morgan."

"All right, Morgan, tell me about this." Whitfield pointed down at the dead man.

"Maybe we should talk without all these people listening."

Whitfield scowled at Jacob. Then he called to the crowd. "All of you go back inside and wait there for me. I've got questions for you."

Whitfield kept his sight on Jacob as he waited for the men and women to move beyond earshot. He caught movement in the darkness and looked past Jacob. A moment later, Glen Kinshaw came into the light of the lanterns.

"So Branham and Shattuck got into a fight," Glen said, glancing down at the dead men. He spoke to Jacob. "When I heard about Shattuck getting shot, I thought I'd come and see if you were part of it."

"Sounds like you might know something about this, Kinshaw," Whitfield said. "But first let's hear what Morgan has to say."

Glen and Jacob locked eyes. "Better start from the beginning, Jacob," Glen said. "Whitfield is a fair man, but he needs to know all there is to know."

"Why are you taking such a big interest in this?" Whitfield asked Glen.

"Jacob is my partner." He stared steadily into Whitfield's questioning face. "I want to be sure he gets a fair shake, no matter what took place here."

"Talk," Whitfield said to Jacob.

Jacob described the meeting with Branham at Fort Laramie where the trapper told about his pelts being stolen by Crows, and his mark on the pelts. Of stumbling onto Branham's marks on pelts at Shattuck's. He poked a finger through the hole in his shirt and told about someone shooting at him. That he knew the gunman was Aasland after he later talked with Branham at Garveen's and found out Shattuck and Aasland had seen Branham arriving in St. Joe. He finished by telling about the ambush Shattuck had set, and the gunfight. He then turned and pointed at the top deck of the River Palace. "I believe there's a dead man up there and it's that boney bag Aasland."

"Let's go take a look," Whitfield said.

Whitfield removed the nearer lantern from the cable and led the way through the riverboat to the upper deck. In the light of the lantern, they found the corpse lying on the deck of the boat. Whitfield turned the man face up.

"Aasland, all right," Whitfield said. "God, he's even uglier dead. He's got a rifle next to him." He stood erect and faced Jacob and Glen. "I knew Shattuck was part owner of the River Palace and was selling the services of whores. But dealing with Indians for stolen furs, now that's something I'm not so sure about." He concentrated on Kinshaw. "Did you see the marked pelts in Shattuck's?"

"No, but Jacob told me what he had seen just as soon as we got outside Shattuck's place."

Whitfield studied the two men for a moment. "Wait here until I ask some questions from the whores and the fellows down below," Whitfield said. He moved away.

Jacob sat down on one of the passenger benches of the boat. Glen dropped down beside him.

"Glen, the marshal may not believe the truth of what happened and try to arrest me. I'm not going to let him do that. Shattuck was an important man in town. If I stood trial, the jury might find me guilty of murder, and put a hangman's noose around my neck. So stand clear, for I don't want you part of any fight I have with the marshal.''

"All right," Glen said simply and fell quiet.

Jacob was glad Glen did not speak further. He forced his mind to think of other things. He listened to the gurgling sound the river current made around the pilings of the dock. More distant on the dark water, a big fish surfaced with a ripple of water, then dove with a splash of its tail.

Jacob's mind jumped farther away still, out on the great prairie west of Florence. Cora was there somewhere in the darkness. The prairie was the edge of civilization, where man's law stretched and broke. White renegades preyed upon the travelers for the first two to three hundred miles west of Florence, and beyond that the Indian warriors raided. Quicksand made the river crossings dangerous, and floods came with the torrential thunderstorms. He knew of a big rattlesnake den under a sandstone ledge near the crossing point of the Loup River. Horses sometimes ran away wrecking the wagons and hurting the drivers. A dozen different kinds of accidents could happen. Jacob felt a deep pain at the thought that Cora might be hurt or in grave danger, or somehow lost from the Mormon handcart company and all alone in the wilderness.

"Glen, I need to talk with you after this is over," Jacob said.

"All right." Glen looked at the young man staring to the west. He thought he knew what Jacob wanted to tell him, and felt a great loss.

The two did not speak again. After a time Marshal Whitfield came back to the upper deck. He stopped in front of them.

"Kinshaw, you and me go back a lot of years. Now

tell me how much I can trust what Morgan has told me?"

Glen looked at Jacob. The face of his young friend held that stony, determined look that it held when he was ready to spring into fierce action. "Jacob doesn't lie. I'd bet my life that he's told you the truth. Shattuck tried to kill him because he didn't want him to tell about the stolen furs. Not only would Shattuck be in trouble for handling them, but if all the trappers heard about it, they'd never sell him another fur."

Whitfield nodded. "Morgan, what I've heard down below bears out what you said about Shattuck setting up an ambush for you and Branham. The whore Corrine told me she saw Shattuck and Aasland talking together before you arrived, and then Aasland went up to the top deck carrying a rifle."

"Does that mean I'm free to go?" Jacob asked. Past Whitfield, he saw Corrine standing at the top of the stairs located midway the boat. She must have followed Whitfield up. The lantern light barely reached her; still, Jacob saw her give him a wave. He thought she also smiled at him, but wasn't sure because of the darkness. Had she truly seen Shattuck and Aasland talking, and Aasland with the rifle? Corrine turned and disappeared down the stairs, and he never saw her again.

"I guess so. Yeah, you're off the hook. I'm going to call it a justified shooting."

"That's just what it was," Jacob said. He glanced at Glen. "You going my way?"

"Just as far as you want."

They left the River Palace and went into the darkness. Jacob guided Glen to Jubal tied to the tree. They stood quietly together in the cloaking night.

Finally Jacob spoke. "Glen, I'm going to catch the steamboat upriver to Florence in the morning."

"Going after that pretty girl, I reckon. You haven't

been the same since you saw her." His young friend was badly smitten by the girl.

"Nothing seems right the way it is. I'm going to California with her. See that she gets there safely."

"Have you thought of what you will do if she turns down your offer?"

"No."

"Well, I have a plan. Renne and me will be going to the mountains in a month. We'll bring enough traps and other equipment for three. You can catch us along the trail and go trapping with us."

"Thanks, Glen, I'll do that if things don't go right. But I'm hoping everything will be okay. Tell Renne I'm sorry that I'm running out on him, you know, about growing grapes and building a winery."

"I'll tell him."

"Well then, goodbye." Jacob held out his hand to Glen. He would miss his two longtime friends.

He rode Jubal off through the night.

Jacob waited impatiently as the ancient riverboat *Providence* churned across the current of the Missouri River toward Florence. The boat was heavily loaded with cargo for the town of some two thousand people, and the other, smaller settlements along the river. She carried but few passengers, six counting Jacob.

The instant the gangway thumped down on the dock, Jacob, leading his packhorse, rode ashore. He went at once to the big general store in the center of the town. The owner was an old friend of his and knew everything that happened in and around Florence.

He entered and crossed the store. "Hello, Lester, you old reprobate," Jacob said and smiled at the aged and stooped storekeeper behind the counter.

"Hello, Jacob," Lester replied and grinned with

pleasure at seeing. Jacob. "Don't be so smart—you're going to be old one day, and you'll be uglier than me."

"I don't doubt it. I didn't see any Mormons around. How long have they been gone west?"

Lester thought a moment, sucking in on his gaunt, wrinkled cheeks. "Ten days now, Jacob," he said. "They camped out on the prairie for better than a week waiting for the workmen to finish building the last of the handcarts."

"They got an awfully late start for a thousand-mile journey."

"I told that big Mormon, Pateman, that they should winter here and then leave in the spring. He wouldn't hear of it. Said the Lord would hold off the snow and let them through to Salt Lake City. Now ain't that tomfoolish thinking? It's been my experience that the Lord goes on and does what he wants without caring for us humans."

"You gave the man good advice, for winter can come early in the mountains. And talking about winter, I hope you've laid in a supply of buffalo sleeping robes. My old one was wore out and I threw it away."

"I bought a hundred or so this spring from a band of friendly Omahas. They're in the storeroom in the back."

"I'll take a look at them."

He entered the storeroom and began to carefully examine the mound of robes that reached nearly to his shoulders. Halfway to the bottom, he chose a hide from a yearling bull, with long guard hairs and a fine, dense undercoat. The Omaha squaw had prepared the hide with excellent care; the robe had no odor and was soft as heavy velvet. With his wool blanket and the robe he could lie down and sleep warmly in the most frigid and snowy blizzard.

* * *

Jacob hurried west, following the trail of the Mormons. The wheel marks of the handcarts and wagons and many human footprints were plainly visible on the worn and rutted route used by immigrants and soldiers going to Fort Laramie, and onward to Utah and Oregon. The way followed the Platte River west to its junction with the North Platte, then northwest along the North Platte to Fort Laramie. There those people going to Oregon went northwest. The Mormons would turn southwest onto the last leg of the journey to Salt Lake City.

The hot sun burned down cruelly and Jacob and his horses sweated. Still he felt light of heart, because for the first time in many days he was pleased with what he was doing, where he was heading. Cora was growing nearer and nearer with each thud of Jubal's hooves on the dusty ground.

Jacob was worried about the dangerously late start the Mormons had made on their journey. The danger was especially great because the last four hundred miles of the trek was the most difficult, for it ran through the towering peaks of the Bear River Mountains and the Wasatch Mountains. He had seen snow in those mountains in October. The Mormons pulling handcarts could travel, with good luck and pushing hard, fifteen to twenty miles each day. The earliest they could reach Salt Lake City would be in late October or early November. Storms and accidents would probably slow them and make their arrival much later. Should heavy snow fall and close the high passes, the people would be trapped, unable to go forward or backward. Many would die of hunger and cold before spring unlocked the land again.

He checked the sun, low on its sky trajectory and falling fast toward the horizon. He must hurry. He raised Jubal and the packhorse to a gallop and raced them straight into the face of the setting sun.

When the last of day burned away to black ash, Jacob

reluctantly halted his running animals. He made a silent camp on the edge of night. For a long time, he sat in the darkness with Cora's beautiful face brightly etched into his memory.

Finally he lay down to a troubled sleep. Several times he awoke and, impatient to again hasten west, checked the position of the stars to know the time remaining until daylight.

Jacob was already riding when dawn arrived from the east. Jubal well rested and wanted to run, but Jacob held him down to a steady gallop. The day would be long and hard, so Jacob would ration the horse's strength.

The morning sun finally climbed above the curve of the earth and its bright yellow rays fought the night shadows and drove them into the hollows and crevices of the prairie and killed them there. The sun caught Jacob and Jubal, and horse and man, like one animal, cast a shadow that lay long and thin on the trail ahead. Jubal chased the shadow on and on.

Fifteen

Cora plodded along beside the horse that pulled her covered wagon across the prairie. She wiped at the sweat on her face with the sleeve of her shirt. The sun was a fireball overhead and the wind lay dead. Walking in the heat was like wading through liquid gravity. She pitied the Mormon people bent in heart-breaking labor to pull their handcarts over the scorching land.

The Mormon caravan of forty handcarts and three wagons were strung out for more than a quarter mile across the prairie. The three oxen-drawn supply wagons led the way. Then came the forty handcarts, one after the other. Cora's wagon followed the last cart. Bringing up the rear was the herd of fourteen steers driven by three of the older boys. There had been fifteen steers until one had been butchered for its meat at the beginning of the week. Another steer would be slaughtered every week or so until the travelers reached Salt Lake City.

The handcarts were two-wheeled vehicles, consisting of a crude wooden box set on an axle between four-foot-tall iron-rimmed wheels. The boxes were three feet wide, four feet long and nine inches deep. Short shafts extended forward from the box for three feet, with a front crossbar to push against. A cart weighed sixty pounds empty. Each person was allowed seventeen pounds of personal items, including bedding and one change of clothing. The remainder of the space was used for the transport of food: oatmeal, rice, peas, potatoes, flour, sugar, salt. Loaded, the carts weighed two hundred pounds. There was a piece of canvas to cover everything.

Clive came into sight, walking along the string of hand-carts toward her. She felt aggravated and angry at the man's frequent appearance at her wagon. This was the thirteenth day on the trail and he was showing up to walk and talk with her more and more often. He was handsome enough, but she had no interest in him, and besides, he was more than twice her age—much too old for her. She noted he always timed his visits when Maude was at the far end of the caravan. That meant he was aware of her sister's strong attraction for him.

"Any problems, Cora?" Clive asked as he fell into step beside her.

"None," Cora said shortly. She had found that the less she said, the shorter the man's visits were.

To her surprise, Clive reached out and caught her hand. He had never done that before. She tried to withdraw her hand, but he held it firmly in his big maw of a fist.

"I'm very glad you decided to travel with us to Salt Lake City," he said.

"How much longer will it take to reach there?" Cora asked. She was certain that she and Maude had made a serious mistake in not waiting in St. Joe for a wagon train to California.

"I estimate we've come about a hundred and thirty miles, which isn't too good. But the people have grown stronger now and we're moving faster than before. Still, we've got nearly three months of travel left. That's if nothing bad happens to slow us down."

Cora remained silent, hoping Clive would leave. However, he continued to walk along beside her, holding her hand.

Clive spoke. "In a few days this heat will be behind us. As we work our way west toward the mountains we'll be climbing higher and higher, and soon we can expect freezing temperatures at night."

"You said we have three months' travel left. Won't it be winter in three months? That old man back at the store in Florence said snow might fall on us. Living in New Orleans all my life, I've never seen snow."

Pateman looked down at Cora. For the first time, she saw doubt in his face. "We don't want snow, Cora. That's the very worst thing that could happen to us."

"I didn't say I wanted snow, only that I've never seen it." She took advantage of Clive's distraction to pull her hand free of his grasp. "I'm sure everything will be all right," she said.

"Yes, I'm sure it will be, too. Well, there are people who need help and Maude can't do it all," Clive said. He left, walking up the line of handcarts.

Clive's possessions were carried in one of the supply wagons. Thus freed, the missionary went among the converts giving encouragement, and pushing where needed on one handcart, or pulling on another. At the fording of the first major stream, the Elkhorn River, Maude had climbed down from the wagon and gone to help Clive. He had smiled at her, and expressed his thanks. Together they helped every cart to climb up the steep riverbank and again onto the prairie. Now each day Maude, like Clive, went along the line of vehicles lending the strength of her big body to those people needing it.

It was at the Elkhorn crossing that it became obvious that one of the supply wagons was much overloaded. The oxen were unable to pull the wagon up the bank. Clive had asked Maude and Cora if they would help transport part of the provisions. Maude had quickly agreed. Thereupon Clive had transferred six one-hundred pound sacks of flour into their wagon. Cora, driving the wagon on, soon discovered the addition of the flour to the load already in the wagon was too much for her single horse. She had climbed down, and now for the past nine days had walked.

Cora had seen many rotting carcasses of cattle, buffalo, and horses along the trail. Vultures fed on the carrion of some of the more recent dead. The bones of other skeletons were picked a pristine white by scavenger teeth.

Cora had not anticipated people dying and was dismayed at the number of graves beside the trail. The Mormons of her caravan had added to the number, for they were now two fewer than when they had started. A baby boy of one year had died of a high fever and convulsions on the fifth day out of Florence. The small body was buried in the prairie sod. A few days later, Mr. Campbell had fallen down unconscious and died of exhaustion in the heat of an afternoon. After the funeral, his widow dashed away her tears. She sorted through their scant belongings and transferred a few articles to the handcart of people who had agreed to accept her with their group. The caravan had journeyed on, the widow pushing at the rear of the vehicle. Her own cart had been left behind on the prairie.

Several of the handcarts had only young women, three or four, pulling them. One of the handcarts had gotten out of control on a steep downslope and ran forward over a girl's foot, badly injuring it. She now rode in one of the supply wagons. Nobody rode except the injured girl and the smallest children.

When the sun dropped below the horizon, Clive halted the caravan for the night in a grove of trees beside a live creek. The tents were pitched in a big circle enclosed by the handcarts. Two men drove the oxen and steers out to graze. One of the men carried a rifle.

Cora parked her wagon just outside the circle of handcarts. She unhitched the horse and led it out to graze with the cattle. The men accepted the new animal with a nod at Cora.

She stopped as she returned to the wagon and stared west across the limitless green prairie. In the shadows of evening, the vast, flat emptiness inspired a disconsolate feeling about a woman's insignificance, a sense that she did not matter at all. However, she felt her destiny lay in that direction. But what was her destiny to be? Was it to be a life of riches, or poverty? Maybe only a short life and then death here in the wilderness? She would go on and discover the future.

Maude came up as Cora reached the wagon. The clothes of the big woman were covered with dust, and just below the mark of her hat band, salt rime made a white band across her forehead. She sank down to sit on the ground and lean wearily against a wheel of the wagon.

"It's hard going," Maude said.

"Yes it is, the way you're doing it," Cora replied. "It's tough enough just walking all these long miles in this heat. I believe we made at least twenty today. Why not walk with me beside the wagon?"

"There are others who need help. And Clive needs me, for he can't do it all by himself."

Cora recalled Clive had used those very same words about Maude. She knew it was Clive that Maude wished to help and please more than the people. She wanted to be near him all the time. Cora was worried about Maude, for Clive seemed to have no interest in her beyond the aid she gave the people. And Cora was terribly afraid Maude would find out about Clive's attention to her.

"How about a bath before we eat?" Cora said.

"That would be nice."

They went up the creek and entered a small cove of woods. In a pool of quiet water, they bathed and then sat silently on the bank as the daylight leaked away into the heavens. As the shadows darkened in the woods, the mosquitoes came out of their hiding places and began to sing their vampiric arias around the faces of Cora and Maude. The sisters left the woods and walked through the dusk to the wagon.

Cora built a small fire beside the wagon and began to cook the evening meal. Maude brought her blankets from the wagon, spread them on the grass, and sat down to rest. Now and again she looked expectantly at the Mormon camp. Cora knew Maude was watching for Clive. Every evening after he had made his round of the Mormon camp, investigating the condition of his converts and their carts, he came and talked with Maude and Cora.

As they finished their evening meal, Clive came out from the circle of handcarts and walked through the growing darkness to the wagon. He squatted on his heels beside the fire.

"Good evening," he said solemnly, as if he hadn't seen them all day.

"Good evening to you," Maude replied and fastened her eyes on the man.

"Hello," Cora said.

"You both are coming to the evening services, aren't you?" he asked.

"Yes, certainly," Maude said.

Clive spoke to Cora. "And you?"

"I'll come," she said. Clive's preaching was not interesting. He preached the same church dogma over and over again.

"Good," Clive said. "I have something important for you both to consider. Don't go to California. Become one of us, become a Mormon. It's the true religion. I can bring the Bible and The Book Of Mormon and explain our beliefs to you. May I do that?"

"We would like to have you tell us about your religion," Maude said. "Isn't that right, Cora?"

"If you want to." Cora did not think highly of Clive's suggestion. However, she could see that Maude was pleased with the idea.

"Make your home in Salt Lake City with us," Clive said. "It's a beautiful place. There is land for the taking. Our people are expanding out from the city in every direction, making settlements in one mountain valley after another. The land is rich and the people make it productive by damming the streams for irrigation water. They plant grain fields and vegetable gardens and orchards. The people are reaping a bountiful harvest. You can also."

"That sounds wonderful," Maude said.

Clive spoke to Cora. "Tomorrow I can take one of the sacks of flour out of your wagon and divide it among the people. That will lighten your load and you can ride again."

"I'll go on walking as long as the others do," Cora replied. She wished the man didn't show so much interest in her in front of Maude, or at any time.

"But there's no reason for you to do that." Clive's eyes were locked on Cora and his voice held deep concern for her. "Ride and save your strength; you will need it in the mountains."

"Some of the smaller children can ride," Cora said. She glanced at Maude, who was intently watching Clive. A light of understanding of Clive's desire for Cora was dawning on Maude. She turned suddenly to Cora; her eyes flattened with anger and her face took on a hard skin. Her mouth opened as if she was about to shout something at Cora, then it closed with a snap of teeth.

Clive saw the anger in the older sister, and the younger, pretty one becoming so tense that she seemed almost rigid. He realized his mistake. Hastily he climbed to his feet. "The service will begin in a quarter hour. Do come." He walked quickly away.

"You bitch!" Maude hissed at Cora the moment Clive was out of hearing.

"Maude, I haven't done anything to make him like me." Cora felt terrible that Maude was angry at her. Clive was the person she should be angry with.

Maude jumped to her feet and towered over Cora. "You lie! I've seen him walking with you. I've seen how you look at him. How you flaunt yourself! Do you think I'm blind?"

Cora sprang erect and stepped back from Maude. The small flickering flames of the fire first lit Maude's face, then the features darkened as the flames weakened. One moment the face showed distinctly, the next moment the face was only a murky form with bared teeth in the opening of her mouth. It appeared as if some animal within Maude was trying to break out. Cora shivered. For the first time in her life, she was afraid of her sister.

"Maude, I never—"

"I know what you're trying to do. You're trying to steal Clive away from me." Maude's voice was shrill, wild. She held up her big hands, bent claw-like. "I should rip your pretty face off."

"Please! Please! I—"

"Shut up! Shut up!" Maude turned and ran into the darkness.

* * *

Cora stood just outside the ring of handcarts and watched the Mormon's evening religious service. A large fire had been built in the center of the area and the yellow flames illuminated the gathering of people, and Clive in front preaching to them. She saw Maude on the far fringe of the crowd, staring with an expression of adoration at Clive. Cora relaxed somewhat. Her purpose in coming to the service was to find Maude, worried about what she might do.

Clive was nearing the conclusion of his sermon. "Brothers and Sisters, Ye have felt the calling to come to the True Church for your salvation. Ye gathered together and came with me to America, the most joyous place on the face of the earth. We shall continue on across the prairie and up into the mountains to the shore of the beautiful Great Salt Lake. There Ye shall be in the Kingdom of God on earth, and it is called Zion."

He lifted both arms to the black sky. "There you can live a righteous life and serve God. You shall surely go to his Celestial Kingdom on high when your time here on earth is finished."

Cora left before Clive finished his sermon and returned dejectedly to the wagon. Her tears came for the pain she knew Maude felt, and for herself also, for she knew Maude would never be the sister she had been before.

She spread her blankets on the ground on the opposite side of the wagon from Maude's pallet. She placed her little .28-caliber Colt within easy reach. How awful it was to be afraid of a sister.

Sixteen

Cora was sitting on her sleeping pallet and pulling on her boots when Clive blew a loud blast on his whistle as he did every morning to awaken the Mormon camp. She looked around for Maude and found her bedroll empty. Then Maude came into sight, carrying a bucket of water from the creek.

Without a glance or word to Cora, Maude emptied the bucket into the water barrel fastened to the side of the wagon. She rolled her blankets and put them in the rear of the vehicle. From the grub box she took a handful of dried apples, and walked away to enter the circle of handcarts.

Cora felt a deep sadness at the gulf that had been created between Maude and her. Though she knew it was not her fault, she still felt somehow responsible. She looked to the east back along the trail to Florence. Would it be better to return to St. Joseph and wait until spring to go to California with a wagon train? Would Maude be agreeable to that? Cora didn't think so.

She went onto the prairie to fetch her horse. The two guards saw her coming and one of them caught the horse and came with it to meet her. She led the animal to the creek to drink, then to the wagon where she backed it in between the shafts. The harness with its thick leather straps, chains, and connecting iron rings was heavy. However, her strength had increased considerably since her journeys had begun and she easily lifted the harness and placed it on the horse's back. As she was hooking the trace chains to the singletree, Clive and a second man came up and stopped near her.

"Cora, we've come to get the sack of flour," Clive said.

"The canvas in back is open," she said, connecting the last trace chain and not looking at the men.

"All right. Won't take us but a minute." He nodded at the man and both went to the rear of the wagon.

Clive lifted the large sack of flour from the bed of the wagon and laid it on the man's shoulder. "Divide it evenly so there won't be any arguments," he directed the man.

Cora heard Clive's words and knew he planned to remain and talk with her. She didn't want his company. Why didn't he realize that and leave her alone?

"Cora, now that the load is lighter you can ride in the wagon," Clive said, walking toward where she stood by the horse.

"I told you that I'm got going to ride. I'll pick up some of the small children."

"Whatever you want, Cora." He moved closer. "But there's something important I want to talk about with you." He looked intently at her. "The Mormon men who go on missions are almost always single. When they return to Salt Lake City, they find a pretty girl and get married in the Tabernacle. I believe you know how I feel about you. I want you to marry me. Will you become my wife?"

Clive reached for Cora's hand, but she quickly stepped back, avoiding him. Her anger boiled up. Didn't he know that should she marry him, Maude would be destroyed? And further, that she had no desire at all to be his wife?

"I'll never marry before Maude does," she said heatedly. "She loves you. Make Maude your wife."

Clive made a step toward Cora as if to catch hold of her. "But she's so plain, while you are—"

"Stop! Stay away!" Cora's voice cut at Clive and her fists clenched at her sides. "I don't want to hear anymore. Maude must be married before I can even consider it."

Clive halted his advance immediately at Cora's vehement outburst. He studied her for a time before looking in the direction of the camp, where they both knew Maude was, then back at Cora. For several seconds more he held his eyes locked on Cora and did not move.

"Have it your way, Cora," Clive said in a hard tone. His face was flushed with anger at the rejection. He pivoted and walked toward the camp.

"Damnation," Cora said under her breath. She and Maude couldn't continue on with the Mormons under these circumstances. She must persuade Maude to return with her to St. Joe.

She went to the front of the horse and connected the shafts to the hames. Then, gathering up her sleeping pallet and a few other loose items, she stowed them away. She looked across the camp to locate Maude.

To Cora's surprise, Maude came running from the circle of handcarts. She was shouting out happily and her face was wreathed in smiles. She grabbed Cora and hugged her, lifting her completely off the ground.

"Cora, something wonderful has happened. Clive has asked me to marry him. And I thought it was you he cared for!" Her voice rose in a happy lyrical tone. "I'm going to be Clive's wife."

Cora looked penetratingly at Maude. "Clive asked you to marry him?" she said, deeply puzzled by Maude's news.

"Yes! Yes! He told me Mormon missionaries always marry upon coming home from a mission. That he wanted a wife. Then he said he wanted me for a wife. Cora, this is what I've dreamed about ever since I met him."

"I know it is, and I'm happy for you." Cora was alarmed that something was terribly wrong, something she could not yet see. What could it be?

"Oh, dear sister, I owe you an apology. I thought you had enticed him away from me. I was so very wrong. He told me that you wanted him to marry me." Maude hugged Cora closely to her bosom. "Thank you for my life. Without Clive, I would have surely died."

"I'm sure you will be very happy."

"We'll be married just as soon as we reach Salt Lake City," Maude said. She gave Cora another hug and ran off like a schoolgirl toward the camp of the Mormons.

To Cora, walking doggedly beside the horse, each mile the caravan covered looked no different from the one before. The flat, grass-covered prairie stretched away in all directions to the faraway horizon without a stream or a tree to break the monotonous sameness. Time could have been flowing backward and she would not have known it.

Nearby in one of the sun's hot updrafts, a dust devil came alive and whirled across the prairie to pounce on the caravan, spinning up the dust and tattered grass in a storm. Cora closed her eyes and stopped breathing until the rotating funnel with its load of trash had passed. Bending and twisting, the dust devil swept away.

The day wore on, the yellow orb of the sun climbing to the zenith and walking slowly down its ancient path across the sky. As the sun neared the horizon, it threw its sharp slanting rays to pierce the eyes of the people like needles. The sun sank lower and the dusk came hurrying, forewarning the near arrival of the night.

The noise of the creaking wheels of the handcarts ahead of Cora ceased as the caravan halted. The day's travel had ended at last. She lifted the five children riding in the wagon, three girls and two boys, down to the ground. "Go find you mothers and fathers," Cora told them. The tykes ran with little shouts up the line of carts.

Maude came up. "Not one sign of water," she said.

"We must ration what we have," Cora replied. Maude had been very friendly since Clive's proposal.

"I'll be gone awhile, for there are some sick people who need help setting up their tents."

"I'll save you a plate of food," Cora replied.

The night seemed to fall with unnatural swiftness and Cora hurried with the chores. She turned the horse out with the other animals and gathered buffalo chips for the evening cooking fire. A simple meal of dried apples cooked with rice, fried bacon, and bread was prepared. She divided the food, placing Maude's portion on a tin plate and setting it aside.

She sat by the dying fire and stared into the darkness lying dense on the awesome, lonely void of the prairie. There was no moon and the stars glittered like ice shards flung across the sky.

She heard footsteps and Clive came out of the gloom and up to the fire. "It's a black night," he said.

Cora looked at him with a cautious, enquiring eye, but said nothing.

"May I sit with you for a moment?" Clive asked.

She hesitated in replying, for she knew whatever it was Clive wanted to talk about would not be to her liking. "Yes," she said, and watched his shadowy form sink down on the opposite side of the fire.

He pulled a handful of dry grass and tossed it onto the fire. The grass caught fire easily and bright flames flared up. He looked at Cora's face in the light of the flames.

"I did as you wanted," Clive said. "I asked Maude to marry me."

"I know. You have made her very happy."

"We will announce our betrothal when we reach Salt Lake City." Clive was silent for a moment. "I want to announce our plan, yours and mine, to marry at the same time."

"What! What did you say?"

"That you and I are also to be married."

"What gave you that idea?"

"You said that you couldn't marry me until Maude was married. Well, now Maude soon will be."

"I never said I'd marry you."

"That's what I understood. Why else would I ask Maude? I never thought of her as my wife until you mentioned it."

Cora was stricken at Clive's interpretation of her words. She certainly did not want him for a husband. And further, it was totally alien to her to even consider sharing a husband with another woman. She had heard the Mormon women discuss plural marriage. Some of the men were said to have two wives, three, ten, and more. Never would she allow herself to become one wife among several.

"I can't be your wife," she said firmly.

Clive pulled back as if surprised at her words. Then his eyes hardened. "But I asked Maude to marry me because of you. And Maude surely wants to marry me." There was a warning in the tone of his voice.

"You misunderstood me. Now let's not talk about this anymore."

"It's not going away that easily. I want you to be my wife."

"I gave you my answer," Cora said, her voice rising with finality. She believed Clive had deliberately twisted her words to suit himself.

"You gave an answer on what?" Maude said, coming out of the darkness and into the light of the fire.

Cora was sorry Maude had heard any of the conversation. She must never know what Clive had said.

"I asked Cora to marry me," Clive bluntly said.

"What! What did you say?" Maude asked in a shocked voice.

"I asked Cora to marry me," Clive repeated, his voice louder and containing a growling undertone.

An expression of disbelief washed over the big woman's plain face. She seemed to shrink into herself. Her features became distorted, growing more homely with each passing second. In a voice tight and raspy, she spoke to Cora. "What did you say?"

Before Cora could reply, Clive spoke to Maude. "I told you that Mormon men often took more than one wife. You said you understood that."

Maude spoke in a voice full of pain and misery. "But you never said you were going to ask another woman to marry you now, even before you and I were wed. And my own sister!"

"Mormon men have found that marrying sisters makes for a happier home. Sisters can share a husband more readily than unrelated women."

Tears glistened in Maude's eyes as she looked at Cora. "What answer did you give Clive?" she asked.

"I told him I couldn't marry him. That he was your husband-to-be."

Clive stared at first one woman then the other. Then his sight settled on Maude. His face was bleak and his voice flinty as he spoke to her. "Maude, you convince her that this is what she must do." He stalked away, his big body stiff.

The sisters watched Clive mingle with the dark and disappear. They did not look at each other. After a long silence and still not looking at Cora, Maude spoke.

"Clive asked me to marry him because of something you said. What did you tell him earlier?"

"He misunderstood what I said. Or at least he acts like he did."

Maude whirled angrily around on Cora. Her eyes were wide with the whites showing around the dark centers. "Damn you! Tell me what you said."

Cora drew back from Maude. "That I couldn't marry before you did. It was my way of telling him I didn't want him for a husband without making him mad."

"So he asked you to marry him before he asked me?"

"Yes. But Maude, I don't want to be his wife. I believe he has deliberately misinterpreted my words to mean what he wants."

Maude's hands rose to clutch at her head. She began to tremble as if she struggled to control some inner battle. She abruptly started to cry. "Now I see it all. He will never marry me unless you also marry him."

"Don't cry, Maude. There will be other men who will ask you to be their wife."

"You're wrong. I will never have another chance, and I want Clive." She wiped her hands across her eyes and looked at Cora. "You must agree to marry him. We can get along, you and I. We have for all these years while you were growing up."

"I don't want to be Clive Pateman's wife. He's too old for me. And I don't even like him."

"You must! Can't you hear me? You must!"

"Even if I should, he may take other wives after he gets tired of us. What then?"

Maude made a deprecating gesture with her hands. "We'll face that when it comes, if it comes. I'm going to tell him that you will marry him."

As if afraid Cora would object, Maude hastily spun around and hurried off in the direction of the Mormon camp.

Cora stared after Maude. She did not call her sister back.

Jacob topped the low rise of ground and spotted the Mormon handcart company less than a mile ahead. The people and vehicles and animals looked small and puny, like a string of bugs lost on the immense prairie. He hoped nothing had happened to harm Cora.

"Jubal, you long-legged bastard, you've caught them," Jacob said in a happy voice. The picture of Cora's face as she had looked at their parting in St. Joe came to him. She had appeared sad at leaving him. Would she now be glad to see him?

He touched Jubal in the ribs with his heels and the horse hurried on.

Cora checked the mass of towering thunderheads not two miles distant and marching like giants upon the caravan. Lightning flashed bright and violent and thunder rumbled. Rain was leaking from the black, swollen bottoms of the thunderheads. Strong winds rushed out from the storm front and buffeted Cora, whipping up the dust from under the wheels of the vehicles and the feet of the people.

As Cora thought that the Mormons should halt and prepare for the storm, the string of handcarts ahead of her stopped. Immediately Clive came down the caravan shouting directions at the people. Swiftly they pulled the handcarts into the usual circular pattern. Tents began to sprout from the prairie.

Cora set the brake on her wagon, moved to the bed and lifted the children she carried down to the ground. They vanished inside the ring of carts like baby quail into tall grass when threatened by the hawk overhead. She unhooked the shafts of the wagon from the hames.

"Do you need help, Cora?" A man spoke behind her.

She turned at the sound of the voice. Her heart began to race with a rich rush of excitement. Jacob Morgan sat with easy grace upon his big gray horse but a few feet distant. He wore buckskin pants and shirt and a broad-brimmed hat, and a pistol and long-bladed knife were belted to his lean waist. He had grown a short blond beard since she had last seen him. She was surprised to see him here, yet at the same time he seemed as natural on the prairie as the buffalo she had seen.

"Jacob!" she cried happily.

"The same," he said. He stepped down from Jubal and came to her. He caught her hands that held the wagon shaft. "Let me finish that," he said.

Cora slid her hands out from under Jacob's. His touch was a very pleasant thing. "All right," she said. She couldn't stop her smiling and hoped it didn't make her look silly.

Jacob lowered the shafts to the ground, and went to the singletree and unhooked the trace chains. Cora followed close behind. The wind blew harder, flapping the canvas on the wagon and popping it on the wooden bows holding it up.

"It'll be storming hard in a few minutes," Jacob said. "Best that we fasten the horse to the wagon so it won't run away."

"That's a good idea," Cora said.

As Jacob tied the horse to the bed of the wagon, Cora spoke again. "What are you doing here?"

Be brave, Jacob told himself. *Tell her what she must be told.* "I have something important to do."

"What is that?"

"To find you."

The expression in Jacob's eyes made Cora's heart

beat even more wildly, until she thought it would break free of its cage of ribs. "You have found me," she said, and was glad that he had.

The storm seemed to spring across the prairie, with the lightning cracking and hissing, and the rain pounding down. The huge drops fell upon the boy and girl, wetting them quickly, cold.

"We'd better get out of the rain," Cora said. She scrambled up into the rear of the wagon.

Jacob swiftly tied Jubal to a wheel of the vehicle, and the packhorse tied to Jubal was thus also secured. He scurried out of the driving rain and up into the wagon under the canvas with Cora.

They sat looking into each other's wet faces in the dim light of the covered wagon. The fierce wind rocked the wagon and the torrential rain flogged the canvas close overhead, creating a mighty din.

Jacob watched Cora, and was oblivious of the world beyond the thin canvas being whipped by the fury of the storm. Never had he been so stirred by a girl. He laid his hat aside. He put out his hand to Cora.

She hesitated but a second before taking it in both of hers. She held it tightly. "I'm so very glad you have come."

"I should never have let you leave without me."

"That is correct," she said and squeezed his hand more tightly.

Her hands on his made his nerve endings strum pleasantly. He pulled her hands gently toward him, so very gently to test her, to find out the depth of her feelings toward him. She came easily, willingly, into his arms. He kissed her, tasting the sweetness of her lips, the fresh raindrops on them. He laid both their bodies down side by side on the blankets on the floor of the wagon. God! How wonderful her rounded woman's body felt against him.

The canvas flap closing the rear of the wagon was suddenly ripped apart. Clive Pateman's big head appeared in the opening. His long arm shot out and caught Jacob by the back of the shirt, yanked him out of the wagon, and flung him down on the rainswept ground.

Seventeen

Jacob rolled on the muddy, sloppy ground where the giant Pateman had thrown him. He thrust out his arms and stopped his bone-jarring tumble. Instantly he sprang to his feet and whirled looking for Pateman in the blinding downpour of rain.

As Jacob spun around, lightning flashed close by like a sun erupting. In the bright glare, he found himself face-to-face with Pateman, and within the man's long reach. He jumped backward as Pateman swung his right fist. The blow barely clipped Jacob's chin; still, it snapped his head to the side and staggered him several steps.

Jacob shook his head to clear it so he could defend himself. The man's fist was hard as a hickory maul. He saw Pateman charging at him with head shoved out ahead and fists cocked to strike. Jacob faded to the side and hit Pateman solidly on the side of the jaw as he went past. Pateman pivoted back and, moving with unexpected quickness, came again on the attack. Jacob was surprised that his blow seemed not to have fazed his opponent. He had never had that happen before. *So give him a couple more!* He dug his feet into the wet ground and hit Pateman with a hard left and right squarely in the face as the man came at him.

Jacob felt the satisfying jolt as his fists thudded on

the man's face. The blows slowed Pateman, but growling fiercely he drove ahead.

As Jacob swiftly back-pedaled, he saw blood streaming from Pateman's nose. Then the man struck out with his long arm and his left fist hit Jacob in the face. The man's right fist followed immediately and slammed into Jacob's chest. He lost his breath with an explosion of air. The power of the blow lifted Jacob off his feet and he landed on his back in the mud.

A tornado of exploding stars spun across Jacob's vision. Through them he saw Pateman lunging forward to fall on him. He hurled himself desperately to the side. Pateman crashed down where he had lain a moment before. One of the man's hands grabbed Jacob by the shoulder, but he wrenched strongly away and the man's hold slipped loose from the wet buckskin. Jacob rolled once more to be beyond reach of the giant.

Pateman was by far much stronger than any man Jacob had ever fought before. Only his quickness had prevented Pateman from catching hold of him, and should the man have succeeded in doing that, the fight would have ended with Jacob badly hurt, or dead.

A cold wind blew through Jacob's mind and cleared it. This was a fight for Cora and he must win. He surged to his feet and pulled his pistol from its holster. He felt the slippery mud on the butt of the weapon and gripped it hard to maintain a tight hold. He leaped at Pateman before the man could climb completely to his feet, and slammed the pistol down onto the man's head. Pateman crumpled pole-axed onto the sodden ground.

Jacob sucked a deep breath of the rain-filled air, and holstered his pistol. What would Cora think about him hitting Pateman with the gun? As he started to turn toward her, a heavy weight rammed him in the back and knocked him sprawling. He heard a scream, wild and shrill, and a booted foot cracked against his ribs.

Jacob scrabbled away on hands and knees. He came to his feet with fists up to defend himself and looking for the man who had hit him. He was dumbfounded to see Maude hurtling through the rain at him. Her face was contorted with hate and she was screaming high-pitched, animal-like. Her hands were balled into fists and she struck roundhouse blows at Jacob left and right, again and again.

"Stop it!" Jacob shouted as he retreated, blocking her blows. He didn't want to hit the woman. However, she appeared deaf to his voice and, screaming loudly, continued to drive in as he hurriedly backed away. If her loud cries should alarm the camp, he could soon have all of the Mormon men on him. He reached past Maude's flailing hands and tapped her on the chin with his left fist.

"Stop it!" he shouted again.

The blow only served to cause Maude to scream more furiously, and strike more wildly. He blocked a blow and struck her hard on the point of the chin. Her forward momentum was halted abruptly and she sat down jarringly on the ground.

"Stay down there!" Jacob warned.

Cora ran up to Maude, knelt and caught her by the arm. "Maude, stop hitting Jacob. You're acting like a crazy person."

Maude turned her rain-washed face up. Cora shuddered as she saw the expression in her sister's eyes. In the murky light from the storm-lashed sky, Maude's eyes were black and staring and tinged with incipient madness. For a few seconds, Cora thought Maude was going to hit her. Then Maude's eyes lost their madness and a haunted, beaten look came into them.

"Help me, Cora," Maude said in a pleading voice.

"Yes. I will help you, Maude."

"Send him away," Maude said. She looked about in

the rain until she saw Jacob, and then pointed a trembling finger at him. "Send that son of Satan away and never see him again."

"I'll do that. Let me help you into the wagon where you can lie down and rest."

"Is Clive hurt?" Maude asked in a little girl's voice.

Cora glanced at Pateman and found him sitting up and rubbing his head where Jacob had hit him. She spoke to Maude. "Clive is all right. Now get into the wagon and out of the rain. Sleep some and you'll feel better."

With Cora's assistance, Maude struggled weakly to her feet. Leaning heavily on Cora, she allowed herself to be guided to the rear of the wagon. She crawled in under the canvas.

Pateman regained his feet. He looked fiercely at Jacob.

"Don't come at me again or I'll break your goddamned head," Jacob threatened.

Pateman wheeled around on Cora. "Do what Maude asked," he ordered hoarsely. "Get rid of that damned gentile."

Tears came to Cora's eyes and she was glad the rain streaming down her face hid them. She took a few steps toward Jacob and halted. "You must leave, Jacob. There can be nothing between us. This is where I must stay, here with Maude."

"Why, for God's sake! What has your sister got to do with you and me?"

"Maude is going to marry Clive."

"Good. That means you can go with me," Jacob said. The situation might work out better than he had hoped. He would take Cora back to St. Joe, and then in the spring they would go together to California.

"No she can't," Pateman bellowed. "She's going to marry me. She has promised."

"Marry you? Why would she, when you're going to marry Maude?" Jacob turned to Cora. "Tell me he lies."

"He doesn't lie. I agreed to it."

"Why would you want to marry the same man as your sister? You deserve better than that. You deserve a husband of your own."

Cora choked with sobs. Jacob was correct and she wanted him to be that man. But Maude must survive, survive as a sane person, and she surely wouldn't if Pateman didn't make her his wife. And he wouldn't, unless Cora became his wife also.

She quelled her sobbing. "Go, Jacob. Leave now, for I will never speak to you again." She turned her back to him, and cried into the tumult of rain and lightning and thunder.

After a time she looked behind her. Jacob and his horses were gone.

Pateman was walking in her direction. He smiled a broad, victorious smile.

Eighteen

Jacob halted when the Mormons stopped their march and pulled their handcarts together on the distant prairie. He sat on his horse and watched the people hurrying to make their camp, throwing up tents and starting evening cooking fires that smoked heavily, their only fuel the damp buffalo chips.

Jacob had not been able to bring himself to ride off and leave Cora. Following the fight with Pateman, he had gone off but a short ways and made a night camp and lay under his tarp listening to the rain. Then come morning, he had trailed the caravan throughout the day. He kept at least a quarter mile away from the Mormons, he was afraid that if he had to fight Pateman again he would kill the big man. Always he had remained close enough that he could make out Cora walking beside the horse pulling her wagon.

After a time he climbed down from Jubal, leaned his arms across the saddle and continued to watch the Mormon camp. Maude had joined Cora at the wagon and they were preparing their evening meal. He saw Maude turn and look in his direction. She said something to Cora and she too looked. He couldn't see Cora's face across the expanse of prairie, but her features were imprinted on his mind and could never be erased.

Finally he tore himself away from his vigil. He made

his own simple camp, spreading his bedroll, unsaddling Jubal and staking him out on the end of his lariat to graze.

Dusk fell upon the prairie, thickening further to become black night. The darkness engulfed the Mormon camp and only the tiny flickering night fires and the outlines of handcarts silhouetted against them marked its presence. How feeble the fires seemed in the immense cave of the black night.

Fragments of a man's voice reached Jacob. He was sure the man was Pateman. A chorus of women's voices rose saying amens. The man must have completed a prayer.

The women began to sing. The female voices, higher pitched than the man's, easily spanned the distance to Jacob. Now that Cora was going to marry Pateman, was her voice among those of the Mormon women?

Jacob leaned forward endeavoring to catch every word and every syllable of the women's song. How brave and beautiful their voices sounded singing against the dark emptiness of the prairie. All around him the night insects ceased their chirp and twitter as if they felt outdone by the women's singing and had become mute.

Jacob listened to the lovely voices of the women down to the last syllable. Then, still wanting to hear more singing by the women, he watched the congregation disperse, their forms passing in front of the fires like dark ghosts.

Jacob, as he did every night after full darkness had fallen, gathered up his camp and led Jubal to a new location. Any enemy who might have watched him bed down should not know where he actually slept. Again he spread his bedroll and staked out Jubal.

Jacob lay and listened to the horse cropping the wild grass and the chitter of the insects. His heart yawned empty and bare, for Cora was lost to him forever. Before now he had thought the great, grass-covered prairie was a beautiful place to ride, to hunt the buffalo, elk, and antelope. Even the danger from the fierce Indian warriors only added spice to the land. But here and now the vast emptiness was so very lonely without a woman. Without Cora. He better understood why the Indian braves never rode far from their squaws. Man was not meant to live alone.

Jacob could not sleep and lay watching the heavens. Nearby Jubal nickered softly, seeming to know Jacob was awake. A moment later Jacob heard the horse moving and it came close, lowering its long, graceful neck until its head was almost touching Jacob, breathing in the odor of its master. Jacob reached up and petted the horse on the neck. Should he do as Cora had ordered him, climb upon Jubal and ride away?

The horse lifted its head and stood looking out over the prairie. Its tail flicked left and right as it contentedly chewed a mouthful of grass. Then Jubal froze and stood stone still with his ears thrust forward in an intent, questioning way. The bores of his nostrils flared as he pulled in a slow breath of air to identify something he saw there in the night.

Jacob sat up slowly and looked in the same direction as the horse. In the deceitful shadows, he could make out something moving and it was coming stealthily toward Jacob.

He picked up the Sharps carbine lying beside him and, muffling the breech of the weapon under his blanket, thumbed the hammer back to full cock. The animal walked upright and so was a man. He could be an Indian creeping in for an attack, or Pateman coming to permanently rid himself of Jacob. He willed it to be Pateman. He felt joyous in a savage way as he anticipated a fight with the man. In the night, with guns,

Jacob felt he would have the advantage. Cora might soon be free of her pledge.

All around Cora the spellbound congregation listened attentively to Pateman's evening service. Maude, seated beside her on a blanket on the grass, was especially enraptured by the man's words. The woman was unknowingly nodding her big head to Pateman's emphatic pronouncements of the goodness of the Mormon religion and the safety and love within its God-given teachings, and the worldly community of Mormons and their churches.

Cora turned inward to ponder her own private thoughts. She had grave misgivings about her decision to marry Clive and it weighed heavily upon her. She remembered the misery and resignation on Jacob's face when she had told him to leave and never see her again. She felt her own sadness at having said those words. All day she had watched him as he rode his horse on a parallel course beside the column of handcarts directly opposite her. She wanted to cry out to him that it was all a mistake and to come and take her away with him. But no sound escaped her lips, for Maude would then have been all alone, with Cora gone, and Clive reneging on his proposal of marriage.

She thought of the Mormon Church's Tenets of Celestial Marriage, a marriage for earth and beyond, for all eternity. How much reality was there to such a belief? Mormon men could have many wives if they wanted them—what of that? What would it be like to share a husband with her sister Maude? Perhaps Clive would be a husband who she would have to share with several other women. He seemed a hard, devious man. Would he beat his wives? So many questions without answers, so many reasons to look at her future life with anguish.

"Let's sing, Cora." Maude's voice penetrated Cora's tormented thoughts.

She snapped back to the present to find the congregation standing. She quickly came to her feet. The hymn "Nearer my God To Thee" began and she joined in with a low, subdued voice. She ignored Maude, who watched her from the corner of her eye.

The hymn ended and Clive closed his hymnbook and looked over the heads of the people at Cora. He started to push through the crowd toward her. Before he could take but a few steps, he was forced to stop when several women closed about him and began to talk with him.

Cora, thankful that Clive had been intercepted, hurried off before he could break free of the women. She reached the wagon and dropped down with a leaden heart on the pallet of blankets she had prepared beside the vehicle.

Maude came up on the opposite side of the wagon where her blankets were spread. She glared through the darkness under the wagon at Cora. "That was rude of you to leave so quickly. I'm sure Clive wanted to talk to us."

"Then why didn't you stay and talk with him?"

"He would want to talk with you, too."

"We'll have all eternity to talk with Clive Pateman," Cora said resignedly. She turned her back to Maude.

"You must be more friendly to Clive," Maude said sharply. "And after our marriage to him, very loving. He must want us as wives." Maude stared at Cora's back for a half minute, then spoke again in a flat, ugly tone. "You *owe* me. *I* mostly raised you after Mother died. Much more than Father did."

Cora stiffened at the stab, but remained silent. She felt tricked by Clive and Maude into the agreement of marriage. Both of them had played upon her sisterly desire to help Maude become Clive's wife. And now she was trapped and must accept the fact she would soon be the wife of the Mormon.

She lay agonizing about her position and staring up into the darkness. The close-by Mormon camp gradually fell quiet as the people sought their beds. Maude stirred on her pallet and then her breathing became deep and even in sleep. Far away on the prairie, a wolf howled, a wild, weird, lonely sound.

The howl of the wolf made Cora think that Jacob, lying all alone on the prairie, must be very lonely. In that same instant of time a daring, awful, delightful thought came to her and she sat bolt upright. She pulled a trembling breath of the black night air as she swiftly evaluated an action that seemed so right, so well deserved. Tradition said that a woman must give herself only to her husband. However, tradition could not change the fact that she loved Jacob and not Clive. And she would not let tradition take away what rightfully belonged to Jacob.

Jacob held his carbine ready and watched the creeping figure materialize, black from black. The range was growing ever shorter and it would be an easy task to shoot the man. The large-caliber bullet from the Sharps would make a hell of a hole.

"Jacob, are you there?" Cora's voice came through the murk of the prairie night.

"God yes, Cora! I'm over here. Come ahead."

Jacob lowered the hammer on the rifle and hurried to meet Cora. She ran into his arms and clung tightly to him.

"I almost didn't find you," she said in a voice between a sob and a laugh.

"I wouldn't have moved camp if I'd known you would come looking for me."

"Well, I did find you—or rather, I saw your horse."

Jacob kissed Cora soundly on the lips, and then took her by the shoulders and pressed her back to look into her night-shadowed face. "I'll saddle Jubal. We can be forty miles from here by daylight."

"What do you mean?"

"We'll go back to Florence and meet with Glen and Renne. Then I'll take you with me when we go to the mountains to trap. In the spring, we'll go to California."

"I can't do that."

"Why not? Didn't you come here to leave with me?"

"No. I came to ask you to go away for I can't stand to see you all day and not be with you."

"That's crazy. You want to be with me and yet you're telling me to leave."

"I know that sounds crazy, but that's the way it must be. I still plan to marry Clive Pateman. For Maude's sake."

"To hell with Maude. I'm going to take you with me."

"It can't be that way. And I know you wouldn't force me against my will."

"I'm not so sure of that." Jacob's hands tightened on Cora's shoulders.

She reached up and caught Jacob's face between her hands. "I am going to marry Clive." Her throat felt constricted, her voice husky. "But I want to spend this night with you. I want you to be the first man to make love to me. Would you want that, too?"

"I want more than one night," Jacob said harshly.

Cora shook her head. "We can have this night and then you must leave. Do you promise?"

Jacob pulled Cora close against him. It would be an easy matter to overpower her and carry her off. As if she had read his thoughts, he felt her stiffen in his arms.

"This one night only," she said sternly. "Do you agree?"

"You have my word on it." Jacob's words almost choked him.

Cora removed herself from Jacob's arms and then caught him by the hand. "Where are your blankets?" she said.

Cora lay with all her naked body along Jacob's. His hands traced the contours of her face, her lips, the mounds of her breasts. They moved lower to explore and caress. She kissed him softly, then fiercely, then softly again, tasting and savoring him. The memories of him and this night must last her forever.

She broke the quietness and said in a shy voice, "Make love to me, Jacob."

"Yes," Jacob replied simply. He slid his hands under her firm, rounded hips. She was goldenly delicious where he entered her.

Jacob was worried about Cora, for she was breathing hard, almost gasping for air. Her ribs were caving in and out at a rapid rate. "Are you all right?" he asked.

"Oh yes! Very much all right! Just hold me close for a little while."

He held her and her breathing slowed. And they made their brief-lived world wrapped in each other's arms.

Cora recalled the battle between Jacob and Clive, how savagely they had fought, striking each other with thudding fists. Then Jacob had pulled his big pistol and knocked Clive unconscious. The battle between the two men had excited, stimulated her. The knowledge came to her full-blown that a man who would not fight for her was of no use in the wilderness. She hugged Jacob more closely to her. The horrible truth was she would be marrying the wrong man.

* * *

"How long before daylight?" Cora whispered, her breath warm against the side of Jacob's face.

He propped himself up on an elbow and looked down at Cora. Even the darkness could not hide her beauty. The polygamist Mormon didn't deserve her. Jacob knew he had been correct when he had told Cora that she should have a husband of her own, a man who would treasure her as his only wife.

He checked the celestial clock in the sky. "About two hours more night," he said. "I'll saddle Jubal and we can be long gone before it's light enough for someone to see us."

"But you promised me. You can't break your word." She drew back from Jacob. "You are going to keep it?"

"My word is good," Jacob said reluctantly.

"Then I must go."

"No!" His imminent loss was an ocean of sadness that was drowning him. He caught her by the hands.

Cora pulled free and climbed to her feet. She began to dress in the darkness.

Jacob stood up and started to pull on his own clothing. "If you must go, then I'll take you back to your wagon."

"I can find my way back. And besides, someone might see you."

She came close, raised up on her tiptoes, and kissed Jacob on the lips. Then, with a sob, she whirled away and ran into the darkness.

Cora's voice came floating back through the night gloom, a fragile sound, as thin as ice breaking. "Good-bye, Jacob."

Nineteen

Wolf Voice lay in the pine trees on the bluff above the North Platte River and watched the three mounted white trappers with four packhorses ride ever closer. He couldn't yet see their faces, but he willed them to be Kinshaw and the two men who had killed his comrades in the Moon of Big Winds near the Big Horn Mountains.

"No shooting until they are directly below us and close," Wolf Voice ordered the five warriors with him. The trappers were invaders and murderers. However, he had noted that only the bravest and strongest of the white men became trappers, and for that reason he would shoot the ones approaching from ambush without giving them a chance to fight back.

Long Running lay on his right, and Big Horse on his left. Broken Arm and his two sons, Elk Piss and Far Thunder, were just beyond Big Horse. Broken Arm wanted revenge nearly as badly as Wolf Voice, for he had lost an older son who had been with Wolf Voice when the white trappers had attacked out of the darkness. All the men were armed with Sharps carbines, the three stolen from the American Army and the remaining from the weapons Shattuck had given Wolf Voice in exchange for the furs the Crows had taken from white trappers.

Wolf Voice looked to the east along the worn white man's trail. Fort Laramie was a day's ride away at the junction of the Laramie and North Platte Rivers. The wagon trains of the white men, heading for the land lying far beyond the farthest mountains, and most of the mountain trappers came by way of Fort Laramie. However, sometimes trappers heading for the Big Horn or the Wind River Mountains, sometimes took a shorter, more direct route lying north of the fort. He wished the three trappers, the enemies he sought, had not taken that northern trail and were indeed the men almost within rifle range.

Wolf Voice believed there would be no more white men with their puny women and children and slow-moving wagons crossing the plains this year, for this was the Moon of Falling Leaves, the white man's November. The Moon of Blowing Snow with its great cold was soon to arrive and any white people caught in the high country would surely die. However, this was not true of the tough white trappers. They would be traveling, they could survive as well in the deep winter as did the Crows.

Before Wolf Voice had left his village to search for his enemies, he had led his braves on the fall hunt and they had killed scores of buffalo and elk for winter meat, and many of the big white wolves that followed the herds for their warm fur. He had examined the pelts and found the guard hairs long and the undercoat extremely dense, a sure sign the winter would be extraordinarily long with much cold and snow.

Below Wolf Voice, the trappers disappeared into a strip of cottonwoods and willows growing along the river. He waited anxiously for them to reappear. Had the wary trappers somehow discovered the presence of the Crow warriors and turned away? That must not be, for he had journeyed far and waited long and must have his revenge.

The horsemen broke from the timber and into view in the meadow below the Indians. Wolf Voice's eyes hardened to black obsidian marbles. The trappers were dead men just waiting to die. Their heavily loaded pack-horses would contain many things the Crows could use.

"Don't hurt the horses," Wolf Voice said. "Shoot when I do. I'll take the man who rides in the lead." He raised his rifle.

He caught his target with the front bead sight of his rifle, and settled both into the notch of the rear sight. He didn't recognize the man and regretted that he was not one of those he sought. But that made no difference at this point. He squeezed the trigger and the Sharps bucked against his shoulder. Instantly came the thunderous roar of the other warriors' rifles.

The trapper shot by Wolf Voice fell sideways from his saddle to the ground. The second trapper, a small man, was lifted from his seat by the impacts of two bullets and fell hard. The remaining man, struck by a bullet from Long Running's carbine, fell forward across the neck of his horse. The animal bolted. After a few jumps of his horse, the rider was jarred loose from his slack hold, and slid from his saddle to bounce along on the ground.

Wolf Voice sprang to his feet and shouted out. His warriors joined him in the wild victory cry. The ambush had been totally successful. He ran down the slope. The others closed in behind him like iron filings drawn to a magnet.

Wolf Voice went swiftly from one dead man to the next, twisting their bearded faces toward him, scrutinizing every one. In angry disappointment, he kicked the last corpse savagely in the ribs. "None of them are the ones we search for," he seethed.

"Maybe they won't come trapping this year," Long Running replied.

"They will come. I heard them talking at the fort and planning to return to the Big Horns again this winter."

"They could have changed their minds, or have taken the northern trail." Long Running was growing tired of waiting, for they had been watching the trail for ten suns. Several groups of trappers had passed, but always too many to attack, until this small group. "We have killed three trappers and have their weapons, horses, and supplies. We should be returning to the village before the great storms, and deep snow falls."

"We'll wait for our enemies," Wolf Voice said, aggravated at Long Running for proposing they leave. "They will come, and we will kill them just as easily as we have these three."

Wolf Voice looked at the other men and saw that they too, except for Broken Arm, would just as soon leave and return to their teepees and women. Wolf Voice's squaw was a crabby woman and he felt no urge to speedily return to the village. However, the other men needed rewards for staying. He swung his arm to indicate the possessions of the white trappers. "I don't want a share of the guns or horses or what is on the packhorses. Divide everything among you. Now we must remove all the sign of what happened here. Hide the bodies in the rocks up there." He pointed at a jumble of boulders on the bluff upstream from them. "Hurry before more trappers come and we are seen."

The Crow braves swiftly gathered the trappers' horses, loading the corpses across the saddles, and left the trail and went up the bluff. Wolf Voice kicked dirt over the blood stains on the ground. He hoped there would soon be more white man's blood to spill on the ground.

* * *

Cora walked beside the horse pulling her wagon stationed at the rear of the Mormon caravan. She was immediately behind the two oxen-drawn supply wagons. This was the afternoon of the first day after leaving Fort Laramie and the Mormons struggled slowly with their handcarts along the North Platte River.

Many days had passed since the people had left Florence, days of hard labor, sweat, and dust. The hard labor continued, however, now the cold of the high plains of the Wyoming Territory in early winter had found them. They had halted for a half day at Fort Laramie, but that short period of rest had done little to restore the people's spirit and strength. They had, however, been able to purchase a small quantity of provisions to supplement their meager food supply.

The sky was crystal blue overhead, but the sun had lost much of its fire and Cora wore her heavy coat over her man's shirt and pants. The cold, blustery wind had stripped all the frost-killed leaves from the cottonwoods and willows along the river. Flocks of ducks, flushed by the caravan, rose up by the hundreds from nearly every pool of water. She noticed that, once airborne, most of the ducks flew south. None of the men with guns stopped to hunt, for the people also knew winter was near and felt the urgency to keep marching toward the valley of the Great Salt Lake where there would be shelter from the frigid mountain blizzards.

Much of the time, the handcarts were hidden from Cora's view as they followed the curving, bending trail that went northwestward following the floodplain of the river. Behind her she heard the boys shouting, they were having trouble driving the herd of steers, much reduced in number because several animals had been slaughtered for meat. The people were terribly exposed and vulnerable to attack by an enemy, penned in as they were by the river on the left and the wooded bluffs crowding the trail on the right. Yet none of the men were out scouting for enemies because all were needed to pull the handcarts.

She came around a bend in the trail and saw Timmy, a boy of six, standing beside the trail. As she came close, he called out to her. "Can I ride a ways, Cora? I'm awfully tired, and I don't weigh much."

"Sure, Timmy, this is nearly level going and I think the horse can pull one more small boy. Hop up in the rear."

Timmy's cold, weary face cracked open in a bright smile. He scampered past Cora to the rear of the wagon and climbed in.

Cora evaluated the condition of the horse. Her wagon, same as the supply wagons, was heavily loaded. Some people had weakened under the grueling task of pulling their handcarts and a portion of the food and other necessities had been transferred to the wagons. In addition, there were now seven children in her wagon. Still, the horse seemed to be pulling the vehicle without too much difficulty. She clucked at the beast and it again leaned into its harness and the wagon began to roll.

Maude and Clive came into sight, moving down the string of handcarts. Maude, like Cora, wore mens' clothing. She easily matched Clive's long, determined strides. During the torturous six hundred miles from Florence, she had lost her soft women's flesh and replaced it with hard muscle. She had always been strong, but now her strength was immense. Several times Cora had seen Maude lift the wheel of a loaded handcart over a rock, or out of a hole.

Clive passed Cora with but a short glance and went to the rear of the wagon. He looked in under the canvas top. "Just as I thought." He spoke to the smallest girl. "Bridget, you have a sore leg, so you can ride. But you—"

Clive's finger pointed at Timmy "—get down and walk."
He pointed at all the other boys and girls. "All of you,
climb down out of there. Don't ever get in this wagon
again. I'm going to talk with your parents to see that you
don't."

With frightened faces, the children jumped down
from the wagon. They warily circled around Clive and
ran past Cora as she and Maude hurried to the rear.

"You can't do this!" Cora raged at Clive. "This is my
wagon and I'll haul who ever I want to."

Clive wheeled around on Cora. "You'll do exactly as
I tell you." His voice was harsh and threatening. His
hand rose to strike her.

Cora dodged back. She saw the anger in his eyes and
knew that he would indeed hit her. She quickly put her
hand into the pocket of her coat and caught hold of
her pistol. Never again would she let someone hit her
without fighting back.

Maude saw Cora reach for her pistol. Clive would not
know Cora was armed, but Maude did. She swiftly
caught Cora around the shoulders and pulled her
tightly against her side, penning Cora's hand firmly in
her pocket.

"Cora, the horse and wagon are overloaded with the
supplies and all the kids riding," Maude said. "They
must walk as Clive says."

Clive dropped his hand. He spoke sternly to Cora.
"No one rides in the wagon unless I say so. And then
only after they have walked as far as they can. Do you
understand me?"

Cora's face was set in rebellious obedience. She did
not reply, for she didn't trust her self to speak. *Damn
you for being so ready to hit me.*

"She'll do what's right," Maude told Clive, still holding Cora.

"All right, Maude." He turned again on Cora. "You

listen to your sister." He stomped away past the two supply wagons and up the line of handcarts.

Maude released her hold on Cora's shoulders. "You must do as Clive says. The provisions you are carrying in the wagon could mean the difference between life and death for people, and are far more important than the kids riding. You've got to know that."

"Maude, I always make them walk going up the hills. On the downgrades and on the flat ground, the horse can pull them easily enough. So I'm really doing no harm."

"Maybe not, but you must obey Clive, soon you will be his wife."

"I won't let him hit me, not ever. I think he will be a mean husband. I know he's stubborn. The colonel at the fort told him he should stop there and build cabins for the people and lay in supplies for the winter. But no! Clive had to go on!" Cora looked beseechingly at Maude. "It's cold and water freezes at night. Already there's snow on the mountains, and we have hundreds of miles yet to go." She pointed at the distant Laramie Mountains. "Look, see the snow."

"I'm sure we won't have to climb that high. And Clive knows what he's doing. He's been over this route before."

Cora spoke with anger and frustration. "Maude, you're wrong. You follow him around like a lovesick puppy. You think whatever he does is true as God's actions."

"You haven't made any effort to get to know Clive like I have," Maude retorted.

"I'm in no hurry to get to know Clive. And you only want to hurry to Salt Lake City so you can be his wife that much sooner."

Maude's face tightened. Her voice came sharp as a

knife blade. "What's wrong in that? Tell me what's
wrong in that!"

Cora saw that strange look again, something
menacing—maybe half mad—lurking behind Maude's
eyes. And she saw her sister's effort to subdue it. She
remained silent, for she dare not push Maude over the
brink of self-control.

Maude glanced up the trail where Clive could be seen
talking to a man at one of the handcarts. Then she
swung back on Cora. Her expression was one of sane
reasonableness again, as if the sight of Clive had
soothed her. "I know Clive's worried about all the people, how far we've got to go, the shortage of food and
warm clothing, and the winter coming on. He's told
me that. Now you add to his problems."

"If he's so worried then he should've done what the
colonel said, stopped and prepared for winter."

"You act this way with Clive and me because we drove
that trapper off."

Cora turned away from Maude to hide her face,
which might give away her thoughts. *Wouldn't you be mad
if you knew Jacob and I made love?* She would never be
sorry for loving Jacob. Her sorrow was in forcing him
to leave. Oh, how she wished she could undo that.

A fresh outbreak of shouts came from the boys driving
the steers. Maude cocked her head and listened. "The
boys are having trouble," she said. "I'll go and help
them. Now you do as Clive says. Let no one else ride in
the wagon but Bridget." She hastened down the trail.

Cora moved to the front of the wagon, grabbed the
rope of the horse, and led it forward to catch up with
the supply wagons that had continued on. Shortly she
broke free of the woods and came out into a meadow,
across which the caravan was strung.

The handcarts came to a stop ahead of her; people
began to call out excitedly to each other and point off

to the right. Cora looked to see what had caused the
people's concern.

Opposite the head of the column on the bluff above
the trail, an Indian sat on a horse and stared down at
the Mormons. He held a rifle across the horse's back
in front of him. Neither horse nor man moved, a large
brown man on a brown horse equal for his size, welded
together into one savage hunting animal. Cora's breath
came shallowly at the sense of menace in the motionless
Indian. How many others were hidden in the trees behind him?

Twenty

Cora watched the Indian sitting his mustang on the bluff above the Mormon caravan. A minute passed, then two, and the only movement he made was to turn his head to look up and down the line of vehicles. Then an understanding of his purpose came to her; he was waiting to see what action the white people were going to take against him.

Cora saw Clive watching the horseman. The Mormon wore a pistol in a holster on his belt, but had made no gesture toward the weapon. Several men from the nearer handcarts were hurrying forward with rifles to stand with Clive. Were they going to shoot the Indian? Maybe they shouldn't do that, thought Cora; maybe the Indian had many others with him.

The Indian gave some signal to his horse that Cora did not see; the animal stepped forward and began to descend the face of the bluff toward the caravan. There was a sudden outburst of concerned cries from the Mormons. Then abruptly they fell silent, seemingly mesmerized watching the Indian.

Wolf Voice reached the flat meadowland, halted, and swung his eyes to view the entire length of the caravan. The people were afraid of him, it was in their faces. He was but one man and yet this entire village of people feared him. Let the Gods persecute all cowards. He

started to ride past the handcarts. He passed Clive and
the armed men grouped around him. These few white
men might fight, but Wolf Voice doubted it and felt no
apprehension when they were at his back.

Cora watched the Indian approach. He sat upon a
buffalo hide saddle, and had a bridle of sorts, a strip
of rawhide passing through the horse's mouth and tied
around the lower jaw, with leads extending up to his
hands. He seemed not to need the bridle to control his
mustang. The temperature was cold and yet he wore
only moccasins with leggings and buckskin trousers and
shirt. He had a wild look about him, smoky bronze skin,
coarse, broad-featured face, and black, shoulder-length
hair that was whipped about by the wind.

Wolf Voice's eyes fell upon Cora and he halted his
mustang. He felt a thrill rush along his spine at the
beauty of the white girl. She was worth many horses.
She stared back at him with a wary, questioning expression. She gripped something in her pocket. Was it a
weapon? Wolf Voice spread his lips in a thin smile, as
white and dead as a bleached bone. He could kill her
easily before she could even begin to draw her hand
from the pocket.

Cora felt a woman's instinct to drop her eyes to avoid
the stare, the direct eye contact of the Indian man. But
at a primal level she knew the Indian was her enemy
and she did not look away from the flat, black eyes. He
had come out of the wilderness and had ridden fear-
lessly past the Mormons with their loaded weapons.
Cora judged him totally capable of carrying out any
scheme that he might devise.

The Indian turned away from Cora and examined
the herd of steers that Maude and the boys had driven
into the lower end of the meadow. He wheeled his mustang about and looked again along the line of handcarts. Then, apparently satisfied with his inspection of

the Mormons, he rode back across the meadow, climbed the bluff to the top, and vanished among the trees.

Maude hurried to Cora. "What did the Indian say to you?" she asked.

"Nothing. He just looked at me."

"Only that?"

"Yes."

Maude scanned the top of the bluff with foreboding. The Indian would be back, and he would come for Cora. Maude didn't know how she knew, only that she did. Men would do savage, awful things to possess her pretty sister. A hot flush of jealousy surged up in her heart. She smothered the jealousy, knowing that Clive's desire for Cora would capture him as a husband for Maude. She must guard her sister very carefully and keep her safe. Should Maude fail to do that, Clive would surely be lost to her.

Cora pulled her wagon into position as part of the ring of vehicles surrounding the Mormon night camp. Clive had insisted that the wagon not be parked off by itself ever since the day Jacob had appeared, and was then driven away. Clive told Cora that the caravan was far enough west to be in danger from attack by Indians. Maude had readily agreed to the new routine. Cora thought there was probably truth in the possibility of danger from Indians, but she knew the main reason for the change was their fear Jacob might again appear and she would go away with him.

She speedily removed the harness from the horse, and the animal was turned out with the oxen and steers to graze in the meadow under the watchful eyes of the night guards. The satchel containing her personal belongings was brought from the bed of the wagon onto the tailgate and she began to dig for her soap and towel.

All around her the Mormon men and women worked swiftly to make camp. Clive had driven the weary people into the evening dusk before halting. Cora saw a man stagger from exhaustion as he worked to erect his tent. A woman leaned on the wheel of her handcart, her shoulders rising and falling as she cried. Children had dropped down on the ground where they had stopped and watched with dull eyes as their parents prepared for the night. Cora was angry at Clive for the block-headed decision he had made not to halt at Fort Laramie. Now, to escape the high country and reach Salt Lake City before the arrival of winter, he pushed the people until they were ready to fall.

She found her soap and towel and hurried off across the meadow toward the river. She must wash and return quickly to prepare supper before total darkness fell in the river valley.

"Cora, don't go far—it's not safe," Maude called out in a commanding voice from where she was helping Clive raise the tent of Widow Mayfield.

Cora disliked Maude's tone, but didn't let that show in her reply. "Just to the river to clean up a little," she called back.

"Watch out for Indians. I'll join you in couple of minutes."

Cora continued on without replying. She drew near the trees growing on the riverbank and warily studied the shadows among them. The dusk was deepening; still, there was enough light to see that she was alone. She moved into the woods and halted at the edge of a pool of water flat and black in the growing darkness.

The full moon, round and pale yellow, floated perfectly lensed in the mirror surface of the water. By looking closely, she could even make out the man in the moon. Was Jacob also looking at the moon this very moment? Cora hoped he was—they would be sharing something in common, even if they did not know it. She recalled the night she had spent in his blankets with him, his arms around her, and his strong, hard body pressing her down. She must not forget that time, that short moment of happiness. Did he have pleasant memories of that night, as she did?

Kneeling, Cora leaned forward over the water and her shadowy face came up out of the earth and stared back at her. The face of the girl in the water was pinched with fatigue and cold, and the eyes were full of sorrow. Cora knew the cause of all that sorrow, and it was the deep regret that she felt from being here with Maude and Clive instead of with Jacob. How could she have been so foolish as to think her happiness had to be forfeited to help Maude become Clive's wife?

Cora regarded the mournful expression on the girl's face in the water. Her debt to Maude should not require a sacrifice so great as giving up Jacob. She was angry at herself for having made such a stupid decision, and no longer wanted to see the image of the wretched person in the water. She stabbed her fingers into the mirror's surface, ruffling the water and obliterating the moon and the second Cora. Oh, how good it would be if she could rid herself of her regrets as easily.

She washed her hands and face in the ice cold water and dried them swiftly on her towel.

Cora awoke to the sound of the horse stomping the frozen ground just beyond the wagon. Though she slept in all her clothes, the cold was like ice needles penetrating her blankets and she shivered. Soon, probably too soon, the food supplies carried inside the wagon would be consumed to the point where she and Maude could sleep inside and close the canvas to keep the cold wind off them.

She hoped nobody would die from exhaustion and the cold, as old man Jeffers had the night before. It wasn't always the old and young who died. Mr. Mayfield, a middle-aged man, had fallen down and died from a burst heart while pulling his heavily loaded handcart over a particularly difficult section of trail. In total, six people had perished since the Mormons had left Florence. Cora wanted no more funerals; she was all cried out.

She raised her head to look at Maude on her bed on the ground nearby. To her surprise, Maude sat with her blankets wrapped around her and propped against a wheel of the wagon. She held her pistol gripped in her hand.

"For goodness sake, Maude, why aren't you sleeping?" Cora asked.

"The Indian," Maude whispered.

"What about the Indian?"

"The Indian is out there." Maude's voice trembled with trepidation.

Cora hastily examined the night beyond the wagon. Where? Where was the Indian? In the moonlight, the meadow was empty. She saw no sign of a man in the shadows among the thick trunks of the cottonwoods near the river. Past the trees, the depression of the river channel was a black sinkhole with nothing visible. Could Maude see something in that blackness?

"I don't see anything," Cora whispered.

"Don't you feel his presence out there?" Maude's voice trembled.

Trying to sense what Maude did, Cora remained very still and let her view drift slowly through the night cloaking the land outside the circle of vehicles. Finally she whispered again. "No. I don't feel that there is someone out there. Anyway, the men are on watch to guard us."

"They won't stop the Indian. Only I can do that. You go back to sleep. I'll see him when he comes, and I'll shoot him."

Cora was anxious about Maude's state of mind. After the Indian had been seen, Maude had not once gone off to the far end of the caravan to help as she often did in the past. Now she remained to the rear where she was always within sight of Cora. Maude was growing ever nearer to a breaking point from her fear that something would happen to Cora that would prevent Clive from marrying both of them.

"I will, Maude. But you sleep too; tomorrow will be another tough day of travel." Cora started to pull her blankets around her, then stopped. Just in case Maude could sense something she couldn't, Cora draped her coat over the top of her blankets and positioned it so she could speedily reach the Colt pistol in the pocket.

Cora tugged on the last of her cold, stiff boots and went hastily to the nearest of the half dozen morning fires the guards had built within the ring of handcarts and wagons. Maude had risen before her and was already at the fire with the pot of tea water heating in the edge of the hot coals.

A few men and women were loading their carts. Most of the others were gathered close around the fires. Clive was rousting the late sleepers out of their beds with no-nonsense commands.

Cora rotated slowly, warming all sides of her by the leaping flames, and then hastened back to the wagon. She rolled Maude's and her bedding and stowed it away. She brought in the horse, harnessed it, and hooked it between the shafts of the wagon. Over the passage of the days of travel, she and Maude had settled into a division of work wherein Cora handled all the chores of tending the horse and wagon and making their personal camp, while Maude helped Clive with the many tasks of keeping the caravan moving during the day and helping to establish the night camp of the Mormons.

Maude arrived and poured two tin cups full of the steaming liquid. She and Cora stood drinking the hot tea and eating cold pan bread, saved from the evening before and spread with jelly.

Bridget came up, huddled inside her thin coat and hobbling on her injured leg. Cora wordlessly broke off a piece of her bread and handed it to the little girl. The tyke began to eat hungrily.

"Did you see the Indian?" Cora asked Maude.

"No, but he was out there hiding and watching us. We must be very careful today."

"Did you tell Clive about the Indian?" Cora asked.

"I didn't have to. I heard him tell the guards to be extra watchful. But I'm the only one who can stop the Indian." She looked piercingly at Cora, as if to see if she understood that.

Cora didn't ask Maude to explain her last statement. She was afraid of the answer. "What do you think he is going to do?"

"He plans to carry you off for himself."

A cold knot formed in Cora's stomach at Maude's words. They reinforced what she herself had felt when the Indian had studied her so closely the day before. He was indeed her enemy. "What do you think we should do?"

"We must be very alert and careful. He will come soon, so stay close to the supply wagons. Will you promise to do that?"

"I will. I believe you are correct."

Clive's booming voice rose above the thin chatter of the people. "We roll in ten minutes."

The temperature climbed a degree or so above freezing as the struggling caravan wore away the morning. Cora was glad for the lessening of the cold for, like herself, most of the people were skimpily clothed. Still there were no voiced complaints. The people toiled on, pulling and pushing on their handcarts. They spoke but little and then only in muted tones. The children plodded along silently beside their parents. Some of the larger ones carried packs on their backs to lighten the load on the handcarts.

From here and there along the caravan came the squeak of wheels rubbing on dry axles. Cora knew Clive would have some strong words for the man or woman who had neglected to properly grease the axles and hubs of their handcarts at the last camp.

The trail straightened and took a more direct and shorter course across a meadow between looping meanders of the river. Several dense stands of pine and oak fingered down from the bluffs and stretched across the floodplain to the river. The handcart caravan reached the far side of the meadow and entered the first strip of woods.

Cora's horse began to limp, favoring its right front foot, and to slow. She reined the horse to a stop so she could examine the hoof for the cause of the trouble. She did not observe the supply wagon in front of her disappearing from sight around a tight bend of the trail. Moving closer to the horse's shoulder, she bent to lift its hoof.

Cora looked up quickly as she caught movement in the corner of her eye, and whirled. An Indian on a big black mustang, holding a rifle in his hands, was riding out of the stand of pines immediately in front of her. Long Running halted, blocking the trail.

Cora's heart jumped and began to hammer, and her breath was suddenly a rapid whistle of fear in her throat. She dropped the horse's hoof and threw a look past the Indian and saw only the empty trail curving away out of sight. Her sight darted back to the Indian and she saw the rifle wasn't pointed at her. Maybe she could shoot the savage before he could shoot her, or at least fire her gun to signal for help. She grabbed for the pistol in her pocket.

As Cora caught hold of the pistol, a second Indian, the one she had seen the day before, jumped his mustang at her from the side. He bent down from the back of his mount and scooped Cora up from the ground in an arm. He jerked her roughly against him. As Cora's hand came out with the pistol, the Indian wrenched it from her grip. He stuck it inside the waist of his buckskin pants.

Cora was panicked at being caught by the Indian, and the loss of the Colt, which was her only means of defense. She began to struggle fiercely, twisting and kicking to break free. Her hands reached backward over her shoulders and clawed at Wolf Voice's face. She felt her fingernails rip flesh.

Wolf Voice ducked his head to escape the raking fingernails, and vised down hard on the white girl's ribs. He clamped the girl's mouth shut with a hand to prevent her from screaming. He wheeled his mustang toward the woods. At that instant, the big horse of a woman he had seen with the cattle charged into view on the trail beyond Long Running. She held a pistol gripped in her hand.

Maude ran at top speed, and she screamed a shrill cry of fury and desperation. The Indian had come for Cora just as she had known he would. He must not succeed in carrying her off. As she rushed forward, she lifted her pistol and pointed it at the Indian holding Cora.

So intent was Maude in rescuing Cora from Wolf Voice that she had ignored Long Running. Now as she ran past, Long Running swung his rifle out in a round-house sweep. The heavy iron barrel struck Maude across the forehead with a resounding whack.

At the smashing impact of the rifle barrel, darkness exploded across Maude's vision. A sickening storm surge of pain washed through her. She ran on for a few steps, fighting the weakening pain and the darkness blinding her. Her legs collapsed and she fell stunned to the ground.

Cora saw Maude fall and lie motionless, and her heart seemed ready to burst with fear that her sister had been cruelly murdered. She began to fight more fiercely, straining every muscle to the breaking point to tear free from the Indian who held her.

"Hold still, or I will hit you," Wolf Voice warned in English, and rapped her smartly on the head with his knuckles.

Cora ceased her struggles with a sob. The Indian was much too strong for her to break free from his grasp. She must bide her time until an opportunity came to escape. She looked at Maude, hoping to see some movement, some sign of life.

"What shall we do about this one?" Long Running asked, pointing down at Maude's body.

"If she is still alive, we will take her with us. She would make a strong slave to help the women."

Long Running sprang down and knelt over Maude. "She is alive."

"Then put her across your mustang. Hurry."

Cora felt a great gladness at the knowledge Maude

was not dead. But her sister was now also a prisoner of the Indians.

Wolf Voice, holding Cora tightly, rode into the thick pine. Long Running hoisted the unconscious Maude up from the ground and hung her over the back of his mustang. He sprang up behind her. Holding the slack body of the woman upon the back of his mount, he followed after Wolf Voice.

Wolf Voice smiled to himself as he held the soft body of the white girl pressed to him. He had been correct in choosing how he could best take revenge upon his white enemies. The pleasure of killing the trappers would have been short lived, but the girl would give him pleasure for a very long time. He shoved his free hand inside Cora's coat and began to fondle her young, firm breast. A strand of her hair, blown by the wind, touched his face and it felt like she was caressing him in return. He would make her his new squaw and she would cook his food, carry wood to keep the teepee fire burning and, best of all, keep his blankets warm. He smiled at the thought. His crabby wife could sleep by herself. He smiled even more broadly.

Wolf Voice and Long Running with their captives came into a small clearing where Big Horse and Broken Arm and his sons were waiting with the property of the dead trappers. They halted their mustangs.

Maude stirred and moaned. Long Running immediately shoved her from the back of his mustang and she fell hard on the ground. She cried out in pain.

"Don't hurt her anymore!" Cora screamed at Long Running.

The Indian ignored Cora as if she had not spoken.

Cora looked down at Maude and saw blood flowing freely from the wound caused by the Indian's strike with his rifle barrel. She started to get down to go to her sister's aid, but Wolf Voice tightened his hold and held her firmly.

Long Running spoke to Wolf Voice. "They will be missed. We must hurry."

Wolf Voice nodded his agreement. "Tie the big woman on one of the mustangs." He stepped down from his mount with Cora still held in his arms. He moved to one of the trapper's saddle horses and lifted Cora astride.

Cora started to quickly dismount on the opposite side of the horse. Wolf Voice reached across and caught her, yanking her back into the saddle. He grunted something she could not understand, and his hand snaked out and slapped her soundly on the side of the head.

Cora's head rang from the blow. *Damn you.* She struck back, but the man dodged and she missed. He appraised her coldly with his black eyes.

"I will beat you if you do not do exactly as I say," he threatened.

Cora wanted to shout at the Indian, to curse him, tell him he had no right to force her to go with him. She clamped her jaws shut and said not a word. *Just give me a weapon, or a chance to flee and we shall then see.*

Cora looked at Maude and paid no attention to Wolf Voice tying her hands to the pommel of the saddle with a length of rawhide. Her sister was mostly conscious now, but still too weak and befuddled to make a fight as Long Running forced her upon a horse. He bound her hands to the pommel same as Wolf Voice had done to Cora. Blood was still flowing from Maude's wound. It was coagulating in the cold to a hideous red mask.

Wolf Voice sprang upon his own mustang and took up the lead rope to Cora's mount. He led his band through the woods away from the white men's caravan and climbed the slope up from the river valley to the mile-high plain. The land, a terrain of low, rolling swells covered with prairie grass, was empty as far as he could see. He raised the band to a gallop to the north, toward the winter camp of his people, many days away on the upper reach of the Powder River.

The cold, stiff wind sprang at Cora, for there was nothing to slow its blast across the treeless plain. Wind tears quickly puddled in the corners of her eyes as she scoured the land. She wanted to find something that would mark the route on which the Indian led them. There was no trail and apparently the Indian was striking out cross-country for some known destination.

Here above the river valley, she now had a better view of the snow-capped Laramie Mountains lying to the southwest. But they were too far away to be of any use as landmarks. Ahead, but many miles away and certainly days of riding, the horizon was broken by jagged mountain peaks. She wished she knew their names; not that that would help her to know her location, for all the land was strange to her. Over the peaks of the mountains, storm clouds were gathering.

She drew her view back from the mountains to scan the terrain nearer to her. There had to be something unique that would identify the route they were taking and she must find it. Maybe, just maybe, she and Maude could somehow escape from their captors; they would need those landmarks to return and find the Mormon caravan.

Twenty-one

Jacob stood on the river docks at Florence and watched the Missouri River as the last of the daylight leaked away into the sky. Only one small steamboat was in sight on the water and it was hurrying downriver at full speed to reach the docks before darkness caught it. Jacob had returned to the town after leaving Cora with the Mormon caravan. For the last five weeks he had been waiting and watching the steamboats for the arrival of Glen and Renne, coming from St. Joe with their winter supplies of food, powder and lead, and a dozen traps for each man.

The waiting was the hardest task he had ever undertaken. He was sunk in deep gloom from the loss of Cora and had morosely wandered the short streets of the town or stood, as now, forlornly on the riverbank, watching the traffic on the water. The loss of Cora was doubly painful because he knew the depth of her beauty after spending the night holding her in his arms. Though he hated Cora's decision to help her sister marry Pateman, he understood her strength, and her loving kindness, in taking that action. Still, he cursed himself for so readily riding away and leaving her to wed the Mormon. She was what Jacob desired above all things in the universe. He should have carried her off, whether she was willing or not. Unknown to himself, his head moved from side to side as if he was trying to turn back the clock.

He left the river as it became heavily shrouded in darkness and entered the town.

Jacob jerked awake to the muted rasp of metal against metal as a key was inserted into the lock of his hotel room door. He scooped up the pistol lying on the bed beside him and rolled to the floor. He raised the weapon and pointed it through the deep darkness at the closed door of his hotel room.

The rattle of metal came again as someone stealthily turned the key and the locking bolt pulled free. Jacob stared hard at the faint outline of the door. One or more of Shattuck's cronies had discovered where Jacob had gone after the shooting. Now they had come to take their revenge. He cocked his pistol. He would send them all to hell the instant they came through the doorway.

The door swung silently open and Jacob saw two men, one behind the other and slightly to the side, framed in the opening. His finger took up the slack in the trigger of his pistol. He could kill them both in less than a second.

"Jacob, you there?" a man whispered.

Jacob caught his finger that was tightening on the trigger at the last possible moment before the weapon fired. That was Glen's voice. Godalmighty! He had come within a hair's breadth of killing his friends.

"Damn you, Glen. I almost shot you and Renne. Why in hell are you sneaking into my room without knocking? Where'd you get the key?"

"Quiet," Glen whispered as he moved inside. "There wasn't a desk clerk. We got your room number from the register and there was a key in your box. Pack your gear. We're leaving."

"What's going on?" Jacob whispered as he climbed to his feet.

"There's hell to pay if the sheriff here in Florence finds out we're in town," Renne replied.

"We'll talk later," Glen said. "Now move. It'll be daylight in an hour and we've got to be long gone from here by then."

Something was bad wrong, Jacob knew. Those two didn't stampede easily. But at least his interminable waiting was over. He hastily dressed, gathered his belongings, and followed the men from the hotel.

The three trappers left Florence and hurried westward through the night lying black on the immigrant trail along the Platte River. The rode their strong mounts and had with them three loaded packhorses.

When the dawn broke, Jacob could not contain himself any longer. He called out to Glen and Renne, "All right, now tell me what's going on."

Neither man responded. The silence stretched as Jacob looked from one of his comrades to the other.

"Are you both deaf?" Jacob said exasperated. "You roust me out of bed and we sneak out of town like thieves. I want to know why."

"We're not thieves," Renne said. "But we did get mixed up in a couple of killings. And the sheriff at St. Joe would like to get his hands on us. I'm sure that he's also sent word to the law in Florence to be on the lookout for us. We rode horseback upriver from St. Joe instead of taking a boat so we wouldn't be seen."

"Why would the sheriff want you, if the fight was fair?"

"Renne, you tell him what happened," Glen said. "You remember it better than me." Glen kicked his mount ahead.

Renne reined his horse closer to Jacob and spoke in a low voice. "You know Glen gets mean when he's drinking."

"Sure." Jacob remembered his first years with the trappers, and the many fights Glen got himself into— got them all into. "But he doesn't drink when he's with the widow woman."

"That's just it. The widow and him had a hell of a row. She got a little lonesome this past winter and took herself some man company, a fellow named Spradling. Glen found out about that. Hurt him something awful. Well, anyway, when he accused her, they got into this bad argument. She told him the winters are too long and if he was going to go trapping again, for him to get out. Well, he's not about to let a woman tell him what he's got to do. He leaves and goes to Garveen's Saloon and begins to drink. He's soon downed several shots and feeling mean. So who do you suppose shows up? That fellow Spradling the widow had over to her house. There was a second fellow with him. Glen just plainly picks a fight with Spradling and shoots him."

"Damnation. I'd hoped Glen was settled down for good."

"That's not all of it. That second man with Spradling sneaked out a gun. Well, I saw him doing that and shot him dead. Time was short and, being in a hurry, I gunned him down without warning. That could be called murder."

"So you and Glen rode for it instead of waiting for the sheriff."

"That's it. We both decided that it'd be a hell of a lot safer for us in the mountains this winter, and then all of us can go to California come spring. There'll be three of us owning that winery."

* * *

"The squaws are hard at work," Renne said to Jacob and Glen.

The three trappers sat on their horses behind the crown of the hill, and cautiously peered over to study the Crow encampment in the valley of the Powder River below them. The Indian village, more than a hundred lodges strong, rested in a broad bend on the south side of the river. The teepees, made of tanned buffalo hides, were stained a dark gray by many fires. Scores of children and dogs romped and played among the teepees.

There was a constant flow of women to and from the dense stand of trees that bordered the river. On each return trip, the women toiled up the slope, packing heavy loads of dry wood in leather straps fastened across their shoulders. Their steps were nervous and hurried, as if some inner instinct warned them that the first great blizzard of the winter was just beyond the horizon and there would be much need of the fuel to hold back the frigid cold.

A short distance downriver from the village, two hundred or more mustangs of a wide range of colors—blacks, roans, grays, and pintos—grazed in a meadow. Three half-grown boys sat upon their bareback ponies on a rise of land above the herd. They talked and laughed among themselves, but their keen eyes frequently scanned the hills above them, and down at the horses they were guarding.

"I don't see any bucks," Jacob said. Apprehensive at the absence of the warriors, he turned his eyes to inspect the land behind them, and then up and down the river.

The three men had followed the immigrant trail to Scotts Bluff, and there they had veered away from the well-used route and took a course northwest. They had passed a hundred miles north of Fort Laramie and now the towering, jagged peaks of the Big Horn Mountains

were visible on the horizon. Two days of hard riding
would bring them to the base of the mountains. Then
one more day would take them up to their cabin in the
high valley where the fur of the mink, marten, otter,
and fox would soon be prime.

Jacob and his comrades always approached every
river crossing with great wariness, and in this manner
had discovered the village of the Crows without being
detected. The Crows spent the summers in the high
country. Then in the late autumn, they took down their
lodges and descended to the river valleys, often five
thousand feet lower in elevation. The Indians were
drawn down from the mountains to these protected valleys where the harsh winter winds blew less fiercely, the
snow was not so deep, and ample wood was available
for fuel. Also buffalo, elk, and antelope sought the low
country in winter and provided a ready larder of fresh
meat for the Crows.

"You're right, only a few old bucks sitting and doing
nothing," Renne said. These were the first words Jacob
had spoken all day, and he had volunteered only the
most necessary comments since they had left Florence.
The girl from New Orleans had bewitched him, and
his heart was somewhere with her to the south on the
trail to Salt Lake City. Glen was just as sour-faced and
untalkative as Jacob.

"Best we go down and buy us a winter woman to sub-
stitute for what we've lost," Glen said to Jacob.

Jacob whirled around on Glen. "What!"

"We all need a pretty girl, and some of those Crow
girls are sure damn pretty."

"You're wrong. I don't want a girl." Cora's face rose
clear and beautiful in Jacob's mind. No girl, no matter
what race or how beautiful, could take Cora's place in
his heart.

"Sure you do. You just don't know it yet—with our

sickness, that's the only cure. You'll be glad later that you got one and took her along with you."

"Nothing doing," Jacob said heatedly. He felt again Cora's lips upon his, and her soft body under him.

"That's a Crow village, not Ute, or Navajo," Renne said. "Those old bucks down there would try to take our scalps rather then sell us some of their young women."

"Then we'll steal them," Glen said, looking at Renne. "Should be easy enough. Just slip up on them in the woods find the prettiest ones, and carry them off."

"Hell no!" Jacob said. "Now let's find a crossing upstream from here and get on to the mountains."

Glen didn't move, sitting and staring down at the Crow village, and the women at work.

"Glen, we shouldn't bother the Indian girls," Jacob said. "Renne, tell him."

"I'm not so sure but what Glen ain't right," Renne said. "But this ain't the right time. The ground is good for tracking and the Crow warriors could trail us easy. Best we leave well enough alone for now."

"I say that we need some women for the winter," Glen replied. "But have it your way, at least for now."

The three men reined their mounts back from the ridge top and rode away from the Crow village. An hour later they forded the Powder on a shallow, rock-ribbed bottom and again headed northwest.

The three men halted their trotting horses when the land fell away abruptly in an oval-shaped depression some forty feet below the plain, extending about a mile left and right and a half-mile straight across. From rim to rim, the huge sink was crowded with buffalo.

Jacob had seen such sinks in the land before. They were places where the water escaped by way of a hidden subterranean passageway. Buffalo often used them as the weather grew colder. He judged this herd of big brown beasts contained at least ten thousand animals. They stood or lay contently chewing their cuds. Some of the spring's calves of the spring frisked about in the cool air. Nearby, two bull calves butted heads, practicing for future combat as adults. Several great white wolves sat on their haunches on the periphery of the herd and watched. The wolves were always with the buffalo, following and feeding off the unwary or the slow, the calves and the crippled.

"They're settled down and not going to spook," Renne said.

"A quiet bunch, sure enough," Jacob said.

"It's shorter to ride straight through them, and I'm thinking we can," Glen said. "The cows have all been bred and the bulls are just lazin'. But still, watch them; they can get cantankerous for no reason."

Jacob pressed his heels against the flanks of his gray and walked it into the herd beside Renne and Glen. The closer buffalo huffed irritably and snorted at the nearness of the men, but still drew back left and right like the parting of a dark surf to let them pass through. The wolves pulled farther back and intently eyed the horsemen.

The men gained the opposite side of the buffalo herd without incident, and the horses lunged up the steep side of the sink and onto the plain.

The three men immediately pulled their mounts to a halt.

"Jacob, there's some of your goddamn Crow bucks!" Glen exclaimed.

A group of mounted Indian braves some thirty strong was coming directly at them. The warriors were close enough that Jacob could see their expressions, and they were as surprised as the trappers at seeing enemies so near. They were armed with rifles and bows and arrows, and most had long lances tipped with iron points, some sticking upward at an angle from scabbards fastened to their mustangs and others held in the warriors' hands. The Indians reined their mustangs to a quick stop.

"Seems like our bad luck hasn't run out yet," Jacob said.

Twenty-two

Jacob's muscles were wound up tightly as he mentally measured the range he would have to shoot to kill the Crow braves, should they attack. His senses sharpened, reaching out to read the Indians, to anticipate their next action.

"Do we fight or run?" Renne asked.

"Neither, just yet," Glen said. "Don't touch your rifles. Let them pick whether it's to be a fight, or just a howdy and we'll be on our way."

"Looks like it might be a hunting party with all those lances," Jacob said, watching the silent band of riders. The lance was one of the Crows' favorite weapons for taking buffalo. The brave on his fast mustang would ride up close to a running buffalo and spear him deeply with the lance, then ride on to catch and spear another. Often the buffalo wasn't killed outright, and would run on a ways before stopping to stand bleeding until it fell. After a hunt, the dead beasts would be scattered over several miles. The lance was also a deadly weapon for close in fighting, after all the firearms were empty and the arrows spent.

"Maybe they don't want to fight any more than we do," Jacob added. He hoped this was true, for in any battle with such a large number of foes, the white men could not win. The best that could happen would be the loss of the packhorses and supplies, and the worst, their lives.

"You could be right, Jacob," Glen said. "If so, they'd not want any shooting to stampede the buffalo. But if they do want to fight, you shoot the man who moves out first toward us. I'll take the second. Renne, you the third. Then we all ride like hell back into the buffalo and shoot our pistols to stampede them. Maybe by riding in among the stampeding buffalo we can get away."

"Or get trampled to death," Jacob said.

Glen raised his hand with the palm out toward the Crows, in the universal peace sign of the plains and mountains. The Indians made no return signal, but sat their strong mustangs and looked at the white men.

The trappers returned the scrutiny for a minute or so. Then Glen spoke. "Let's ride out of here. Move slowly now along the edge of the sink and stay close to the buffalo."

Jacob fought the urge to look behind as they walked their horses away from their enemies. They must not show concern; that could be interpreted as a sign of weakness and fear and could draw an attack when otherwise none would be forthcoming. However, his ears were cocked to the rear and straining to hear any sound made by approaching horses.

A hundred yards were made good, and another hundred. He heard nothing from the Crows and his breath began to come more easily. He turned and looked at the Indians.

The band of Crows were riding toward the sink. As the braves went, they began to spread out left and right in a long, single file. Lances and bows and arrows were taken into their hands and made ready for use. The Crows reached the brink and vanished down into the sink.

The low rumble of a thousand hooves thudding on

the prairie came to Jacob. "They're going after the buffalo instead of our scalps," he said to his two comrades.

"Maybe they need meat more than they need a fight," Glen said. "Best we get out of here."

"I want to be long gone by the time they get done killing buffalo," Renne said. "With their blood hot, they might come hunting us."

They rode hard through the remainder of the day. A fireless camp was made in night darkness.

Jacob took the first guard and sat lonely, watching the drift and prickle of cold, distant stars.

The bitter cold wind slapped Cora's face raw and wind tears were frozen on her cheeks. Her head was pulled down into the collar of her coat and her hands were shoved to the bottoms of her pockets. Wolf Voice had untied her hands from the saddlehorn after the band had ridden several miles from the Platte River and the Mormon caravan where they had taken her prisoner. Her clothes were woefully inadequate to protect her from the driving wind and the temperature that was dropping swiftly. She was numb with cold and barely able to maintain her seat on the back of the trotting horse.

The Crows and their two captives rode steadily north. Wolf Voice guided the way, leading Cora's mount. Long Running came next, towing Maude's horse. Big Horse and Broken Horn and his sons, Far Thunder and Elk Piss, came behind with the horses and possessions of the dead trappers. All the Indians now wore wolfskin coats and caps taken from the packs tied to the backs of their mustangs.

Wolf Voice looked back at Cora to evaluate how well she was enduring the journey. She rode slump-shouldered with ice on her cheeks. She wasn't as tough as the Crow women. They could have followed him for days without such a look of miserable weariness. Still, her white beauty more than compensated for her white weakness. Then, to his surprise, he saw her turn her head and scan the land ahead and to both sides, and check the position of the sun. She was marking the route and, by the sun, the direction they traveled. She was tougher than she appeared at first glance. He would guard her closely to ensure that she never had the opportunity to escape from him. He knew she would try.

Cora studied the terrain they traveled through. The land was becoming ever more broken. They rode across shallow valleys that ran off to the right; that was to the east, she judged, observing the sun setting on her left. Here and there short hills reared up between the drainages. Copses of pine, oak, and juniper capped some of the hills. She saw a herd of fifteen of more elk trotting from in front of them.

She looked backward at Maude. Her sister's clothing was as poorly suited for the weather as Cora's. Maude stared straight ahead into the cold, gusting wind, from a face streaked with crusted blood that had flowed down from the wound the Indian had given her across the forehead with his rifle barrel. Her dark hair had come loose from its bun on the back of her head and whipped and flicked in the wind like a horse's tail. Her eyes were unreadable, all thought hidden. Cora returned to studying the land, the shape of the hills, the directions the streams flowed, hoping to see something unique, like an oddly shaped rock outcropping that could be easily remembered.

When the pale, weak sun abandoned the land and fell behind the faraway horizon, Wolf Voice called a halt for the night. He chose a patch of pine on the lee side of a hill where there was some protection from the frigid wind. Some of the Indians immediately set about unloading the horses and hobbling their legs, and the others to gathering wood for a fire.

Cora climbed stiffly down to the ground. Holding to the saddle, she stomped the ground trying to get some feeling back into her cold, numb feet. She almost fell when Elk Piss came and led the horse off while she still held to it.

She moved to Maude, who had dismounted and stood looking dejectedly back in the direction from which they had come. "They're building a fire, Maude. Come and let's get warm."

"I've lost Clive," Maude moaned. "The damn Indians made me lose Clive."

"Don't think about that now. We must get warm before we freeze."

Maude looked at Cora. "Clive will follow us and kill the Indians?" she said in a hopeful voice.

"He will try to find us," Cora replied. She knew Clive would never leave the Mormon people to fend for themselves while he pursued the Indians. If Maude and Cora were to survive, they must do it all by themselves. "I'm terrible hungry. I hope they'll give us some food."

"I'll never eat any of their heathen food," Maude retorted.

"Don't be stupid. We must eat so we'll be strong enough to escape if the chance comes to us. Maybe even tonight, after the Indians go to sleep."

"Do you think we can find our way back?"

"I've been watching the route we came, and I think I can lead us back to the river. Then we will follow and catch up with the caravan. Now, don't you make the Indians mad so that they'll tie us up for the night. We'd better not talk anymore, for that one who led my horse is watching us."

Wolf Voice saw the two women stop talking and come toward the fire. The big, homely one was taller than he was and appeared very strong for a woman. Were she and the pretty one relatives? From the way she had come to the defense of the smaller one, it seemed to indicate they were. That wasn't important now. He would question them later.

The Indians gave way to allow space for Cora and Maude to come up to the fire. Cora stood very close to the flames and spread her hands over them. She shivered with pleasure as the fire ate into the pine wood and flared higher, showering her with its warmth.

The Indians took jerky and pemmican from a large leather pouch, and began to eat standing around the fire. The pemmican was made of shredded dried meat, suet, dried berries, and nuts molded into small cakes. Cora smelled the aroma of the food, and her hunger surged. She had eaten nothing since a very small breakfast. She held out her hand to Wolf Voice and pointed at the pemmican.

Wolf Voice stared at Cora, his expression betraying nothing. Then he handed a pemmican cake to the pretty white woman.

Cora accepted the food with one hand, and then waited with the other outstretched for a second piece for Maude.

"She doesn't need food," Wolf Voice said, smiling without mirth. "She's too big already."

"Yes, she does," Cora said firmly.

Wolf Voice shifted his piercing eyes to Maude and grinned wickedly. "Come here and get food," he commanded.

Maude looked down at the fire and did not move.

"Come here!" Wolf Voice shouted. His eyes glittered with a murderous light.

Cora was instantly afraid for Maude. From the flat,

ugly way the Indian spoke, she knew he would do something awful to Maude, maybe kill her if she didn't do exactly as he ordered. "Maude, get your food," Cora said quickly. She caught Maude by the arm and turned her to face Wolf Voice.

Maude took the pemmican cake, but she simply held it in her hand and made no move to eat it.

"Go away," Wolf Voice growled, and motioned with his hand for Maude to leave.

Maude went slowly, obviously taking her own good time, to the opposite side of the fire. She stopped near Broken Arm and looked across the fire at Cora.

Wolf Voice put the last of the pemmican cake into his mouth and walked to the bulging pack saddles piled on the ground by the horses. He took two buffalo hide sleeping robes from one of the packs and came back to the fire. He threw one of the robes at Maude's feet. The second, he held out to Cora.

As Cora came close to take the robe, Wolf Voice's hand jumped at her like a large brown spider and clasped her around the back of the neck. He shoved his face close to Cora's. "You will become my woman when we reach my village," he said, his eyes glittering with lust.

Cora's heart cramped at the threat. Her worst fears had been confirmed. She tried to back away from the Indian, but he held her fast by the nape of the neck.

Wolf Voice brought up his other hand and caressed the soft skin of the white girl's face. He grinned in anticipation of the pleasure she would give him. Then he remove his hands from Cora. "Go sleep," he ordered, with a sweep of his eyes that indicated both women. "There," and he pointed at a spot on the ground within the light from the fire.

Cora pivoted around, glad to be free from the Indian. She joined with Maude and they spread their robes very close together where the Indian had pointed. Without a word, they lay down in their clothing and wrapped themselves in the thick, hairy hides.

Cora pulled the robe up over head, but left a small peephole to stealthily watch the Indians. Her pulse raced for neither she nor Maude had been tied. As soon as the Indians were all asleep, she and Maude would steal horses and slip away into the darkness. If they could not acquire horses, they would strike out on foot. Anything to escape.

The Crows prepared their beds on the ground around the fire. They talked together for a few minutes and then all of them, except for Wolf Voice, rolled themselves in their robes. He threw more wood on the fire, and then sat down on his robe and began to leisurely hone his long-bladed skinning knife on his leather leggings.

Cora's hopes of escape sank, for she realized the Indian was on guard; another one would take his place, and then another, until the night was spent. There would be no opportunity for she and Maude to escape.

Cora whispered to Maude. "They're going to keep guard. I don't think we're going to get away tonight."

"The bastards," Maude whispered back. "I wish I had my pistol."

"I'll stay awake," Cora said. "Maybe he'll go to sleep."

She lay watching the Indian, the firelight glinting off the knife blade with each stroke he made to put an ever sharper edge on it.

Twenty-three

"Dammit! Make up your mind," Renne growled at Jacob. "It's either ride up into the mountains with me, or ride with Glen and steal an Indian girl. And my advice to you is you should go with Glen—he's going to get himself an Indian girl no matter how many bucks are guarding that village. With your help, he might get it done without getting himself killed."

The two men with their packhorses were halted at the base of the Big Horn Mountains where the mouth of the valley that held their trapping cabin widened and merged into the flat plains. They sat their saddles, and the cold north wind buffeted them as they watched Glen, nearly out of sight, galloping his horse to the southeast, toward the Powder River.

Jacob turned toward the aged sun flaming weakly in the cold, blue sky above the snowy spires of the Big Horns. He stared up at the high, rocky ramparts which were home for nothing but hermit eagles. He felt a soul-bending loneliness, a gulf his two friends could not fill. He was no longer satisfied with where he was, and who he was, now that he had lost Cora. Life yawned empty and bare ahead of him, and he was drawing back from it, from the chase that had at one time so thrilled him.

He had an immediate decision to make. He studied

the sky and knew Glen was correct—a storm would soon arrive that could perhaps provide cover for a raid on the Crow village they had found two days before. Over the crest of the mountains, high, thin clouds of ice crystals were heralding the storm's approach. Already a faint gray nimbus was gathering about the sun. One day, two at the most, and arctic cold and snow would fall upon all this land. He shivered with dread, for he knew firsthand the frigid emptiness that held the mountains prisoner in winter, and would soon close again upon them. He was not yet ready to be penned in the valley, and often driven to seek shelter within the confining log walls of the cabin.

A hard recklessness born of a loneliness that squeezed his heart, came upon Jacob. Some daring venture was needed to put some zest back into life. What better way to accomplish that than to help a comrade capture a valuable prize from a worthy enemy? Also, Renne was correct; what Glen planned held odds that were all wrong. If Jacob went with Glen and stayed alert, maybe he could keep old man death away from his friend. He twisted and gave Renne a rakehell grin. "What the hell. I'll go help Glen steal a girl. Maybe two—one for you."

He spun his gray stallion to the east and ran the big brute across the plains after Glen.

Cora watched the blizzard, a wall of blowing snow roaring down upon her not a quarter mile distant across the sere emptiness of the high plains. Hours earlier, dark, heavy clouds had driven over the Indians and their prisoners and assassinated the sun, forcing a feeble, dusk-like light upon the earth. Now the storm would be upon them in seconds and Maude must be signaled to be ready to try and escape under its cover.

Cora cautiously checked the six mounted Indians rid-

ing with her, the leader, Wolf Voice, and three others
in front and the two youngest behind. How alert were
they to her actions? All were staring at the approaching
storm. She reined her horse to the side, closer to
Maude's mount. When Maude turned and looked, Cora
silently mouthed the words, "Get ready." She made a
short hand gesture at the white mass rushing at them.

Maude looked at the storm, then back, and nodded
her understanding. Her jaws tightened into hard ridges
of muscle.

Cora and Maude had been captives of the Indians
for five days. During the first part of their captivity, Cora
had been greatly worried about her sister. Maude was
sullen, belligerently shouting at the Indians, and refus-
ing to obey their demands. That had brought brutal,
bloody blows upon Maude from the Indians. The anger
of Wolf Voice was so great that Cora thought he would
surely kill Maude. By the end of the third day, Maude
had come to the full realization that Clive was not pursuing the Indians. With that understanding, Maude had
become pliant, quickly carrying out the orders of their
captors. The Indians interpreted Maude's silence and
hurried obedience as a sign of her surrender to them.
But Cora knew differently, for she could read the look
in Maude's eyes. It was very dangerous to underestimate
her strong, tough sister.

The wind was growing in intensity and Cora pulled
the wolfskin coat around her more tightly. After the
first day of cold riding, she had told Wolf Voice that
she and Maude needed warmer clothing for the frigid
weather, and asked him to give them the sleeping robes
to use for warmth while they rode horseback. He had
looked at Maude and laughed derisively, but had given
Cora a fur coat from the packs of the dead trappers.
Cora had almost refused the coat because Maude would
not receive one, but then logic took control. She knew

that should she and her sister escape from the Indians, even one coat they could share would be of the utmost importance to prevent them from freezing to death while they searched for the Mormon caravan.

The storm's frontal winds struck Cora and the others, knocking them about and staggering the horses. The winds howled past them, sending the tall, frost-killed grasses running like waves of a broad, gray sea. And onward still the winds rushed, trying to blow themselves off the face of the earth. A handful of seconds later, the snow torrents of the blizzard swirled upon the Indians and women.

The storm surge of snowflakes blinded Cora. All around her the world was an ocean of streaking, tumbling white. She was floating in a void totally without color. Even as she fought to stand against the storm, she knew its very ferocity would aid in her escape.

She flung a look at Maude beside her. Maude was watching her expectantly.

"Now, Maude! Now!" She motioned with her hand for Maude to follow, and jerked her horse to the left. She began a frantic drumbeat on the beast's ribs with her heels. The horse bolted away from the Indians and into the maelstrom of white.

She heard a man shout behind her. Then another, who she knew was Wolf Voice. A chilling fear ran along her spine as she waited, expecting a bullet to strike her. Then the racing horse buried itself and her in the bosom of the snowstorm and she was hidden from the sight of her enemies. At least for the moment.

Cora gripped the heaving back of the horse tightly with her legs as the brute made a score of lunges through the cascading torrents of snow and then settled into a flat-out run. She risked a glance behind to see how her sister was faring. Maude's mount was charging hard on her heels, with the big woman clinging fast to the pommel of the saddle with one hand and hammering the animal on the neck with the other.

Cora turned back to the front and leaned forward into the wind and snow. She was a fair rider, having ridden astride her family's horse in New Orleans, and had also learned much from the long days upon the Indian's horse, but none of that had prepared her for the breakneck race through a blinding snowstorm. She feared the horse would stumble on some unseen object or step into a hole in the ground and fall, or that she might lose her precarious perch upon its back. But there was no alternative. She lashed the straining beast between her legs with the ends of the leather reins.

She must not continue along the same course upon which the Indians had last seen them, and were surely pursuing them. She looked to the side at Maude, who had drawn up parallel, and thrust her arm out to the side to signal that they should make a turn. Maude chucked a thumb in the same direction.

Cora whirled her horse steeply to the right, and tore on. Maude held her station at Cora's side, and continued to pound her straining mount with her fist.

They raced through the tumult of the storm for what Cora judged was nearly two miles. The snow was building on the ground, but had not yet accumulated sufficient depth to hold a track that was not quickly erased by the wind. She considered making one more turn to elude the cruel brown-skinned men. However, not knowing where the Indians were, another course through the driving snow might just as likely bring them again within their enemies' sight.

As Cora stared hard ahead into the cataracts of falling snow, a gaping fissure opened along which she could see for several yards. In that alleyway of extended vision were the dark forms of two horsemen. They immediately brought their mounts to a halt and lifted rifles. Cora's heart froze with dread. In this remote land, the men could only be Indians. And they were blocking her path.

Jacob and Glen rode in the blizzard, with the fierce winds pounding their backs and snow frozen to the tails of their horses. The storm overran them at daybreak as they were climbing out of their sleeping robes. They had mounted their horses, and let the strong north winds blow them along with the snow toward the Powder River.

Jacob's vision was restricted by the falling snow to but a short pistol shot and he watched warily ahead. He calculated they were getting very close to the Crow village. They must not stumble into squaws gathering last-minute fuel, or warriors returning to camp from a hunt.

Both men held their rifles across their saddles in front of them wrapped in a sleeve of buckskin. The sleeve protected the firing caps from becoming damp; Now Jacob peeled it away and poked it into a saddlebag. He gave the breech of the rifle temporary shelter with his cupped hand. Beside him, Glen performed the same action.

The snow fell heavily, the wind whipping it off ahead of the riders. Just before him the downpour of snow was jammed together by the wind in a white wall impenetrable to his eye. From that opaque surface sprang two horsemen racing pell mell. They drove straight at Glen and Jacob.

The reckless speed of the oncoming horsemen surprised Jacob. Surely they could not have been any more able than he to see through the snowfall. Only men riding for their lives would risk such a dangerous pace.

The two horsemen reined their mounts to a stop barely twenty feet away from Jacob. He saw the frightened, white faces of the riders. Instantly he recognized Cora, and beside her, Maude.

"How in hell!" Jacob ejaculated.

"Son-of-a-bitch!" Glen said.

Cora, squinting into the wind-driven snow that bit at her face, did not immediately know the man was Jacob. She saw only that one of the horsemen was coming toward her. Then she heard the man shout, "Cora!" and she knew the voice.

He brought Jubal in against Cora's horse. With both of them still astride, he encircled her in his arms and pulled her tightly to him. "God, Cora, how did you ever get to this place?"

"Jacob! Jacob!" Cora cried. She pressed herself to his chest. She shivered with the pleasure of his strong arms around her. Tears came to her eyes.

Maude started to ride forward to tear Cora away from Jacob. But then she looked at Glen, who was steadily watching her. She halted. She needed the trappers to help Cora and her to escape from the Indians. Her sister could be taken away from Jacob at a more opportune time.

"Don't just sit there," Maude called out above the howl of the wind. "The Indians are coming. They had us captive and are probably just behind us out there."

Cora pulled back from Jacob. "Please help us, Jacob," she said.

"You know I will," Jacob said. He turned to Glen. "Things have changed now."

"So I see," Glen replied.

"I think back toward the mountains would be the best direction to go."

Glen started to answer, then something caught his eye, and he hastily looked past Jacob. "There they are," he shouted, and lifted up his rifle.

Jacob twisted to look. Half a dozen ghost-like riders were indistinct forms not but a few score yards away in the dense white snowfall. They were stopped and every eye was examining the two women who unexpectedly had become four people.

"Go, Jacob!" Glen barked. "Get the women out of here. Go! Go!"

"Follow me," Jacob called to Cora and Maude.

He gouged Jubal off into the teeth of the storm. Cora and Maude kicked their mounts into a run behind Jacob.

Glen brought up his rifle and aimed at the Indian offering the most clear target. He fired, saw the man sway backward as the bullet plowed into him.

Immediately Glen spun his horse and sent it racing after his friends. He threw himself forward on the animal's neck. Several rifles exploded at his rear. And the blood roar of a hunting pack, deep and savage, reached his ears.

He glanced back at his foes. They were only fleeting forms, now seen, now vanished. No sound came now from the phantom pursuers. He looked to the front and straightened in the saddle.

Glen felt a blow on his back and a shaft of pain lanced through him. He had been shot, for he knew the feeling from old wounds. The pain grew, huge beyond agony.

He pressed his hand against his stomach where the lead ball had torn free. He had seem men gut shot, as was he. It was a hell of a way to die.

He pressed harder on the exit hole of the bullet, trying to staunch the flow of blood that he knew was pouring from his body. The shock of the terrible injury came crawling up on him, a black mist growing and condensing on the borders of his mind. *Hold on, Glen*, he told himself. *Don't fall out of your saddle before you catch up with Jacob.* He grinned a pain-filled grin into his snow-filled, frozen beard. He was a dead man.

Twenty-four

Jacob led Cora and Maude straight into the maw of the blizzard. He knew their chance of escaping from the Indians was slender. The snow was now deep enough to hold horse tracks. Given a few minutes, the strong winds would erase the tracks, but the Indians were already upon their trail and chasing swiftly after them. To make it more difficult for his pursuers to follow, he should be running a course that continually changed, but he dared not until Glen caught up with them.

Jacob cast a glancing look behind; A moment passed and Glen came barreling out of the boiling white cauldron of the storm. He sped up and pulled in alongside Jacob.

"You hurt?" Jacob called out, noting Glen's sagging body.

"Just nicked in the side," Glen called back. He straightened his body as best he could, and hid his grimace of pain at the movement. Nothing must cause Jacob to slow the group's fast pace. "We'd better make some turns and lose the bastard Crows," he said. "You lead the way."

Jacob rode Jubal to the front and guided them on an irregular, unpredictable path, swerving, running straight for a distance, then veering off again. They came upon an exposed rock spine of the earth where the snow had been blown away. He whipped Jubal to the side to ride along the rock outcrop for more than half a mile. He always worked north, into the brunt of the storm and away from the Powder River, and paralleling the Big Horn Mountains some one hundred miles away. Should they elude the Indians, then they would turn west to their cabin.

The blizzard continued its onslaught on the land. The snow accumulated on the ground and ran in tumbling white streams before the wind. Drifts grew in the swales and in the lee of every raised rock and bush.

Jacob led the group on with miles passing under the swiftly flying hooves of the horses. When the day grew old, he stopped the weakening and blown horses. He looked through the falling snow at Cora. She appeared frozen, and fatigue showed in her strained, haggard face, in her every movement. He felt sorry for her, yet there were many miles to ride.

Cora saw Jacob watching her and gave him a frail smile. Her head felt light and woolly. She must not let him see how exhausted and cold she really was.

Jacob reined Jubal to Glen's side. "That old horse jolting you too much?" he asked the slumped figure.

Glen raised his pain-filled face to Jacob. "His step is as soft as the bounce of a woman's tit," he said. He tried to smile, but didn't have the strength to stretch his lips. He began to lean to the side and reached out to clutch Jacob's arm. "I'm all done in. Best you help me down before I fall."

Jacob, holding Glen in his saddle, swiftly dismounted. He helped the wounded man down to lie on the ground. He saw for the first time the red wetness that soaked Glen's clothing from his waist to the tip of his moccasins.

"Damn you, Glen, why didn't you tell me how bad you was shot?"

"It's a killer all right. And there wasn't anything you could do for me."

"Let me look." Jacob reached to open Glen's coat.

Glen feebly shoved Jacob's hands away. "No. It's no use." He was silent for a moment. "Jacob, something's come plain to me during these past few hours."

"What's that, Glen?"

"Man wasn't meant to last forever, or even for very long. I've lived a half century—a good, interesting fifty years. Now this is the end of me."

Jacob stared down at the man who had taught him so much, and had fought so many battles beside him. And he was dying and there was absolutely nothing Jacob could do to save him.

"I don't want to die lying like a dog on the ground in the snow," Glen said. "Sit me up. Death likes a shining mark."

Jacob lifted Glen and propped him against his shoulder. "That better?" he asked.

"Better," Glen said, his voice a whisper barely heard above the noise of the storm. "I always thought dying was but a one-man job. But it's better to die with a friend holding you up to meet death face to face."

Glen's voice ceased. He stiffened as a whirling, black tornado sucked him up and the world vanished. He went limp in Jacob's arms.

Jacob turned and looked off over the plain, watching the swirling, wind-driven snow, but not seeing it, for a long time.

"Is there anything I can do?" Cora asked.

"No, nothing," Jacob replied, roused by Cora's voice.

He removed Glen's wolfskin coat and gave it to Cora. "You look frozen, so put this on—it's better than the one you've got."

"It's large enough to fit Maude. I'll give it to her." She handed the coat to her sister.

Jacob gathered Glen up in his arms. Gently, he placed the dead man across the saddle of his horse, and tied him securely there.

"What are you doing?" Maude called. "You're surely not going to take that corpse with us."

"Sure as hell am," Jacob retorted. "I'm not going to let him out here for the coyotes and wolves to chew on. He'll get a proper burial, just as he would give me."

"He'll rotten before we find the Mormon handcart company," Maude said with disgust.

"We're not going to look for the Mormons."

"What do you mean!" Maude's voice was a shout. "That's where we must go right now."

"The Mormons are days of hard riding south of us. And the country is covered with a foot of snow. More is sure to fall. We'd probably have to travel all the way to Salt Lake City."

"That's where Cora and I want to go."

"We're going up into the mountains to our trapping cabin. The Indians will never find us there, for they don't know about it. In the spring, we'll figure out what to do."

"I'll not go there with you," Maude cried out shrilly.

Cora saw that strange, twisted expression come surging into her sister's face. Did Jacob see it also? He seemed not to. He shrugged his shoulders and mounted his horse.

"That's your choice," he said. He turned to Cora. "You're going with me—its much safer," he said matter-of-factly.

"Maude, we've got to go with Jacob, because we could never find the Mormons on our own with snow on the ground," Cora said.

"I say we can," Maude snapped back.

Jacob had had enough of Maude. "Cora is going with

me. And that's final. You can too, if you want. Just shut your mouth about the damn Mormons."

He grabbed up the reins of Glen's horse and, leading the animal with its burden, went off through the turbulence and murk of the storm. Cora trailed close behind.

Maude sat her horse and watched the two riders fade into mere silhouettes in the falling snow. Then, with an angry, crazed look in her eyes, she kicked her mount off after the hazy figures in the white curtain.

Jacob stopped and the two women halted behind him. He watched ahead across the frozen prairie. The snowfall had stopped, however the wind still blew strongly, sending streams of snow flowing and rippling around the legs of the horses. He examined the bank of water vapor rising up from the ground three hundred or so yards away. It froze quickly to ice crystals and moved off with the wind. He had never heard of hot springs in this part of the country. Yet there were many thousands of square miles white men had never seen. Such a place of heat, if it existed, would make an excellent spot to rest during the fast approaching night.

Jacob urged Jubal onward, and as they drew nearer to the ground cloud, a dark mass became visible at its base. A moment later, he identified the source of the water vapor. It was rising from a vast, closely packed herd of night-bedding buffalo. The animals' breath, condensing rapidly in the super-cold air, was creating the ice fog.

There must be thousands of the big, shaggy beasts, thought Jacob as he roved his sight over the multitude of bodies. He dismounted and motioned for the women to do likewise, and they edged forward. The wind was from the animals to them, and they came to the perimeter of the herd and were not detected.

The wind picked up its vigor and the snow began to fall again. The dusk was almost night. No better location could be found to sleep the darkness and the storm away than among the shelter of the herd. . . . if it could be done without stampeding the lot of them.

Two cows lay side by side and facing off ninety degrees from the wind. In the ice lee between their bodies, the snow had drifted, nearly burying a calf of the past spring.

Jacob, moving slowly and crouched low, secured the front legs of the horses with short hobbling ropes. He removed his buffalo robe and, motioning to the two women, whispered, "We sleep here tonight. I'll spread the sleeping robes."

Jacob, still moving in slow motion, spread Glen's robe on the snow between the cows and beside the calf. The calf raised its head, looked at the crouched humans, and then sniffed at the tanned, smokey hide robe. A strange-smelling buffalo, yet still the friendly, safe scent of one of its own kind. The calf again rested its head beside its dam and went back to sleep.

Jacob motioned for Cora to lie down, and pointed where Maude should lie beside her. He had chosen Cora's place next to him. God, how he wanted to be close to her.

"I'll not sleep under the same covers with you," Maude said sharply. "And neither will Cora."

"It's up to you whether or not you sleep under the robes," Jacob retorted. He was tired and would not argue with the disagreeable woman. "But there's just two robes and there's three of us. Anyone who tries to sleep without one will freeze before the night is over. That means you, for Cora is going to use one. And I sure as hell plan to."

Cora caught her sister by the arm. "You know Jacob is correct. I'm frozen just standing here. I'll sleep next to Jacob and you won't have to get close to him."

"You sleep next to him!" Maude exclaimed. Her hands clinched at her sides. "I'll not have that."

"You must, for there's just the two of us."

Maude considered that for a moment. She looked at Jacob with disgust. "You do it," she told Cora. Maude would be alert to anything they might try that was improper.

Jacob was glad the problem was resolved. However, Maude's actions were unreasonable. "What's wrong with your sister?" he asked Cora, uncaring whether Maude could hear. "We're being chased by Indians who want to kill us, trying to stay alive in a blizzard, and yet she acts as if we were somewhere civilized back east."

Cora did not want to explain the reason Maude behaved as she did. "She will do whatever is needed," she replied.

Without delay, Cora lay down where Jacob had indicated. Maude, with a surly expression, did likewise.

Bringing his rifle with him, Jacob took the section of the ground robe on the opposite side of Cora. He spread his sleeping robe over all three of them.

Cora lay listening to the arctic wind moaning an endless dirge as it walked the dark world. She felt its cold fingers clawing at the protective covering, searching for an opening so it could come inside with her. She smiled. She felt good, deep down where her real being lived. Her enemies had failed to kill her, and the frigid storm was held at bay an inch away. Best of all, Jacob and Maude, the only people she cared for in all the world, lay one on each side of her. If only Maude would accept Jacob. A deep worry swept over Cora. Suppose Maude never did, and insisted on them going to Salt Lake City in the spring, and the arranged marriage to Clive? *No, that can't happen. Maude must accept Jacob. She must.* With that thought, Cora fell into a sleep of exhaustion.

Beside her, Jacob heard her breathing become slow

and steady, denoting sleep, and withdrew the hand that he had started to extend to her. She must be allowed to rest; tomorrow would be a rough one. He lay in the black wintry night, and pondered what the future might bring. He knew he would do his utmost to take Cora to California with him. But what of Maude?

In the cold, gray dawn the herd of buffalo began to stir in their snow beds. Here and there an animal rose and shook off its snow covering in a miniature blizzard. The storm had gone off to the south with its winds, leaving a blue-domed sky arching over a white world.

Jacob had been awakened by the first sound of the buffalo stirring. He did not want to move because Cora lay turned toward him and her soft breath fanned his face. His heart beat with pleasure at her nearness and the woman smell of her. For days he had been afraid he would never see her again. Now she lay within a hand's width of him. For the moment he was content.

Still, daylight could mean danger, for their enemies could be near and see them. He shoved the robe aside and cautiously raised his head to look around. The horses stood grouped together where he had left them just beyond the perimeter of the buffalo herd. Nearby three gray-white wolves hungrily eyed the hobbled mounts. Jacob tossed aside the robe and climbed erect with the rifle in his hands. The wolves swapped ends and lunged away through the foot of snow blanketing the prairie.

The rush of cold air brought Cora awake and she quickly sat up. She saw Jacob standing holding his rifle. "Do you see the Indians?" she asked hurriedly. "Are we in danger?"

Jacob looked down at Cora, looked into her eyes, to the shore of the unknowable world of the female. He wished he could read her inner thoughts, especially about him.

Maude came up out of the robe and fastened her view on Jacob. Jacob paid her no attention. He knew she was going to be big trouble.

He spoke to Cora. "No danger. There's nothing in sight but the buffalo and a few wolves. I'll get the horses and we'll head west to the Big Horns."

Maude swung her view over the snow-covered land. Then she fastened a hard stare on Jacob. "We can just as easily go south and find the Mormons," she said forcibly.

"I told you what we're going to do," Jacob growled. "Chasing the Mormons is just what the Indians would expect us to do. And Salt Lake City is too long a distance to cross with horses in the winter."

"That Indian Wolf Voice is smart enough to figure out what we'd most likely do," Cora said to Maude.

"Wolf Voice, is that what you called one of the Indians?" Jacob asked.

"Yes, the one who seemed to be the leader," Cora said. "Do you know him?"

"Glen, Renne and I fought him once and hurt him bad. Then later he tried to shoot us. I don't like to hear that bastard is still out prowling around." He recalled the first fight with Wolf Voice and his Crow braves not far from the mouth of the valley where his two friends and he had their cabin. Wolf Voice would know of that valley, for that was his land. Might he not reason that the trappers, heavily loaded with furs, had just left that place when he discovered them? And further that they would return there, if possible to escape him, and to trap furs again this winter? He had a hell of a hate for the trappers and that could drive him to search the valley even with deep snow on the land. Renne was there and would not be expecting an attack.

"We've got to ride," he said. "Roll the robes up."

He stomped off through the deep snow toward the horses. They watched him, the bores of their nostrils smoking like fumaroles in the frigid air. He lifted Glen's stiff, frozen body up and carried it with him. As he drew close, the horses huffed at the smell of death and pulled back.

"Whoa. Whoa." Jacob commanded the skittish beasts, and they stood still.

He lashed the corpse upon the back of the horse.

Twenty-five

The three riders—with Glen's corpse—hurried over the frozen, snow laden plain. They rode single file with Jacob guiding the way. Cora followed close behind in the trail that Jacob's horse had broken through the foot of snow. Maude brought up the rear. Ahead of each rider paced long, dark shadows, cast by the morning sun at their backs.

Cora burrowed more deeply into the wolfskin coat. The garment kept the top of her reasonably warm, but her scantily clad legs and feet felt the bite of the immense cold. She would never complain to Jacob. She looked up from following her mimicking black shadow to the two hungry hunting hawks wheeling back and forth across the winter sky of pale blue. They were the only living things, except for her group, in all that cold, white world. As they glided back and forth on the wind, they seemed to her to be weaving an invisible cloth in the sky. She wondered wherever on the open, snow-cloaked prairie did sky hawks put themselves at night.

She lowered her sight to the earth, for she felt Jacob's eyes upon her. He was watching her with a man's look at a woman he had loved, who knew the many pleasures she offered. The look sent a thrill through Cora.

Jacob shifted his view past Cora to Maude. She was focused intently on him. An iron-headed woman, and she hated him, he knew. He had observed Cora watching Maude with a worried, almost fearful expression. Did Cora know something about Maude that Jacob didn't? He recalled Maude's attack upon him when he was fighting Pateman, after the two had discovered Cora and him together. She was a powerful woman and one to be reckoned with. He would be on guard, for he thought her capable of committing murder, and his death would not displease her, at the right time.

Jacob hastened the women onward toward the Big Horn Mountains until the blood-red sun vanished into the bottomless pit behind the rim of the world. As the gray, evening dusk swarmed over them, the temperature began to drop rapidly. A wind rose and started to run with the snow, swirling it about the legs of the horses.

A short time later, he halted the group in a range of low hills covered with pine. He quickly surveyed the area close around them. They were in a narrow, crooked valley where a fire could not be seen but a few yards. A fire was desperately needed with such intense cold and the wind whipping away their body heat. In the bottom of the narrow valley, the wind blew less strongly; however, above his head, it whistled in the tops of the pines.

"We camp here tonight," he called to Cora and Maude. "Spread the sleeping robes there." He pointed at the space beneath a pine with dense foliage where less snow had accumulated on the ground.

Jacob dismounted and quickly hobbled the horses. He took a leather pouch containing his fire-making tools and went to a down and dead pine near where the women were spreading the sleeping robes. He began to strike sparks from his flint and steel onto a piece of punk screwed into a nest of fine, dry grass. After a few attempts, the punk caught fire. He blew gently on the tiny embryo and extended the fire to the grass with a small flame curling up. He placed the nucleus of a fire under a pile of twigs broken from the pine. Upon this was piled a huge quantity of dry limbs. Soon tall yellow flames were leaping and driving back the dark and cold.

Cora waded through the snow to the fire and spread her stiff, frozen hands to the flaring flames. The flames shone like splinters of the sun. The radiated warmth striking her body was so grand she wanted to cry.

She looked across the fire at Jacob, silently squatting on his heels on a little patch of snow he had tramped down. He was staring into the fire and his palms were turned outward like a penitent. What secret thoughts did he ponder? She knew with certainty that she felt safe with this young man of the plains and mountains. She still wondered why he had not reached out and touched her during the past night when they lay so close together under the robes. Tonight she would reach out to him. But it could go no farther than that, not with Maude under the same robe with them.

Jacob rose to his feet. "Cora, please find us some food in the pack behind Glen's saddle," he said.

"Yes, Jacob," Cora said.

He went into the dark to the horses. He came to Jubal and ran his hand along the horse's neck. Jubal nickered softly at Jacob's touch and its skin ran and quivered under his hand. The horse nuzzled Jacob while he checked the hobbles on its legs, until the man moved out of reach.

Jacob moved to Glen's horse, and the Indian horses Cora and Maude had ridden, feeling their hobbles. All were holding.

He checked the sky. The moon had broken free of the horizon and rode unbridled in the vast, clear sky.

Without cloud cover to retain what little heat the land had gathered from the sun, the night was going to be terribly cold.

He turned back to the camp where the fire made a small yellow bubble in the cave of the black night. In the light, Cora was visible sorting through Glen's pack. The big, hulking Maude was staring into the darkness in Jacob's direction as if she could see him.

In that unguarded moment, Maude's expression was villainous.

Cora extended her hand under the sleeping robe and found Jacob's. He started to draw her close, but she held back. He relented at once, understanding her reasoning, that Maude would feel the movement. He lay happily holding the soft hand.

Cora rested, contented. She looked out from under the robe and into the night. To her surprise, beyond the fire she saw several shiny, golden lights floating in the blackness. She quickly identified them. The horses had drawn near to the humans. The beasts' eyes were catching the fire and burned like gate lamps to another world.

A last yellow flame candled up from the dying fire, then all was black as the darkness of night raced in. Cora squeezed Jacob's hand and, still holding it, went to sleep at once.

Cora's breath smoked pale in the cold air, as if she burned with an inner fire. Jacob smiled at his imagination and leaned toward her. To his delight, she leaned to meet him.

They kissed, their cool lips crushing together, clinging, and their breath mingling in a small, white cloud about their faces. When they pulled apart, both were smiling, and they sat looking into each other's eyes.

Night was being shoved aside by morning dusk as they rested on the ground robe. To ward off the cold, the end of the top robe was wrapped around them. At Cora's back, Maude slept soundly. A moment existed for Cora and Jacob to steal a little love.

"Once more." Cora's lips silently coined the words.

Jacob willingly obliged her, tenderly cupping her face in his hands as their lips met. He held Cora for several seconds. Then Maude stirred, and Cora hastily withdrew from him.

Jacob looked at the awakening Maude. Damn bitch ruined a good thing. He climbed to his feet and walked off through the snow to the horses.

Cora's spirits lightened as the sun ballooned up above the horizon and took the world from darkness. However, the sun did nothing to lessen the arctic cold, so intense that it seemed like she was moving through liquid gravity.

Ahead of her, Jacob glanced at the rising sun, but did not alter course. He, like the Indians, Cora noted, seemed to have an excellent instinct for direction, day or night.

Jacob had begun the day's journey well before daylight. Cora knew he was worried about his friend Renne somewhere in the mountains. She hoped they would find him safe.

She looked at the mountains that Jacob had told her they would reach that day. The tall peaks were white from a deep blanket of snow, and blended into the clouds that hung over them so that it was nearly impossible to distinguish earth from sky. She would live the winter in one of those high valleys with Jacob and

Maude—if they could escape from the Indians. She turned to the rear and anxiously looked for pursuers chasing across the land after them.

They climbed up a thousand-foot high ridge where the sky was an ocean of swift wind. The snow had been swept from the stony backbone of the ridge; still, it had been a heart-bursting climb for the horses. Jacob halted the laboring beasts in a partially sheltered place below the crown of the hill. The horses spread their weary legs and stood pulling breath with hoarse, sawing sounds. Jacob had driven them hard all day, yet he knew Wolf Voice and his braves could have beaten him to the valley that held his cabin.

Jacob had not approached the valley by his usual route. He had held north four or five miles and then had come up over the foothills that merged into the Big Horns. Should the Indians have reached the valley before him, he didn't want to be trapped by them in the narrow bottom.

He dismounted and waded the snow to the crest of the hill and warily surveyed the valley lying below him. A small herd of wintering deer were in a brushy draw downhill from him. They had not seen Jacob, and he was glad for that. Their flight would have warned anyone who saw them of his presence.

He scanned up and down the snowy valley. Nothing moved against the white background. He searched on, looking for stationary objects that could be enemies. Again he saw nothing that caused him concern.

He returned to the horses and spoke to Cora. "We may have gotten here before the Crows."

Cora nodded, showing her understanding. Jacob's face was strained and crinkled against the wind, and snow, caught in his beard, now more than an inch long, had made it white. For that brief moment, Cora saw what he might look like when he was an old man. Should he live a long life in his dangerous world, he would be a striking old man.

Jacob mounted and led up and over the crown of the hill. The deer spooked away in front of them. As the riders neared the bottom, they encountered a broad trail of trampled snow where a herd of some half hundred buffalo had crossed the valley. Jacob fell in on the trail and followed it down out of the timber and onto the meadow floor of the valley.

"Damnation," Jacob cursed as he stared down at the tracks of more than half a dozen unshod horses in the snow.

"Could they have been made by wild horses?" Cora asked, knowing from Jacob's expression and words that they had not been.

"I wish to God they were the tracks of mustangs," Jacob replied, looking up the valley along the tracks. "But they're being ridden. See how straight they go? The Crows have beaten us. They passed here some time this morning."

"What can we do?"

"Nothing. I just hope Renne spots the Crows before they see him, so he can get into the timber. If he can do that, he'll give them a tough run."

"I told you we should have ridden after the Mormons," Maude said, her tone showing she was pleased at the discovery of the tracks of the Indians. "Now let us get on our way to Salt Lake City."

"What do we do, Jacob?" Cora asked. She was angry at Maude's words.

"First thing is to get back into the timber before the Crows come back down the valley and see us. Our tracks

are mixed in with the buffalos', so the Crows won't notice we've been here. We'd better do it fast for they
could be coming back any time."

"Then after they've passed, we can start for Salt Lake
City," Maude said, obviously happy with the turn of
events.

Snow was falling steadily when the seven mounted
Crow warriors came into sight. They rode single file
beside the frozen stream in the center of the valley. The
last man led an extra horse with a saddle, and Jacob
recognized it as Renne's mount. He gripped his rifle.
Renne was most probably dead. If the women had not
been with him, he would have trailed after the Crows
and killed some of them in the night. Their lives would
have been short, he would have seen to that. In the
snow and darkness, he could have killed them one by
one.

The Crows passed like ghosts in the snowfall a hundred yards from Jacob. He was certain the man that led
was Wolf Voice. Jacob could do nothing except let them
ride past. With his blood hot for revenge, he watched
as the Crows quickly faded into the snowstorm.

Jacob found Renne crumpled against the log wall of
the cabin near the door. He had been shot several
times, and scalped. Jacob gently lifted Renne's cold,
snow-covered body in his arms. "The sons-of-bitches!
The sons-of-bitches!" he cursed.

Cora was with Maude near the horses. She saw the
misery in Jacob's eyes. She started to move toward him
to offer comfort. Then she halted; what could she say?

The cabin had been built in a grove of huge ponder-
osa pines growing beside the creek. Snow had drifted

deeply around the trunk of the largest tree on the outside perimeter of the stand. Now Jacob carried Renne to the snowdrift and laid him down. He brought Glen's corpse and placed him beside Renne. He would bury them in the snow until the ground thawed in the spring and he could dig graves and have a proper burial.

Jacob stared down at the dead, frozen bodies of Glen and Renne. A cold wind blew through his young mind. Once he had thought a man who had no fear could do anything he wanted. How bitter was that thought today, with his two comrades dead. Glen had been correct. Man was not meant to live for very long, no matter how brave and strong he might be. He realized fully why a man took revenge for wrongs done against him or his friends. That was all there was.

He looked at Cora. No, there was something better than revenge—that was love for a woman.

Twenty-six

Jacob surveyed the destruction the Crow Indians had done to the interior of the cabin. The structure was twenty feet by twenty-five feet and made of logs. The cracks between the logs were chinked with mud that had been strengthened with grass mixed into it while it was wet. The floor was of earth, pounded hard.

The belongings of the white trappers had been flung about. He saw some of their possessions were missing. The three pole bunk beds were in pieces, the leather thongs that held them together cut. The webbing of the three pairs of snowshoes had been slashed. Some of the legs of the table and chairs were broken. Only the stone fireplace was intact.

"I can put it all back together in a few hours," Jacob said, looking at Cora, and casting a brief glance at Maude to include her in his comments. The cabin and furnishings were crudely built and thus easily restored.

"What can I do to help?" Cora asked.

Before Jacob could reply, Maude spoke. "Why bother? We'll be leaving right away for Salt Lake City to find Clive."

Cora saw Jacob's gray eyes take on a distressed look at the mention of Clive Pateman. Then his expression hardened. "Maude, we're going to spend the winter here in this cabin—it's too dangerous because of the Indians and the deep snow to travel. In the spring, soon as the weather breaks, we'll go south to Salt Lake City." He would not now tell the woman that never again would he permit Cora to leave him. In the spring was soon enough for that. They would have to travel through the land of the Mormons on the way to California. He would leave Maude there, glad to be rid of her.

"We must go now and find Clive," Maude shot back in an urgent voice. "It's almost dark now, but we can leave first thing in the morning."

Jacob's nostrils became white with sudden anger. Damn contrary woman. Before he could speak, Cora stepped toward Maude and looked up into the face of her huge, towering sister.

"Don't talk about Clive again," Cora said with heat. She hated to see how much the name of the Mormon agonized Jacob.

Maude thrust her head belligerently forward and smiled satanically. "Our marriage to Clive, yours and mine, should take place soon as possible."

"I don't want to talk about that." Cora was galled at Maude's provoking manner. "I don't even want to hear his name."

"I'll say his name as often as I want. Clive! Clive! Clive!"

"Cora, let's fix the cabin." Jacob spoke hurriedly to forestall further argument between the two sisters. Cora was his and nothing Maude could do would change that. His heart beat nicely in his chest in contemplation of what that meant.

"All right," Cora said. She was glad he had interrupted. Further argument might antagonize Maude into some kind of craziness.

Jacob saw a sly, victorious smile cross Maude's face as Cora turned away from her.

"What will we do for food?" Cora asked. "And won't the Indians come back?"

Jacob pointed out the open door at the storm. "Look there. The snow is falling an inch an hour. The Crows will camp at the mouth of the valley for a time, then, when we don't show up, they'll think we're not coming and go to their village for the winter. As far as supplies, we never have kept all of it in the cabin for fear of someone raiding it while we were gone. I'm sure Renne has food and other provisions in our cache back in the woods. I'll go check it out once I have a fire started."

With the fire burning strongly, Jacob left the cabin and circled to the back. He halted for a handful of seconds beside the snowdrift that held the bodies of Glen and Renne. They had been good friends and he felt a terrible loss.

He went on along the cabin wall. The rear quarters of an elk hung from the branch of a pine, high up where predators could not reach it. Here was enough meat for three weeks or more, thanks to Renne, and thanks to him also was a large rick of fireplace wood.

Jacob struck off through the unmarked snow among the trees to the usual place for their cache. There was no sign the Crows had even bothered to look for such a hidden place.

The snow on the limbs that camouflaged the cache, which hung some ten feet above the ground in the big pine, was undisturbed. No ground cache would be as safe, for it would have been impossible to fool the sharp noses of wolverines and other meat-eaters and they would have quickly dug up and eaten or destroyed all provisions.

He climbed into the pine and hoisted up the tarpaulin-wrapped bundle of supplies. Sugar, salt, dried ap-

ples, raisins, and flour, and a few tins of canned goods
were extracted and placed into the leather bag he had
brought with him. The remaining provisions were re-
wrapped in the tarpaulin and again lowered to hang
from the limb of the pine.

Jacob shinnied down the trunk of the tree to the
ground. He was pleased that he could provide Cora with
a variety of food. He had once lived for two months on
meat alone and had found it a very undesirable and
tiresome diet.

He started back to the cabin, then froze; on the mountainside close above him, a scream like a woman in terror
tore a hole in the cold evening. The cry mounted and
peaked and echoed back and forth between the valley
walls before it reluctantly died. A mountain lion, and a
big one from the volume of its cry. Jacob grinned into
the falling snow in the direction of the big cat. It was
enjoyable to hear the lion scream. The previous year he
had seen the tracks of a lion several times; this one might
be the same one. However, he would have to be on guard
to see that it didn't attack the horses.

He pulled a deep breath of the snow-laden air, and
felt the tiny spot of coolness as each snowflake he had
drawn into his mouth melted on his tongue. He was in
a domain that he had thought he had grown tired of,
but now, here with Cora, his love of the mountains came
again to him. Oh, if only the bitch-woman Maude wasn't
here.

While Cora cooked supper, Jacob set about repairing
the furniture. Maude sat with a sour face on the floor
in front of the fireplace.

The pole beds were easily reassembled and tied with
strips of rawhide. The legs of the table and chairs were
going to be more difficult. However, he temporarily

splinted the legs with split lengths of wood and bound them firmly in place. Later he would do a proper job by making new legs. He finished and seated himself on one of the chairs.

He turned to watch Cora by the table. At that very instant she raised her view to him. They stared at each other, their eyes consuming the distance that separated them. She conspiratorially glanced at Maude and found her facing away. She gave Jacob a sweet look. Jacob felt the wonderment of a young girl's eyes, pools of promise, deep and dark.

Cora's mouth curved into a smile. Her smile lifted his heart and he could only smile in return.

This is dangerous, thought Cora. She dropped her sight to the food on the table and, when she had controlled her smile, called out. "The food is ready."

Jacob could not sleep. He lay listening to the wind walking the dark world and arguing with itself outside the cabin. The fire had long been dead in the stone and mud fireplace and the frigid cold of the blizzard had invaded the cabin. Cora lay not more than a body's length from him on the bunk against the wall opposite to his bed. He yearned to go to her. But he dared not, for Maude lay even closer, having cannily chosen the bunk nearest to him. She was undoubtedly awake and would hear any movement Jacob would make toward Cora.

The storm raged on and the snow would be deep come the morning. That would not prevent him from searching for the steel traps Renne would have set. Jacob would find most of them, for he knew his friend's method of trapping. Many furs could be trapped during the winter and taken to California with him. He would continue with the plans he had worked out with his friends and purchase a large tract of land for his vineyard.

Jacob sensed someone near his bunk. He folded his fist and prepared to strike. Cora's crazy sister might be stealing close to crush his skull with a stick of fireplace wood. Surely Cora would not be so reckless as to come to his bunk with Maude so near.

A hand came out of the deep gloom of the cabin darkness and touched Jacob's shoulder. He grabbed the hand and prepared to strike, but the hand was small and he stopped his swing. A second searching hand touched his cheek, then shifted, and a soft finger was placed across his lips as a sign to be silent.

Cora was now just above him and he could make out the white cloud of her body. Only her naked body could be so visible in the darkness. He lifted his sleeping robe and drew her down beside him.

Cora trembled with the cold, but more from her daring. Twice now she had come uninvited to Jacob's bed. What would he think of her? Would he be pleased this time, as he was the first? She knew what she wanted. He must want the same—he must. Then he wrapped her in his strong arms and kissed her again and again.

Jacob tasted Cora. His hands caressed her soft, smooth skin. He felt the warmth building swiftly and chasing away the cold of her body.

"Be very quiet," Cora whispered, her mouth pressed to Jacob's ear.

How did a man love a woman he so desired and do it quietly? Jacob wondered. He would try, but if he should involuntarily cry out and awaken Maude, then so be it. He would face that problem if it came.

He felt Cora positioning herself to receive him. She tugged gently on his hands.

* * *

The visible world within the ice fog was completely silent. It was a little world of a few hundred feet, circumscribed by misty white.

Jacob had discovered the snowfall had ended and the mountain valley full of the ice fog when he had risen at the first fading of the night. Carrying his weapons and an ax, he headed out to check on his horses, the ones they had brought with them and the packhorses Renne had taken up into the valley. All had been found safe. He leaned his ax against a tree and continued on downstream a ways.

He stared through the masking ice-laden air along the creek with its every drop of water frozen solid. The scattering of pine and cottonwood trees were also frozen, to their very hearts. The super-cold air stung his nostrils with every breath he drew. That was but part of the mountains in winter and not to be complained about. His pulse raced with how alive he felt with a grand night just past and now the perfect morning after.

The mountain lion came into the fringe of Jacob's vision, moving stealthily upstream on the far side of the creek. It raised its big padded feet up and then put them straight down in the deep snow. The huge cats did not remain in the high country when snow buried the land. The mule deer, their favorite and principal food, migrated to the low country in winter. The lion must follow its food source or starve. This lion did not look starved. But he had delayed a long time in making his departure.

The lion was forcing a trail through the snow that reached nearly to its stomach. It ceased trying to walk and made two long bounds. The second leap brought it directly opposite Jacob and it caught his scent. Its big, tawny head swung and the yellow eyes fastened on the man.

Jacob had lifted his rifle and was looking down the

sights at the lion. He could have easily hit it with a rock, so close was the animal. They stared at each other through the ice fog.

Jacob's finger tightened on the trigger of the rifle. The lion's pelt would be worth four or five wolf pelts, or two or three mink or marten pelts. Also, there was the danger that if the lion lingered in the valley it might attack the horses.

But then he lowered his rifle, and returned the lion's gaze. The seconds passed and neither the man nor the lion stirred.

"Get on with you for I'm getting cold just standing here," Jacob called. "And don't hang around, for then I'll reconsider letting you go." He motioned at the lion with his hand.

The lion pivoted away as if understanding the safe dismissal. With long leaps, the snow flying from its plunging legs, the great beast vanished into the frozen ground cloud.

Hell, the Crows might've heard the shot anyway, Jacob told himself as he rationalized his decision not to kill the lion. In the confined chasm of the valley and with the total silence, the crack of the big bore rifle would carry for miles.

He returned upstream to the horses near the cabin. All were pawing in the snow trying to find grass. Jacob saw they were having little success due to the depth of the snow. After placing his rifle in the crotch of a pine tree, he went to a thickly limbed cottonwood. Jubal and the other horses watched him expectantly.

Jacob swung the ax and struck the trunk of the cottonwood a hard blow with the sharp bit. Instantly an ear-splitting explosion sounded and a deep crack ran up the trunk of the cottonwood a dozen feet. The strike of the ax had added to the pressure already within the

super-frozen tree trunk and had caused it to split with
the resounding noise.

"Like to have busted my ear drums," Jacob called
out to Jubal.

The horse eyed Jacob, its ears pricked forward.

"You don't care," Jacob added. "You're just hungry."

He resumed chopping and soon had dropped the
tree with well aimed blows of the ax. "Come and get
it," he called.

The horses went immediately to the downed cotton-
wood and began to eat the tender tips of the limbs.
They munched contentedly on the sweet, soft wood.
The less desirable bark they would eat later.

Jacob waded through the snow to a second cottonwood and began to swing his ax.

Cora sat abruptly up in bed at the loud noise of the
cottonwood splitting. Maude jumped from her bunk
and into the center of the cabin.

"What was that?" Maude cried to Cora.

"I don't know." She looked at Jacob's empty bed,
then at the fire burning brightly in the fireplace. The
cabin was warm, so he must have been up for some
time.

She climbed out of bed and padded barefoot to the
door. A dense fog lay cloaking everything. Jacob's tracks
led away downstream. At the limit of her view, she saw
Jacob swinging his ax. Half hidden by the gray fog, he
seemed to be some mountain spirit. A pleasant, com-
forting feeling at his presence coursed along her veins.

"Jacob is chopping with an ax on a tree," Cora said.

"Chopping never made such a sound." Maude replied. "What could have caused it?"

"I don't know. We'll ask Jacob when he comes in."

Cora quickly dressed and began to prepare breakfast.

They would have elk steak, hot bread, and stewed apples. As she worked, she began to hum a merry tune.

Maude stopped buttoning her shirt and focused on Cora. Why would her young sister be so happy locked in the mountains? Why so early in the morning? Maude looked at Jacob's bunk, studying it intently.

Fear seized Maude. "Cora," she called and advanced swiftly upon her sister.

Cora turned, still humming. She was smiling softly to herself in remembrance of the night when Maude grabbed her by the shoulder.

"What did you do?" she demanded. "Did you sleep with that bastard?"

Cora tried mightily to control her reaction to the sudden, unexpected challenge. She felt guilty for what she had done with Jacob. But why should she? Her face grew warm with a blush that she could not prevent. Then she let anger boil up at Maude's grabbing her so roughly. Her anger would mask the emotion she had because of loving Jacob.

"Let me go," she ordered and tried to pull away.

Maude's grip on Cora's shoulders tightened. For just a moment she thought she had seen guilt on Cora's face. She shook the smaller woman. "You're to be married. Did you sleep with that dirty trapper?" Maude's voice held growing desperation, and something much more terrifying.

Cora saw Maude's control of herself weakening. She was approaching the precipice beyond which lay madness. She was being crowded there by Cora's actions. Cora would have to lie to stop the fall. "No, Maude. No!" Cora fought to hold her voice firm, to reassure and convince Maude that she and Jacob had done nothing. She reached and caught her sister by the wrists. "You know I would never do that to you. Like Jacob told us, we will go to Salt Lake City in the spring."

Maude stared down into Cora's eyes. She wanted to believe her little sister. But she knew something had happened. Perhaps just a touch between the two, or worse, a kiss. She would watch them very closely, and every minute of the day and night.

"All right. I believe you. But stay away from him." She released her hold on Cora's shoulders. The big hands rose quickly to vise Cora's face between them. With her eyes boring into Cora's, she spoke, her words brittle and sharp as shards of glass. "Or I will kill him."

Jacob leaned the ax against the wall near the door and entered the cabin. He took in the tableau of Maude holding Cora by the face, and her menacing, threatening expression.

"What's going on?" Jacob called.

Cora looked to the side past Maude's hands at Jacob. "Nothing. We're just having a sisterly talk."

Maude's grip on Cora's face relaxed, her hands falling away. Cora stepped back.

Jacob knew there was more to this than a sisterly conversation. Maude could hurt Cora with ease. He would never let that happen. The women parted, Cora going to the table where food was laid out. Maude went to her bunk and sat down.

With one last look at Cora, Jacob took off his fur coat and moved to the fireplace where he spread his hands to the flames. Something was wrong. He must find a way to talk alone with Cora.

Maude watched Jacob with a malignant glare.

Twenty-seven

Jacob often looked at Cora as he restrung the webbing of the bearpaw snowshoes the Indians had slashed. She sat by the fireplace, and her pretty face was burnt umber in the glow of the fire's embers. Her chin rested on her bosom, and her expression was sad, pensive.

He had tried to talk with her all day. She could not be drawn into conversation, and her answers to his direct questions were brief almost to the point of being rude. He was prevented from talking with Cora alone by Maude's constant presence. She was his foe and somehow responsible for Cora's behavior.

Maude observed Jacob's vexation at Cora's lack of response to him. She smiled into her hand. She had Cora's promise never to go near the trapper again. That promise was very important, for now Maude was positive Cora had lain with the man. The depth of the change, the drawing away of Cora from Jacob, and his hangdog, lovesick expression told her what had happened in the night. Just to be certain they never made love again, Maude must not allow them to be alone together.

She looked at Cora. Her sister's eyes were half closed and she was tracing the outline of her lips with a finger. What was she thinking? Probably about the trapper.

Jacob finished attaching the new webbing to the pair of snowshoes and stood them in the corner next to the other two pairs. His friends and he had made the snow-shoes the winter before. The devices were necessary if a man was to move about in the deep mountain snow.

He twisted suddenly and caught Maude watching him. The hatred in the big woman's eyes was ageless and ugly.

To hell with you too, woman. For what you are doing to Cora, I should abandon you here in the mountains and take Cora to California. But you are Cora's sister and I can't do that unless she tells me that it is all right with her.

In the frozen dawn of the new day, Jacob left the cabin. He carried his rifle, pistol, and skinning knife, and in a pack on his back a sleeping robe and a small quantity of food. His course was down the valley. He would try to find the traps Renne had set in that direction. At the same time he might discover whether or not the Crows had given up their search for the women.

The crunch of Jacob's snowshoes on the crusted snow awoke the sun. However, the fiery orb hung far away, dimmed to a pale, one-candle moon by the ice fog.

He had lain all night, sleeping fitfully, awakening often, waiting for Cora to come to him. Once, for just a brief moment, he thought he saw her white, spectral body standing in the frail light of the cabin. Then the pale form was gone.

Several times he had swung his legs out of bed and sat with his feet on the cold earthen floor, tempted greatly to go to her. Because of the way she had acted toward him during the day, he had not taken the first step from his bunk. He cursed the damnable gods who would put the beautiful Cora so near, but prevent him from making love to her.

As Jacob had reflected upon Cora's behavior, and Maude's part in it, his pace over the snow had been

fast. Now he halted and stood catching his wind, his
white breath pluming out in the sub-zero air. The ice
fog seemed less dense than earlier in the morning.
There was a slight motion in the mist. Perhaps it would
soon move out of the valley.

The stillness was broken by the sound of running animals. He wheeled about to look in the direction of the
sound. A band of nine elk, cows, calves and a big bull,
came into view trotting across the valley. One of the
calves limped badly from an injured right front leg. The
elk frequently glanced apprehensively to the rear.

The bull, carrying a huge spread of antlers, veered
off from the cows and calves and went into a stand of
pine not far from Jacob. The remainder of the animals
hurried on. A few seconds later, a family of wolves, two
adults and four pups of the spring, broke out of the
fog on the trail of the elk.

The wolves ran in great leaping bounds through the
snow, moving as smoothly as streams of flowing mercury.
The young ones did not appear to be taking the chase
seriously. They tunneled their noses in the snow, mouth-
ing a little of the frozen wetness, and shouldering each
other in a playful manner as they ran. Then one of the
pups saw the older wolves drawing away and leapt off
after them with determined speed. The remaining pups
gave up their foolery and fell in behind. Jacob knew the
wolves would soon pull down the injured elk calf.

The bull elk had not detected Jacob's motionless
form a short distance away. Jacob killed him with an
easy rifle shot. Within a few minutes, he had field-
dressed and quartered the elk. He hung the quarters
in a tree. With long strides, spraddle-legged strides to
keep the bearpaw snowshoes from becoming tangled
and dumping him in the snow, he continued on.

* * *

Jacob had found eight traps by the time the black wave of the night came stalking. Five of them held animals, their legs penned between the steel jaws of the traps. He had slain them with a club and skinned them while they were still warm. Frozen, they would have been impossible to skin without damaging the pelts. He reset each trap.

In the edge of darkness, he made a lean-to of pine boughs and built a fire close in front so that it would throw heat inside. On the ground, he carefully placed more boughs, overlapping them for a soft bed. On this he spread his sleeping robe. He would sleep as warm as did a bear with his fur and fat in a cave.

Seated on his robe, he began to roast a piece of fresh elk meat over the fire. With Cora acting as she was, and the surly Maude watching his every move, he had no desire to return to the cabin. He would make a diligent effort to locate all the traps and take the pelts of every game animal that had been caught. In three or four days, he would go back to the cabin and see if things had changed for the better.

The top of the pine tree above his head started to sway under the press of a slow, cold breeze. The ice fog stirred. Gradually the breeze became more boisterous, growing into a wind. The wind swiftly became a violent blast, shredding the ice fog and ripping it from its cloaking hold on the valley. High above, a yellow-eyed moon came into sight orbiting the earth.

Jacob looked around at the moonlit snow and forest. The tops of the trees were gilded with silver. The snow seemed to glow with its own light, against which the trunks of the trees were sharply outlined. It was a fine thing to see a goodly distance over the land again.

It was not long before shadows began to ripple through the night as clouds chased across the heavens. The wind that had removed the fog was the forerunner of a new storm. Within an hour, the many shadows had become but one that blanked out the entire sky. The snowstorm fell on the mountains like a big, white dog.

Jacob pulled his robe more tightly around his shoulders to ward off the cold. The flames of his little fire sawed about in the stiff wind. The snowflakes fell steadily, hissing as they died in the yellow flames.

Jacob reached into a pocket of his mind where he had stored the memories of the two wonderful nights Cora had spent in his bed, and relived both grand experiences staring into the fire. He felt her warmth as he had felt it those nights, and neither the cold nor the buffeting wind could reach him to disturb his reverie.

Cora loaded her arms with wood from the rick behind the cabin and stood erect. In the dusk that was deepening to darkness, the fog was coming alive, wispy streamers of it beginning to undulate back and forth. Still the valley was totally silent, as it had been for two days. She strained to hear the wind that could be stirring the fog, listening for anything that would break the stillness of the wilderness.

Jacob was out there someplace making his bed in the frigid snow. Had he become ill? Had he gotten hurt where no one would ever come to his aid? The thought of him dying sent shivers through her.

She had lost Jacob because of her fear that Maude would lose her mind if Clive would not marry her. The Mormon was a hard man and cared nothing for Maude. Cora was certain of that. He would not take Maude as wife if Cora did not also become one. She believed she must marry Pateman to save Maude's sanity. As Maude had said, she had contributed more to raising Cora than had any other person in the world, and Cora owed her a very great debt. That to only a very small degree lessened her pain from the loss of Jacob. Cora's head ached with the sorrow of her loss. Her sorrow tore tears from her eyes.

She blinked aside her tears so she could see, and circled the cabin to the front door and entered. The cabin was illuminated only by the flames in the fireplace. With head lowered so Maude would not see her tears, Cora crossed the room and laid the wood on the floor by the fireplace.

Maude arose from her bunk and dropped the bar across the door to secure it behind Cora. She then re-seated herself on her bunk. Cora went to her own bed and lay down without a word. She turned her back to her sister.

Maude sat motionless and watched the fire die. She waited for time to pass. With the trapper absent from the cabin, she felt more at peace, more in control of Cora, and of herself. His presence greatly disturbed her, for she sensed his liking for Cora, and his hatred for her. It was becoming ever more clear that she would have to kill the trapper. He was very strong and she must prepare well. She had slain two men in New Orleans, maybe three men if the third one she shot had died of his wounds. She would not fail to kill the trapper.

She heard Cora's sobs come out of the gloom of the cabin and echo off the walls. It did not matter that she cried. It mattered only that she marry Clive.

Jacob felt joyous in a ferocious sort of way. He lay in the blowing, streaming ground blizzard at the mouth of the valley and spied upon the camp of the Crow Indians. He had found the camp in late evening and now it was full night. It consisted of a big lean-to of pine boughs located at the base of a narrow ridge of land extending out from the mountainside and onto the valley floor. He knew the area from past travels past it.

Near the camp, the ridge was pine-covered, while higher up it was but a rocky spine.

He had stashed his pack of skins, sleeping robe, and snowshoes some five miles back up the valley near the last trap he had found. Knowing the snow would be considerably less deep at the lower elevation near the edge of the plains than in the mountains, he had decided to leave the snowshoes behind. Carrying only his weapons, he had stolen downstream to search for the Crows, should they still be in the valley.

As he had worked lower and came out of the wind-shadow of the mountain, he found a ground blizzard in full raging fury. The snow was being picked up by the strong wind and carried a ways, dropped, only to be picked up and carried again, the motion repeated endlessly. A multitude of turbulent snow currents raced eastward away from the mountains.

The tumbling streams of snow reached to Jacob's waist. Above that, the air was clear. Overhead the frozen, full-faced moon was slowly climbing the black wall of the sky. In the moonlight, he could see for miles across the snowy land.

The size of the lean-to the Crows had erected indicated to Jacob that there were several men using it. He counted six Crow horses tethered close by the shelter. How many were packhorses and how many were mounts?

He noted the ridge of land hid the camp from anyone who would be approaching the mountain from the plains. The Indians must expect the women, and the men who had rescued them, to come from that direction. After the Indians had raided the cabin of the trappers and killed Renne, they had set up camp in the mouth of the valley. Now they were waiting for their prey.

The hot blood of battle raced through Jacob's veins. The Crows had killed Glen and Renne. Now revenge for his comrades' deaths was possible, here close at hand, and he couldn't just walk away. Before the night was over he would kill some of the murdering bastards.

A chill went through him as a voice seemed to call to him, a voice from the void beyond life; "Kill all of them, Jacob." The voice sounded like that of Glen, gruff and matter-of-fact, as if it would be an easy thing to kill the warriors.

Jacob shook his head. He could have only imagined the voice. And anyway, he had already decided from the number of horses that there were too many of the Crows for him to kill them all. But they must not be allowed to remain within the valley, for then they might decide to ride up the stream and investigate the cabin again. Was there a way to slay some of them, and at the same time, in some manner, cause them to leave the valley?

There was danger for Cora in any move he made against the Crows. Should they reason correctly that the attack came from someone in the valley, they would immediately ride on the cabin. But surely there must be a way to trick them.

Slinking low and slow and hiding most of his body in the ground blizzard, for the moonlight would outline him against the white snow, he stole in a circle around the Crow camp. There would be a warrior posted on lookout and Jacob must find the man before he spotted Jacob.

Jacob thought the lookout would be on the top of the ridge above the camp, where he could have a good view in all directions. He crept forward, taking a step, then pausing, his eyes probing the blowing snow and the night.

Drawing closer to where he reasoned the man should be, he dropped down into the ground blizzard on all fours and crawled. He could see little, but in turn, little of him could be seen by an enemy. The stream of running snow had a discernible body, and to Jacob gave the sensation that he was doing a slow-motion swim in a thin, white fluid that was very cold.

A few minutes later, the trees took shape in the snow. He lifted his head above the ground-blown snow.

Jacob saw the movement of the Crow lookout as the man shifted his back to a new position on the boulder against which he sat and rested. He was wrapped in a buffalo hide. Snow had drifted around him, covering him halfway up his chest. Had he not stirred, Jacob would have mistakenly taken his form in the darkness for part of the boulder. The brave had chosen a good location. From it he could see the wide mouth of the valley, the plains beyond, and also his camp below.

Jacob angled off to the side to come up behind the brave. The swish of the wind and hiss of the moving snow masked the small sounds he made. The woods closed around him, and he climbed the rise to be above the Crow, who would be looking down over the land.

Close at the rear of the man, Jacob leaned his rifle on a tree and pulled his skinning knife. He snaked forward to the boulder and raised up to look. The mere top of the man's head protruded above the rock.

Jacob lunged upon the rock and reached across to clamp the man about the face in the crook of his arm. Instantly he snapped the man's head back and slashed the knife across his neck.

The heavy buffalo hide wrapped about the brave deflected Jacob's knife and kept the sharp blade from slicing the man's throat. The man surged upward, trying to gain his feet. But Jacob's weight forestalled the effort, holding him pressed down in his sitting position. Jacob swung over the boulder, and as he fell upon the Crow stabbed through the robe and into the man. The knife plunged deeply, grating off bone.

Jacob's momentum flung the two men down to roll on the snowy ground. Jacob stopped their roll with him on top of the thrashing body of the Crow. He held the man firmly. The Crow cried out and desperately fought to throw off Jacob and the entangling robe. Jacob thrust the knife to the hilt in his opponent. He felt the man shudder with a terrible spasm of pain. The man's struggle weakened rapidly, then ceased as he died.

Jacob lay breathing hard on top of the dead Indian. That was for Glen. Now one for Renne.

He sat the man up where the moonlight shone on his face. He was a young man about Jacob's age. Too bad he wasn't Wolf Voice or Long Running, thought Jacob. He dragged the limp body to a nearby snowdrift, scooped out a trench in the drift, and buried the body.

Going back to the boulder, he found the Crow's rifle. He seated himself where the man had sat and wrapped himself in the buffalo skin. But not tightly, not trapped so he could not move quickly, as had been the Indian. Having laid aside his brimmed hat after first reaching the cabin, he now wore a fur cap similar to the Indian. With the snow and the darkness, he could easily be taken for the dead man by the next Crow lookout until he was very close.

Holding the dead man's rifle, he prepared to wait. The snow had drifted deeply around the Crow indicating he had been on guard for a considerable time. His relief should not be long in coming.

The wind droned over the boulder and talked in ragged sounds in the pines. It began to build a drift around Jacob. The cold increased.

The ghost of Renne came and sat in the snow beside Jacob. He was not visible, nor did he speak. Yet Jacob sensed his presence. "All right, old friend, I understand what you want me to do," Jacob said into the wind and the night.

He saw below him the dark form of half a man, the bottom half hidden in the swirling ground blizzard, leave the camp of the Crows and move toward him.

Twenty-eight

The Crow warrior climbed up the slope through the ground blizzard toward Jacob. He trailed a rifle in his hand and scanned up and down the moonlit valley. Detecting nothing threatening, he focused on the figure propped against the boulder in the snow.

Jacob lowered his face when the Indian looked directly at him, and parted the buffalo hide to free his arms. He had gathered his feet beneath him upon first seeing the Crow leave his camp, and now he could rise swiftly. He took a firm grip on the stock of the dead Indian's rifle.

"Elk Piss, are you awake?" Far Thunder called.

Jacob grunted and shook some snow from his shoulders.

"Well, get up and go get some sleep."

Jacob rose, shoulders hunched, head still tilted downward. In a slow, sleepy manner, he shoved the rifle outside the robe that hung loosely around him.

"This is all foolishness, this waiting for the white women to come," Far Thunder said. "And Wolf Voice thinks the men who took them from us are the very same white trappers who killed so many of our warriors. He burns with hate for them and he has convinced our father to stay here with him. As for me, I'm ready to return home. It's too cold to wait longer. What do you think?"

Far Thunder was three steps away and slightly below when Jacob raised his head and looked at him. Far Thunder took one additional step as he peered through the night's murk, trying to better discern the features of the face rising toward him. Then the moonlight fell upon the face and illuminated it. The man was not Elk Piss, but a bearded white man. Far Thunder hastily jerked up his rifle.

Jacob straightened swiftly to his full height and struck a powerful roundhouse blow with the rifle. The heavy iron barrel of the weapon crashed into Far Thunder's temple. The dull crushing sound of skull bones breaking came to Jacob. The jar of the blow vibrating up the rifle and into his arms was so damn satisfying.

Far Thunder collapsed, long slivers of bone driven deeply into his brain. His body rolled a few times down the hill, then stopped and lay in a crumpled, dark heap in the blowing snow.

Jacob went to the body of the Crow and turned it face up in the moonlight. The dead man was another young buck Indian, like the one before. They had been brothers, Jacob knew, for he could understand enough of their language to have learned that from the man's words.

He had killed the man for Renne. Yet as he knelt by the slack body, some of the gratification he had felt when he had struck the man down washed away. If only the two dead men had been Wolf Voice and Long Running, then the killing would have given Jacob total satisfaction. Still, he had gained much, for now Cora and he had two less enemies searching for them.

For half a score of minutes, he looked down at the Crow camp watching for men moving. The camp remained quiet. No one there had taken alarm.

Now to complete his plan for misleading his enemies.

All of his previous tracks had long since been blown away by the wind and the Crows would not know the direction from which he came. However, they must know the direction by which he left. The sign that would mislead them must be quickly and properly laid.

He retrieved the rifles of the two braves he had slain and then carried them up the ridge above the tree line and cached them there. He recovered his own weapon and dropped back down to the pine woods near the Crow's lookout. There he hurried to the east through the snow lying among the trees. With the wind blowing gently and drifting the snow but little, his tracks would last for hours before they were completely blown full of snow.

He hurried from the woods and onto the plains. Now the wind had a broad, open sweep and filled his tracks almost as swiftly as he made them.

Four miles later, he entered the last stringer of woods jutting out from the mountain. The wind was slow here and he left well-defined tracks.

The snow had grown more shallow as he worked downward. Now as he left the woods, he increased his pace to a trot. The night was half spent and there was much land to travel over if the false sign was to be well laid. When the morning came, the wind might die, as oftentimes it did on the plains. He needed the wind for completion of the deadly game he played.

Two hours later, he reached a narrow strip of woods bordering a creek where the snow was drifting but slightly. There too he left his tracks. He hoped the Crows would wrongly interpret the sign he had made and believe the attacker of their camp had gone onto the plains, and follow him there. They would not be easily deceived, because they were men who had spent their lives hunting animals, and men.

Beyond the woods, the wind was blowing strongly

over smooth, open terrain and the ground blizzard was swiftly filling his tracks. Jacob turned north. He trotted for an hour, then turned ninety degrees and headed back to the west and the mountains.

The valley was still held captive by the night as Jacob climbed to the top of the high ridge three miles north of Wolf Voice's camp. He had been traveling steadily for most of a day and night and had covered a large expanse of country, all of it through snow, some of it deep. His legs trembled with weariness. Still he could not rest.

With the strong wind clouting him, he made his way along the descending crest of the ridge. It was difficult to maintain his footing, for the ridge's flesh of soil and trees had been stripped away, leaving only its rock bones. The snow was whipped away, unable to lie on the smooth stone.

He recovered the rifles of the two Crows he had killed. With all his weapons ready, he concealed himself above the tree line in a spot where he could watch the Crow camp.

He had left three groups of tracks to lead Wolf Voice away from the valley and the mountains. Should the man not find the signs, or not be fooled by them and instead lead his warriors up the valley, Jacob must try to stop him.

The wind died abruptly around him, as if a great door had been closed to shut it off. The snow ceased swirling over Jacob. He was glad for the arctic wind to stop blowing. The rock upon which he lay was cold enough to send shivers through him.

The valley was shaping itself out of the morning dusk when three Crow warriors came out of the lean-to.

* * *

Wolf Voice shoved aside his sleeping robe and sat up under the lean-to. He turned his head first one direction and then another, trying to focus on some sound that could have awakened him. He heard nothing. Even the ground blizzard had blown itself silent. But there was something out there in the night, something dangerous and menacing.

He listened to the warnings that sometimes came to him. There had been no warning when the white trappers had attacked his camp moons ago. Perhaps he was being warned now of their presence. The hate for the white men raced through his veins like molten lead. He had to slay them.

The rays of the low-hanging moon shone in under the roof of the lean-to. In the light, he saw snow had blown in and lay in shallow drifts around his bed, and the beds of Broken Arm and Long Running. The beds had been built on mats of boughs broken from pine trees. The sleeping robes of Broken Arm's sons Far Thunder and Elk Piss were gone and snow drifts lay over their pine mats.

With growing concern, Wolf Voice rose and pulled on his moccasins, coat, and cap. He had slept in his other garments. Both of the men would be gone from the lean-to at the same time when they were changing places at the lookout. However, the thickness of the snow on their mats showed they had been gone much too long for just that single purpose.

"What is the matter?" Broken Arm asked, awakening at the sound of Wolf Voice stirring about.

"Far Thunder and Elk Piss are both gone. And there is snow on both beds."

Broken Arm hastily rose from his bed and began to pull on his fur coat. "We must go and see if anything is wrong," he said with mounting worry for his sons.

"Maybe the two of them are on guard together and

talking," Long Running said. He too was swiftly drawing on his outer garments.

"They argue some, but don't talk much with each other," Broken Arm said. He took up his rifle and slung the ammunition pouch over his shoulder.

"I don't like this," Long Running said. "I remember what the white men did the last time we thought we had them trapped."

"Let's not stand here talking," Wolf Voice said. He hurriedly left the lean-to and went into the night. Broken Arm and Long Running followed close behind.

Wolf Voice scanned quickly around into the night as he waded through the snow up the slope. What was threatening them? Where was it? The round moon rode low in the western sky, showing the night was mostly spent. It was a huge ball, magnified as it neared the horizon. Its silver light showed only the unbroken snow around the camp. The dark pines on top of the ridge above the camp stood starkly outlined. He couldn't make out the boulder in the edge of the pines which all had agreed was the best place for the lookout to be stationed.

Wolf Voice slowed as the boulder came into sight. Try as he might, he couldn't make out anyone near it.

"I don't see anyone," Broken Arm said. He increased his pace and moved ahead of Wolf Voice.

"Careful now," Wolf Voice cautioned the impatient man.

Broken Arm hurried on, not heeding the warning. He lessened his pace only as he came close to the boulder rearing up out of the snow. The snowdrift around the stone was large and its surface smooth and unbroken. His worry became fear for his sons.

He stepped on something buried in the snow not far from the stone. He ran his foot along the object. With a horrible certainty, he dropped to his knees and began to fling the snow aside. Far Thunder's face came into view. Broken Arm felt the cheek of his son, and found it cold and stiff.

Broken Arm raised his head to the black sky and howled a shrill, keening call of agony. He cried out again, a long piercing cry full of great sorrow.

Wolf Voice and Long Running ran up and stopped beside Broken Arm, kneeling over the body in the snow.

"Who is it?" Wolf Voice asked.

"Far Thunder," Broken Arm answered his voice tightly controlled. "Help me look for Elk Piss."

Wolf Voice and Long Running began to wade about, circling out from the stone in ever widening circles. In but a short time, Wolf Voice halted with his foot touching something heavy buried under the snow. He squatted and started to dig.

"I've found Elk Piss," he called, chilled with anger. The white men had come in the night as they had before. He looked down at his camp. They hadn't attacked the men who had lain there sleeping. Why was that?

Broken Arm and Long Running came up swiftly and knelt beside the still body in the snow. Broken Arm ran his hand in under the coat of Far Thunder who lay so still. The body was cold.

"He is dead," Broken Arm said, his gut clenching.

"We will kill whoever did this," Wolf Voice promised. "I'm certain it was the white trappers for they like to fight in the night."

"I agree with you," Long Running said. "This has their smell."

"Find their tracks," Wolf Voice said. "Look in the woods. Perhaps not all of them have been blown away by the wind there."

Jacob saw the three Crows climb up the ridge from their camp and find the bodies of the men he had

killed. They began to search for his tracks, and soon
one of them shouted out to the others from the pine
woods. They talked among themselves, then swiftly
broke camp and headed off on horseback along the
trail he had left. The corpses of the dead men they took
with them, tied across the backs of mustangs. His plan
was working, at least for the time being.

Jacob dropped down from the ridge and hastened
up the channel of the frozen creek. An hour later he
retrieved his pack of raw skins and sleeping robe from
where he had concealed them. He must rest for a time.
The cabin was miles away and it would be nightfall by
the time he could reach it.

Wearily he hacked boughs from a pine tree and
spread them to keep his robe off the snow while he
slept. He dropped down, wrapped himself in the soft
robe, and went immediately to sleep.

Maude caressed the cold iron barrel of the rifle that
had once belonged to Glen Kinshaw. What a lovely,
deadly weapon it was. She raised it to her shoulder and
aimed it through the trees at the path beside the creek.
Yes, she could hit a man at that range.

She was hidden in a thick grove of pine trees some
three miles downstream from the cabin. She had se-
lected the location because the valley narrowed there
for a short ways, and anyone traveling along the creek
would have to come within rifle range. Also, the distance would be great enough that Cora, inside the
cabin, would not hear the shot that killed the trapper.

Maude lowered the rifle. She had loaded the weapon
with an extra heavy charge of powder. There must be no
chance the man would survive the wound. Maude chuckled happily at the thought of the bullet tearing into Jacob, and the horrible pain he would experience before

he died. Soon the trapper would no longer be a threat to her.

This was the second day Maude had waited for Jacob to return. She waited patiently, for return he would, because of Cora.

Twenty-nine

Jacob trotted upstream along the frozen creek. The sun had already fallen cold and sullen behind the snowy mountains. Dusk was gathering among the big cotton-woods and pines of the valley bottom, welding them all together into a world of gray, murky shadow. He hurried, for he didn't want to sleep another night in the snow.

What kind of welcome would he receive from Cora? Most probably she would be the same distant, untalkative girl he had left almost four days before. He would not like that, but simply being near her would give him pleasure. At the thought of seeing her pretty face again, he increased his pace.

Maude came instantly alert in her hiding place in the pine thicket when she spotted something moving through the woods. A second later she identified the trapper trotting in her direction. He had a bulky pack on his back. Two rifles were tied to the outside of the pack. He carried a third in his hand. Where had he acquired the two additional rifles? The load must be heavy; still, he ran easily on his snowshoes.

The man was very strong. She recalled the hardness of his fist and the power of his blows when they fought each other on the prairie. He must never be given the chance to hit her again. She raised the rifle to her shoulder.

Maude caught the trapper with the front post sight of the rifle, and then settled both post and man into the notch of the rear sight. Holding her aim on his chest, she tracked him as he drew ever nearer. She ignored the trees that passed between her gun and target. Just a few more paces along his course and he would be at his closest point to her. At that place, there was a small opening in the woods; she had chosen her shooting stand carefully.

She felt her pulse speeding as she looked across the sights of the rifle at the trapper. He should have been killed long ago, before he had made love to Cora. That could not be reversed, but never again would he have the opportunity to be near Cora.

Maude squinted through the grainy light of the thickening dusk. The trapper was almost at the opening. There he would die. Her finger took up the slack in the trigger. *Not too much pressure, Maude, don't get overanxious and fire before everything is perfect.* She chuckled in anticipation of seeing the man fall, and the sights of the rifle bobbled a little. *Stop that.*

The trapper came into the opening. Then, to Maude's surprise and consternation, he suddenly sprang ahead at a faster pace. The sights of the rifle fell behind him. In three long strides, and before Maude could shift her weapon to bear on him again, he was into the trees beyond the clearing.

Maude shook with angry frustration. How had he known she was there with a rifle trained on him? Why else except to escape from her would he have so abruptly increased his speed across the opening? Damn him to hell.

She gripped the rifle and watched the woods where

Jacob had disappeared. Would he now be hiding behind some tree along the path up the valley and shoot her as she passed? She must be very cautious as she returned to the cabin.

Cora straightened from stirring the food in the cooking pot hanging in the heat of the fireplace. She listened for Maude, who should have returned by now. The only sound from the outside was the wind whistling around the cabin and clattering the wood-shingled roof. The wind found the chimney and came tumbling down into the fireplace. The fire arched its back and hissed at the wind.

Cora went to the door and opened it to look outside. The cold wind rushed over her, forming goose pimples on her bare arms and she folded them across her bosom. She glanced both ways along the creek channel. In the deep mountain valley the days were short and the night was falling rapidly. There was only the snow, and the frozen trees, and the darkness filling in the spaces between them.

She was worried about Maude being lost in the woods in the black night. For the past two days, Maude had left the cabin early with one of the dead trappers' rifles to hunt for game. Always she returned by evening dusk. She had killed nothing the first day. Perhaps she'd had better luck today and that was why she was late. Still, if she did not return very soon it would be too dark to see to travel and she would have to spend the night in the snow. Cora shivered at the remembrance of sleeping outside in the bitter cold. She closed the door.

Through the trees ahead, Jacob saw light spilling out the open door of the cabin. Then the light winked out

as the door was closed. He slowed and came on at a
slow walk. Now that he was at the cabin, he was reluctant
to enter. He expected coldness from Cora, and from
Maude, total hatred. Both would be awful to face.

To hell with both women. He was tired and hungry.
He removed his snowshoes and leaned them against
the cabin wall. He went to the door, shoved it open,
and stepped inside.

Cora was near the fireplace. Maude was nowhere in
sight. At least he would have a moment without that
woman's baleful eye upon him.

Cora heard the door open and spun around. Jacob
stood just inside the doorway. She waited, looking at
him and, since Maude was not present, expecting him
to smile at her. But there was no smile for her. His face
had grown a harder skin, and she sensed a farawayness
in him.

She knew she was responsible for the change in him.
She had caused him to become someone else, a sad
man who did not smile and masked his feeling toward
her. Or maybe he no longer cared for her. Regardless
of that, he needed cheering up. She gave him a smile.

Jacob was surprised at the lovely, wonderful smile of
welcome that Cora gave him. His tight face softened
and a broad smile of his own broke through. All his
love for the girl welled up and sent his blood rushing.
From the expression that came into Cora's eyes he knew
she understood his emotion. She continued to look
steadily back at him, but her smile became uncertain,
and then faded away entirely.

He dropped his pack to the floor, laid his rifle across
it, and moved toward Cora. His desire for her was so
strong he could not resist it, no matter if Maude should
come through the door the next instant behind him.
He caught Cora up in his arms, and crushed her to
him.

Cora knew she should be resisting Jacob. However, she seemed to be burning, but a cold burn, like foxfire in some dark wood. She was sure her skin was cool to Jacob's touch. He began to kiss her, his lips finding hers through his beard.

Cora leaned back from Jacob, and put her hands on his chest to push him away. But it was too late for that. Her cold fire had burst into bright flame.

Jacob looked down at Cora. Her eyes seemed on the point of ignition.

Maude crept along the path leading to the cabin. The imprints of Jacob's snowshoes were very faint in the frail light. She trembled, fearful that a rifle would explode and send a bullet slamming into her from the trees rearing darkly on all sides. A second great fear crowded the first in her mind, a fear that Jacob was at the cabin alone with Cora.

She gripped her rifle and wished for more light to drive away the murk in the woods so she could see her enemy. At the same time, she was glad for the growing darkness so he could not see to shoot her. All the conflicting thoughts made her head ache. Damn the trapper to hell. Her headache, all her problems, were his fault.

The square, squat form of the cabin came into sight, and she halted and straightened to her full height. She had not been shot. *My God!* That meant he was in the cabin with Cora.

Maude rushed across the snow to the cabin. Strangely, the door stood partially open. Silently she shoved it open further and looked inside.

The light of the flames from the fireplace showed Jacob on his bunk with Cora. They were locked in each other's arms. Maude heard Cora's passionate whispers as she and the trapper took their love. Their strong, young bodies were thrusting quick and hard at each other, as violent as a knife fight.

Anger boiled up in Maude and raced like molten lead through her veins. She felt the throbbing of her heart to the very tips of her fingers. Her breath came scalding in her lungs. She jerked the rifle up to her shoulder and through a dark haze aimed it at the center of Jacob's back. Cora's promises were nothing, for she could not resist the man's advances. *I'll kill the bastard and then there will be no temptation for Cora.*

Thirty

Maude aimed the rifle at the entangled bodies of Cora and Jacob on the bunk. She tried to align the rifle sights on Jacob in such a manner as not to also shoot Cora. Several times she was on the point of firing, but held her finger. So close were the lovers embracing and so swift their movement, there was always the strong likelihood the bullet would pass through Jacob and also hit Cora.

Then a horrible thought came to Maude. She must endure what Jacob and her sister were doing. For should she slay Jacob in front of Cora, what then? Would Cora still marry Clive? Maude had to destroy the trapper somewhere away from the cabin, make him permanently disappear. Cora must never have any suspicions that Maude was connected with him not returning. Maude lowered the rifle, pulled the door shut and backed away into the night.

She bumped into the trunk of a tree and, startled, dropped the rifle. She sobbed a guttural cry and clutched at the tree. The two lovers did not know the dimensions of the misery that she suffered because of their love-making. She did not think they would care had they known. However, her time would soon come to get what she wanted. For now she must subdue her burning urge to murder the man. Maude began to strike the tree with her fists, hammering the hard, rough bark again and again.

Her mind refused to acknowledge the pain, and her thoughts were becoming fragile and difficult to hold, like puffs of smoke. Then her grip on the world slipped away entirely and she fell unconscious in the snow.

Maude came to her senses lying shivering in the snow. She raised her head and looked around in the night. Where was she? What had happened?

A short distant away light showed among the trees. That must be the cabin, she thought. Then it all came flooding back, the memory of Cora and the trapper wrapped in each other's arms flaming up in her mind.

She rose to her feet and moved a few steps toward the light and saw Cora standing in the doorway of the cabin, staring into the darkness. Cora spoke over her shoulder to someone inside behind her. "I'm worried about Maude," she said.

Jacob came into view beside Cora. "It's too dark for me to find her. I can fire my rifle. Maybe she will hear that and know the direction to make her way to the cabin."

"No need for that," Maude called from the dark woods. "I've found my way back." She came into the light carrying her rifle. She slowed, glancing at Cora to see if any visible change had occurred in her. Then she pushed past Jacob and into the cabin.

"Maude, there's food in the pot by the fireplace," Cora said.

Maude made no reply. She sat down on the floor in front of the fire and stretched out her hands to the warmth of the flames.

"You're hurt," exclaimed Cora. She came quickly and took hold of Maude's bloodied hands.

Maude pulled roughly away. "I fell in the dark, that's all. Leave me alone." She turned back to the fire. Cora's fingers had felt dirty from touching the trapper.

Cora drew back. She looked questioningly at Jacob.

He shrugged his shoulders at Cora's silent query. But he knew what bothered Maude. He had left the door open when he entered, but it had been closed when Cora had gone to look outside. Maude had spied upon them, and had seen all that they had done. The knowledge of it was in her actions. He thought it was best that Cora not know.

He would not say or do anything that might set Maude off into some kind of a tantrum. He opened his pack of fresh pelts. The flesh and fat that remained on them after skinning must be removed and the pelts stretched to dry.

Jacob saw Maude raise her hands and wipe her knuckles across her eyes, as if wiping away cobwebs. Blood from the bruised knuckles left red smears, like fresh wounds on her flesh. Her face hung like a death mask.

Wolf Voice halted his exhausted and faltering mustang when the frigid moon rose above the flat horizon. The sere, snow-covered plain stretched away empty in every direction. They had ridden fast all day. Since mid-morning, they had found no sign of the man who had slain Broken Arm's two sons. At that time a strip of timber along a stream had held tracks. The man's course had been toward the place where the sun was born each morning. There lay Fort Laramie of the white man's army. Wolf Voice had judged that would be the man's most probable destination.

After losing the trail for several miles, the Crows had separated, Broken Arm and Long Running fanning out left and right of Wolf Voice, and riding zig-zag courses in an attempt to again discover the man's tracks. No sign was found and now darkness was falling. Wolf Voice had thought they could easily ride the man down, traveling as he was on foot. That was why they had brought the bodies of Broken Arm's sons with them. After slaying the man, they would have journeyed on to their village in the lower valley of the Powder River.

As the day had worn on, Wolf Voice's doubts about his decision to race after the man onto the plains had grown ever greater. Now those doubts were perched on his shoulder with talons of iron and could not be shaken off. Why was the man they chased on foot instead of being mounted? Was it to mislead the Crow into thinking they could catch him? After killing Broken Arm's two sons, he could have stolen a mustang easily while the other Crow slept. Also, the man, by altering his course to the side by only half a mile or so, could have avoided the woods where his tracks remained to guide anyone pursuing him.

Long Running and Broken Arm rode in and stopped near Wolf Voice. "Have you found some sign of the man?" Broken Arm asked.

"No," Wolf Voice replied. "We have been tricked." He pointed to the rear, at the distant Big Horn Mountains. "The murderer of your sons is back there. We have ridden all day in the wrong direction."

"Why do you say that?" Long Running said.

"If you had no mustang, would you have gone onto the plains where your mounted enemy could catch you?" Wolf Voice asked. "And he made no attempt to hide his tracks? No, he is in the mountains."

"But where in the mountains?" Broken Arm asked. "They are very large."

"I think I know," Wolf Voice replied.

* * *

Maude crept upon Jacob kneeling in the snow and setting one of his steel traps. She moved easily, gliding over the ground totally without sound, and drawing close to his back. She aimed the big Sharps rifle and shot him through the spine. The bullet exploded from his chest with a gush of blood and flesh. But the trapper did not seem to feel the wound. He jumped to his feet and whirled toward Maude. His face was twisted with anger and his teeth were bared in a ferocious snarl. He raised his big fist to strike her.

Maude awoke from her evil dream with her mind full of terror, and the feeling she had failed twice to kill the trapper. She cautiously rolled her head to look with hooded eyes at his bunk. The man had already risen and was near the door of the cabin with Cora. Maude pretended to be asleep and listened to their conversation.

"I'm going up the valley to look for traps Renne might have set in that direction," Jacob told Cora. "I should be back by nightfall."

"All right." Cora glanced at Maude and, deciding she was sleeping, turned back to Jacob. A gentle, loving smile came out of hiding.

"You are more beautiful than anything I have ever seen in the world," Jacob whispered. Before she could reply, he picked up his rifle and went out the door.

Maude lay in bed for a few minutes, then stretched and yawned, acting as if just now coming awake. She threw back her cover and stood erect on the earthen floor.

"Good morning," Cora greeted Maude. She was worried that her sister would be the same ornery, distant woman she had been the evening before.

"And to you, too," Maude said, forcing a light tone in her reply. She wanted no conversation and went to the food Cora had prepared and placed on the table.

Maude had no appetite, so intent was she on her plan for the day. She forced herself to eat a small amount.

She took up the rifle she had carried the day before. The weapon had fallen in the snow and the powder might be damp. She drew out the old powder and recharged it with fresh. A new cap was slipped over the nipple.

Maude pulled on her coat. She took up a pair of snowshoes from the corner and strapped them on. The deep snow was difficult to wade through, so today she would try out the snowshoes. She retrieved her rifle and turned to Cora.

"My luck was bad yesterday. I have a feeling my hunt will be successful today and I will kill something." She laughed pleasantly.

"I hope it is," Cora said. "Don't stay out too late. I worry about you getting hurt, or lost."

"Don't worry about me. I can take care of myself. And nobody can get lost in the valley with mountains on all sides."

Maude held the aim of the big bore rifle on the trapper as he came through the trees along the creek. The sun had fallen behind the western shoulder of the valley wall; still, the daylight was ample, and the sights of the rifle easily found. He was farther away from her than she wanted. She had searched, but had been unable to find a shooting stand as favorable as was the one the day before. This place had to do.

The wind was falling down the mountainside and swaying the limbs of the trees. It made a rasping sound on the limbs of the tree above Maude's head. The noise sounded like a death rattle to her, and she believed it was an omen that she would succeed in slaying the trapper. A grin of incipient madness cracked across her face. She laughed a short string of chuckles.

She stopped laughing. Pressed her cheek tightly to the stock of the rifle. Squeezed the trigger. She felt the solid jolt of the gun kicking back against her shoulder as it fired. Saw the trapper fall.

A great joy rushed through Maude, for she had succeeded in killing the trapper.

Thirty-one

"Sorry, girl," Jacob said to the yearling female wolf that lay trapped and bleeding in the snow.

The jaws of the steel trap had broken and splintered the bones of her left front leg. The sharp ends of the bone had cut through the skin and the snow was stained bright red with her blood. She struggled to three legs and came toward Jacob to the end of the chain that secured the trap to a nearby bush. She rolled back her lips, baring her long white teeth, and her yellow eyes followed his every movement as he approached.

Jacob halted within striking distance of the wolf. He saw her fur was long and fine. Her pelt would bring a premium price in California. He struck her down with the hard wooden club he had cut from a nearby tree.

He skinned the wolf quickly and put her pelt in the pack on his back. He snowshoed on, winding a course down the valley through the woods.

Jacob swung along at a goodly pace. He was returning early, for he knew he could have searched more thoroughly for traps. He readily admitted to himself that he had cut the day short to hurry back to Cora.

A rifle exploded ahead and off slightly on his left. The bullet passed his ear with a suck of air like a whisper from the void. Immediately came the small jar of the after-shock.

He hurled himself down in the snow, and rolled twice to bring himself up behind the trunk of a tree. Mostly buried in the deep snow, he remained perfectly still, tense and waiting. He was in a place of few trees, and should he move he would be seen.

The shot had been fired from a dense stand of timber nearly a hundred yards distant. Lying as he was behind the tree, he was hidden from the shooter. The man would have to come into the open to investigate his kill. He would be noisy on the crusted snow, and so too would Jacob if he tried to move.

He raised his head and cautiously probed the woods, searching for a sight of the man who had shot at him, for anything that would indicate the location of his foe. There was nothing to shoot at. Jacob must outwait the shooter.

His right ear burned and he reached very slowly to feel of it. His hand came away bloody. The bullet had cut a small notch in the outer rim of the ear. It was not a wound to worry about. The worry was who had shot at him.

He concentrated on the woods, staring hard in among the trees. He breathed slowly, quietly through his mouth. The minutes passed.

Half an hour passed and Jacob remained stone still except for his eyes prying into the woods. Try as he might, he saw no sign of the man.

A crow came down on quiet wings and perched on a tree limb above Jacob. The bird examined the man with its keen, liquid eyes, saw that he was alive, twice cawed raucously with disappointment, and climbed up and away with his black wings on a soft ladder of air.

Another half hour went by. The shadows of evening dusk were gathering. Perhaps the man was not going to come. He might even have abandoned his position.

Jacob rose, hoping not to hear a shot and feel the

punch of a bullet. There was no sound except the wind in the trees. Bent low, he crept off to the right of the shooter. He thought the man, had he left, would most likely have gone down the valley, so he would look for his tracks there. Should he not find tracks, then he would steal upon the woods from where the man had fired.

After a short search, Jacob found the shooter's snow-shoe tracks. The man had left walking exactly in the footprints he had made going to his ambush. That was why Jacob had not heard the man moving.

Maude put a sour expression on her face as she drew near the cabin. It was a difficult task not to smile because she felt so happy at the death of the trapper.

Cora was singing "Listen To The Mocking Bird" in a sweet, contented voice as Maude opened the door of the cabin and came inside. She must be thinking about the trapper. *Well, that is all ended, for he is dead and gone forever. Now your pretty face can get us Clive for a husband.* She had to fight the urge to laugh.

"You seem in good spirits, little sister," Maude said.

"It isn't all that bad here," Cora replied. "And we'll be leaving in three or four months for Salt Lake City."

"Maybe sooner than that."

"What do you mean?" Cora studied Maude.

"The trapper could decide to take us there this winter." Maude had to be careful what she said.

"I don't believe he will, not as long as there's so much snow on the ground."

"You're probably right," Maude said. She felt strong and was certain she could take them safely to Salt Lake City. She placed her rifle in the corner by her bunk. After taking off her coat and boots she lay down on her bed. A sound, pleasant sleep found her almost at once.

* * *

Jacob halted a few yards from the cabin. The tracks he had followed had led him directly here. Now he knew with certainty that crazy sister of Cora's had been the shooter. The bitch must think she had killed him. What of Cora? Was she in danger from Maude?

He hastily jerked off his snowshoes. He ran to the door, flung it open, and sprang inside. Cora was at the table. She whirled around at his sudden entrance.

Maude heard the door slam back into the wall and heavy footsteps. She leapt from bed. Her thoughts were that they were being attacked by Indians and she must fight them off.

Instead the ghost of the dead trapper stood in the center of the room. His face was tight with rage.

"What's wrong, Jacob?" Cora cried. She saw the blood on his shoulder, and then his injured ear. "You're hurt."

"Maude tried to kill me," Jacob said, his voice fierce. He spun toward Maude and advanced upon her.

Cora turned upon her sister. "Maude, did you . . . ?"

Maude's eyes were wide and staring, the whites showing. Then they narrowed, locking with an insane light on Jacob. "Bastard, you're dead! Dead!" she screamed, foam and spittle spraying from her mouth. She threw back her head and shrieked, an animal sound that peaked at an intensity of madness that made Jacob's spine tingle.

A red haze cloaked Maude's vision. Through it she saw the trapper coming toward her. He appeared to be increasing rapidly in size, and his big fist was drawing back to hit her. She snatched up her rifle leaning against the wall close by and swung it at the trapper.

Jacob dodged back and the blow missed. He reversed his direction and jumped at Maude, catching hold of the rifle as she again swung it at him. The two reeled across the room wrestling for the weapon. Jacob tightened his grip on the rifle and spun, shouldering Maude and staggering her. At the same time he wrenched powerfully on the rifle and tore it from the woman's hands.

Maude whirled away from Jacob. She had to escape from him. She ran blindly, tripped over a chair, and fell full length. She sprang up immediately and ran again, crashing into the wall with a resounding thud. She pivoted around, crouched like a caged animal, and began to flail her arms wildly in Jacob's direction. Blood streamed down across her mouth from an injury to her nose.

Cora ran to Maude and tried to grab her by the arms. But the big woman shook her off.

"Jacob, help me," Cora cried. "She'll kill herself."

Jacob rushed across the room at Maude. She struck at him and darted past. Jacob's reaching hand caught a momentary hold on Maude's shoulder as she went by and spun her partially around. She staggered and slammed into the wall again.

Jacob sprang upon Maude and captured her around the waist with his arms. She twisted swiftly and hit him viciously in the face.

The crazed woman was immensely strong and Jacob felt the sting of the blow. He shoved her back to arm's length, and struck her two rapid blows, one to the stomach that took her wind, and one to the side of the head that addled her.

Maude fell backward to the earthen floor. Jacob leapt upon her and quickly flipped her to her stomach. He twisted her arms behind her back.

"Get me some of those strips of rawhide I used to repair the snowshoes," he called to Cora.

Cora hastily brought the pieces of hide to Jacob.

Maude struggled weakly as Jacob bound her arms and legs. Finishing, he stepped away.

Maude raised her head and looked at Jacob. "Dead! Dead!" she cried. She jerked her sight from Jacob and screamed, a piercing cry not even half human.

Cora came toward her with hands extended. "Maude, please don't carry on so."

Maude fell silent and her eyes shifted to Cora. She began to laugh, a lunatic's laugh.

"She's gone completely mad," Jacob said. "I guess she thought she had killed me, then when she saw me alive, it sent her over the edge."

Cora knelt beside Maude and reached out to touch her bloodied face. Maude thrust her head out at Cora and her teeth snapped together like rocks hitting, barely missing Cora's fingers.

Cora snatched her hand away. "Oh, Maude, what has happened to you? I never wanted you to be hurt. Why do you hate Jacob so much? And me?"

Maude stared at Cora, her eyes glittering crazily. Cora looked into her sister's eyes. She saw no reason there, only the insane world where her sister now lived.

Cora turned to Jacob with a sob. "Will she ever be all right again?"

"I don't know, Cora. I just don't know. Maybe later, maybe after she sleeps. Let's see how she is tomorrow."

"I pray that she becomes her old self again."

I hope not, thought Jacob. *For then she'll try again to kill me.* "Help me lift her onto her bunk," he said.

Jacob stood with Cora in front of the cabin and watched the winter night settle into the valley. The black shroud of darkness was thickening quickly, closing off their view of the mountainsides above them. They remained silent and unmoving, finding pleasure in each other's company. And the night deepened further, wrapping itself around them close and soft.

Cora's hand crept inside Jacob's and rested small, warm, and trusting within his clasp. "We are in a terrible situation," she said. "What shall we do?"

"I don't know. It's a sorry thing that Maude feels like she does about me. And that helped drive her crazy. But I have the right to love you."

"Yes, you do." She squeezed his hand.

Jacob looked over his shoulder and into the cabin. The room was almost dark, the fire burned down to a small bed of coals. Maude lay on her bunk with her eyes closed, making no sound. Jacob didn't know if she was asleep, unconscious, or watching them through some insane veil. He would soon find out.

He led Cora inside and closed the door. He put his arm around her and guided the way across the dark room to his bunk.

"What if Maude hears us?" Cora whispered.

"She won't. I don't think she knows what is happening around her."

"I'm so sorry for her. I feel I'm to blame for what has happened."

"Don't feel guilty. Maude is Maude's enemy, not you, nor me. Believe me about this."

"All right, Jacob." Cora pressed her body to Jacob's. Her hands rose and caressed his bearded cheeks. She rose on tiptoes and kissed him on the lips.

"Cora!" Maude's scream, shrill and strung taut as piano wires, sliced the cabin's darkness. "Cora! Cora! What are you doing?"

"Oh, my God, she's watching us," Cora whispered. "I can't do it with her there." She jerked away from Jacob's arms and into the gloom of the cabin. Jacob heard her throw herself onto her bed.

Damn the crazy sister, thought Jacob. He went outside

the cabin and stomped up and down in the snow. What
was to be done now? He couldn't be locked in the cabin
all winter with Cora, who wouldn't love him, and the
insane sister who was the cause of it, and had to be kept
tied.

He broke into a pounding run down the valley with
the snow crackling and crunching under his driving
feet. A mile passed behind him, then two and three.
The low-hanging branches of the trees, hidden in the
darkness, often struck him. He floundered in deep
drifts of snow and fell, only to jump back to his feet
and race on. He finally stopped running, his heart hammering and his breath rushing with a hoarse sawing
sound into the hollows of his lungs.

He stood for a time catching his breath. Then longer
still, wrestling with his problem and watching the cold,
uncaring moon come up over the shoulder of the
mountain and throw its light down into the frozen valley.

With the cold cutting him with its icy sharpness, Jacob
turned and trudged back up the valley. He still had no
answer to his dilemma.

Thirty-two

Maude wasn't going to be sane again when morning arrived, Cora knew it. Her sister's loss of reason had been coming on for months and wouldn't suddenly disappear. She believed Jacob thought the same as she did. It was all so unfair to him. She wouldn't blame him if he abandoned them.

Cora sat in her bed with the buffalo robe wrapped around her. She stared into the darkness of the cabin, unable to sleep. Jacob had returned through the black night hours ago and, without uttering a word or building up the fire to make a light, fell into his bed. A decision had to be made about him, and Maude, who wanted him dead. In her madness, did Maude also want Cora dead?

Something moved in the murk of the cabin. It was more sensed than seen, for the darkness was so dense that it seemed to have weight. Cora strained to see. A patch of a lighter shade of darkness was moving near the door. It floated there for a moment, and then drifted soundlessly toward Jacob's bunk.

Either Jacob or Maude was moving about. Maude? Cora threw off her cover and sprang to Maude's bed. She ran her hand over the bunk. Empty.

"Jacob!" Cora shouted. "Maude's loose!"

She hurled herself across the narrow width of the

cabin, and sprang upon Maude looming over Jacob's bed. Her arms encircled the woman's broad chest and she yanked backward with all her strength. Her sister's big body seemed made of stone, and gave way to her pull not at all.

Jacob snapped awake with Cora's cry ringing in his ears. He saw the dark form of Maude above him. He hurled himself from his bunk onto the floor. He heard something heavy crash down on his bed where he had lain but a moment before.

He made a roundhouse sweep with his arms through the blackness, found Maude's legs, and a second, smaller pair he knew was Cora's. He shifted his arm to encircle only Maude's legs and jerked them out from under her. Maude thumped down with a cry near him. He threw himself on top of her.

Jacob immediately struck Maude hard on the ribs with his fist. The breath left the woman with an explosion of air. He swarmed upon her and penned both of her arms to her sides. Beneath him, Maude's chest heaved as she fought to draw breath.

"Cora, hurry, see if there's any hot coals under the ashes," Jacob said. "Make a light."

Cora rose and hastened to the fireplace. She found the poker and raked through the mound of ashes left by the evening fire. A few live coals came to the surface and glowed red in the darkness. She placed thin wood shavings on the coals and blew on them. After a few breaths, the shavings burst into flame, and their yellow light shoved the darkness into the corners of the cabin.

Cora looked at Jacob sitting astride Maude on the floor. Then she saw the chopping ax embedded in Jacob's bunk where he had lain. That was why Maude had been near the door, to get the ax.

"Oh, my God," she exclaimed. What a horrible, demented act Maude's deranged mind had conjured up. "I'm so sorry, Jacob, for what she tried to do."

Jacob looked to see what Cora saw. The ax had cut through the furs he used as a mattress and was stuck in the slats of the bed. "She is totally mad, so you don't have anything to be sorry about. You saved my life."

"I don't want you to die. Not ever."

"Well, someday it'll sure happen," Jacob said. "Now we'd better tie her up." He examined the lengths of frayed rawhide fastened to Maude's wrists. "She must've worn into them rubbing on the wood of the bunk. This time I'll use stronger pieces. Bring me a piece of the elk hide."

Cora did as Jacob asked, and then knelt down beside him as he bound Maude's wrists and legs. "We must do something for Maude," she said. "Maybe a doctor could help her. I heard of doctors in New Orleans that sometimes could help people like Maude."

"I think all big towns would have them."

"We must take her to one. And they must not fail to help her, for I don't want her locked up in an insane asylum."

"The nearest town is Salt Lake City. It's small and I doubt that there'd be a doctor of that kind there. We'll have to take her to St. Louis, or San Francisco."

"When can we leave?"

"Cora, there's deep snow in all this high country. The ground for hundreds of miles in every direction will be covered with it."

"I know there will be snow. What I want to know is, which city should we go to, San Francisco, or St. Louis?"

"San Francisco is my choice, for I want to end up in California." *And I want you there with me,* Jacob thought. "But there are many snowy mountains to cross to reach there."

"I understand it would be difficult. But can we do it?"

Jacob believed he could make it to San Francisco if he was alone. But could Cora stand the grueling journey? He didn't want to allow her to die in the snow on some frigid mountain. And what of crazy Maude, who he would have to keep tied?

"The hardest part is getting down out of the mountains to lower country where the snow isn't so deep. Then there's high desert country to cross, and a range of mountains to climb over to reach California. We would have more than a thousand miles of the damnest, toughest traveling you can imagine. The horses won't be able to carry us through the country with deep snow, and that part we'd have to snowshoe."

"Then you think we can do it?"

"We don't have any other choices." Jacob said "We've got to chance it."

The snowflakes were huge, floating down like dead, white birds. They landed silently, clinging to everything they touched. After only a few minutes, they were piled an inch thick on Jacob's shoulders as he worked loading and saddling the horses in front of the cabin.

The storm was a wet one and Jacob knew it would drop much snow on the mountains. He must get the women down on the plains as swiftly as possible. Even there the snow would be falling, just not as much.

He finished with the horses and went to the open cabin door and called inside, "Cora, bring Maude and let's be on our way."

"Come, Maude, we're going to Salt Lake City and then on to San Francisco to get a doctor for you," Cora said.

Maude looked straight at Jacob, standing in the doorway. She was dressed, as was Cora, in her heavy clothing and fur coat. Her hands were tied in front of her. She gave Jacob a feral animal look and did not move.

"Maude, listen to me," Cora said insistently. "You can see Clive in Salt Lake City. Jacob is going to take us there."

Maude slowly shifted her sight to Cora. Her face twitched as she concentrated on what Cora had said. "Marry Clive?" she asked in a dull voice.

Cora was startled by Maude's words. She hadn't spoken for hours. She exchanged glances with Jacob. Maybe here was a way to control her sister. "Maude, would you like to marry Clive?" she asked.

"Marry Clive," the big woman said in a slightly brighter tone.

"If you want that, then we had better go with Jacob," Cora said. "You do what he says and you'll see Clive in a few days. Do you understand me?"

Maude looked back at Jacob. Her face twisted and her mouth worked as she fought some battle with herself. Finally she spoke. "Marry Clive."

"Jacob is your friend, Maude. He wants only to help you. You mustn't hurt him. Do you understand that?"

"Marry Clive," Maude intoned.

"Maude will soon marry Clive," Jacob said "Now we must go and find him."

Jacob watched warily ahead as he led the women and horses through the snow pouring down through the limbs of the tall pine trees. He wore snowshoes as did Cora and Maude, trudging along beside him. He towed behind him seven horses, tied nose-to-tail in single file.

The first two horses in line were unloaded animals Jacob was using to break trail through the deep snow. Next came two packhorses carrying sleeping robes, food, and spare weapons. Saddle horses for Cora, Maude, and himself came last.

The lead horse struggled with the snow, so deep that the animal couldn't walk. It lunged forward time after time to keep up with Jacob. With each lunge, its narrow hooves plunged to the bottom of the snow. The second horse had somewhat less difficulty in moving forward. With the snow becoming ever more packed with the passage of each horse, the one that followed had an easier time of it.

Jacob looked to the side at Cora. She appeared so small and vulnerable in the flood of falling snow. She was brave and sturdy, and was speedily adapting to the snowshoes. Still he worried. She couldn't know how severe would be the hardships that they must overcome on the long journey that lay before them.

He snowshoed ahead, trailing his rifle in his hand. He kept a taut rope on the lead horse, forcing the animal to come with him. In a few days, both lead animals would become so exhausted they would drop. He would sacrifice them to save the strength of the horses that must carry the two women and him to Salt Lake City and beyond.

In the cascade of falling snow a few yards ahead, Jacob saw an Indian astride his mustang take form like a bad spirit. Behind him and even less defined in the snow, a second mounted and approaching Indian became visible. There was the merest shadow of a third rider farther back in the forest. How many more were there just beyond sight?

Jacob dropped the lead rope, and grabbed his rifle with both hands. He recognized the nearest Indian, who was breaking trail for the Crows—Wolf Voice. The Crow had not been fooled for long by Jacob's false trail on the prairie. There were at least two other warriors with him. Jacob had little chance to win a battle against all of them.

Jacob was pleased that Wolf Voice was closest to him. At least he could shoot that Crow sonofabitch. Jacob swept his rifle up and brought it to bear on the man.

Wolf Voice knew his danger the instant the white man called Jacob appeared out of the snow. He remembered how very quick the man was. He jerked the reins of his mustang and spun the animal to the side. He dropped down to hang on the animal's side opposite Jacob, a heel and one arm holding him in place. From there, protected by the body of his mustang, he would shoot from under the neck of the animal at the white man.

When Wolf Voice disappeared behind his mustang, Jacob immediately shifted his rifle to the second Crow, Broken Arm. The man's view had been blocked by Wolf Voice's body and he was only now seeing Jacob. The range was very short and Jacob fired at once. The bullet struck Broken Arm in the sternum, shattering the thick bone. The impact of the bullet knocked the man tumbling from the back of his mustang.

The moment Jacob fired his rifle, he threw himself sideways and down into the snow, for Wolf Voice had taken aim on him As Jacob fell, Wolf Voice's rifle crashed and a bullet tugged at the shoulder of his coat.

Jacob sprang to his feet and, holding his empty rifle like a club, ran forward on his snowshoes at Wolf Voice. The Crow swung back into his saddle, and jumped his mustang to meet Jacob, to ride him down.

As the Crow's mustang came into reach, Jacob swung his rifle and struck the charging animal a powerful blow across the nose. He instantly jumped to the side to avoid the hard hooves of the beast.

At Jacob's savage blow, Wolf Voice's mustang came to an immediate stop and reared up on its hind legs. It whinnied in pain, reared still higher, and kicked the air. It slipped in the snow and fell backward.

Wolf Voice reacted swiftly, shoving himself away from the falling horse. He landed agilely on his feet a few steps in front of Maude and Cora. He pivoted to face Jacob, and plunged his hand inside his clothing for his pistol.

Jacob surged to his feet and dug for his own pistol under his buttoned coat. As he ripped the weapon free from the binding coat, the third Crow, Long Running, was charging his mustang at him. Long Running held his rifle to his shoulder, aimed at Jacob and ready to shoot.

Jacob knew he was going to be much too late to kill both Wolf Voice and Long Running. Which to shoot? The Crow that remained alive would easily kill him, for the range was so short that it was impossible to miss his target.

Maude came into Jacob's sight, snowshoeing forward with long, awkward strides. Her bound arms were outstretched toward Wolf Voice, her hands spread like talons to grab him.

The Crow, intent on Jacob, did not see the woman at first. Then he heard her feet on the snow and whirled in her direction. With a fierce cry, Maude slammed into Wolf Voice. They went down in a tangle of arms and legs.

Jacob whirled, the barrel of his pistol making the arc that brought its sights onto Long Running. He shot the man in the center of the face. A round black hole appeared in the bridge of the Crow's nose. Long Running fell from his horse and plunged into the deep snow.

Maude fought Wolf Voice on the ground in a flurry of snow. As they rolled and thrashed, she held the Crow's gun hand with both of hers and screamed in a high-pitched voice.

Wolf Voice slugged Maude in the face with his free hand, then again and again repeatedly. The savage blows stopped Maude's screams. Yet she continued to resist with all her strength Wolf Voice's efforts to force the gun down to point at her.

Jacob rushed to aid Maude. Before he could reach her, Wolf Voice's pistol exploded. Maude cried out in pain.

Wolf Voice shoved Maude's slack body aside. Still lying in the snow, he raised his pistol toward Jacob.

Too late, Wolf Voice, Jacob thought. He shot the Crow through the heart, driving him backward in the snow.

Cora rushed up and dropped down in the snow beside Maude. She lifted her sister in her arms. Blood was gushing from a gaping wound in her throat. Her face held a tortured expression as she tried to pull back the life that was escaping her. Her eyes found Cora's, fastened on them. "I want to marry Clive," she gasped. She shuddered, and died.

"No, Maude! No!" Cora sobbed. She pulled Maude to her bosom.

Jacob knelt beside Cora and put his arms around her shoulders as she cried. He wanted to say something that would comfort her, but no words came to him. He laid his head against hers and hoped his nearness would help. After a time he released Cora's hold on Maude and lay the body down in the snow.

Cora reached out and closed Maude's eyes with her fingers, eyes that were mere holes into nothingness. "It's all so awful," Cora said, looking up at Jacob.

"Maude saved my life," he said.

"She did, didn't she?" Cora said, stifling her sobs and looking up at Jacob. "I'm glad she did that. I'll remember her as she was before she changed, before all this happened."

Jacob wiped away the snowflakes that had fallen onto Cora's cheeks. He gazed into her eyes and saw his future universe in creation. A beautiful universe it was.

AUTHOR'S NOTE

The Mormon handcart migration lasted five years, from 1856 through 1860. In total, ten companies containing 2,962 converts and 653 handcarts crossed the wilderness of the Great Plains and the Rocky Mountains to Salt Lake City.

The converts, mostly young women from England and Scandinavia, bent their backs in heart-bursting toil to pull the handcarts through the wilderness. Meager food rations and fierce storms falling upon the unprotected people added to the misery. Many weakened and died and were buried in the prairie sod or the rocky soil of the mountains.

The most terrible loss of life occurred in the fifth handcart company. The company was poorly organized and started late from Iowa City, Iowa. Dressed in summer clothing, and with their food gone, the Mormon converts became stranded by a winter snowfall in the high mountains far north of Salt Lake City. Three out of every ten people perished from exhaustion, hunger, and the cold before a relief party of young Mormon men, sent by Brigham Young from Salt Lake City, could reach them.

The handcart companies of 1856, 1857, and 1858 began in Iowa City. The journey was 1,300 miles and took approximately four months. With the completion of the railroad to St. Joseph, Missouri, in February 1859, the route was shortened to 1,000 miles and took about three months. The Mormon immigrants organized at

St. Joseph, then caught riverboats up the Missouri River to begin their handcart trek from Florence, Nebraska. (Florence is now part of Omaha.)

The Mormon Church halted the use of handcarts after 1860. Thereafter, the new immigrant converts traveled by wagon train, until the completion of the transcontinental railroad on May 10, 1869. The journey that had required three to four months of great hardship could now be accomplished in relative comfort on the train in less than two days.